Mixed Medicines in Geneva

Al Logie

AOS Publishing, 2024
Copyright © 2024

Al Logie

ISBN: 978-1-990496-76-9

Cover Design: Chanelle Poupart

Visit AOS Publishing's website:
www.aospublishing.com

Table of Contents

Continued

1.
The Doctor

"I don't want you making a fuss. I have the doctor's recommendations."

Some interfering dinner guest of my guardian had arranged this unlikely consultation. The physician in question was, so the front pages assured us, a national hero. I was a small, dark-haired thirteen-year-old, named Jean-Marc Montabeille, and not in obvious need of medical assessment. Orphaned in the aftermath of the devastating 1923 earthquake in the Mediterranean island of Amphora, I now resided in Geneva with my guardian, a member of the charity which had rescued me. I had not yet found my bearings in my new city with its important international organizations and theological institutions: I only knew that everyone seemed to advance a different theory on how I might be formed into an exemplary citizen.

The doctor's reputation came from thousands of saved lives in foreign territories. He would identify the sources of diseases and, with his talented wife, would cajole and entertain the authorities until stagnant ponds were drained, waters filtered, and sewers built. A typical editorial ran:

As one applauds the honours bestowed on Dr Auguste Weygand by dignified monarchs and governors, one reflects that our confederation is a fountain of those humanitarian impulses required to retrieve the world from disease, famine and the barbarity of modern war. But now, while Dr and Mme Weygand take a well-deserved pause from diphtheria-infected hospitals, perhaps we can benefit at home from their indomitable vigour.

The elegant doctor's vigour persisted. However, now approaching his fiftieth year, he was exploring new domains where he might make an even more spectacular contribution to human welfare. I was to be afforded a role in these endeavours.

Weygand's success came from analysing cause and effect and not becoming lost in bureaucratic and scientific detail. As a result, he had kept thousands from the morgue. Would it be possible using this methodology to identify the causes of delinquency and intervene in advance?

The Weygands had been deeply disappointed by the moral fibre of the young men that they employed on their return. The chauffeur submitted fraudulent fuel expenses. The gardener was dismissed for inappropriate overtures to the daughter of the neighbouring industrialist. The chef was convicted of trafficking stolen truffles. And yet, all three had come with sincere references. As with disease, the challenge would be to determine why some individuals were susceptible to corruption, what triggered the onset, and what preventive measures would be effective.

This audacious initiative was not announced publicly. Better to have a result than a theory. The doctor corresponded with friends, wardens, educationalists, and psychologists. The problem was clearly urgent. This was no time to get bogged down in analysis and tiresome Poisson distributions. As he explained to the guardian, common sense and observation were the surest guides. Did Servetus or Harvey[1] need to consult government statisticians before proving the circulation of the blood?

The rest of Switzerland was enjoying a warm June evening. I was in an airless room with the setting sun in my eyes. Dr Weygand, in a crisp white summer suit, and his taciturn assistant had just completed a physical examination. This was cursory for every component except my head, which they measured with gauges before studying my pupils and irises.

---

1 William Harvey, died 1657, is credited with discovering the circulation of the blood. Servetus, died 1553, had also observed this, but his books were destroyed, and he was burned as a heretic in Geneva for his views on the Trinity.

"You are very fortunate, Jean-Marc. A rigorous regime will be necessary, but we may be able to get you on the right path. I will give the details to your guardian so he can help you adhere to it."

"I don't feel ill. Is this because of the wax in my ears? I can try to clean them more often."

"It is better that you talk to your guardian tomorrow. But the wax is unattractive. Make sure you use cotton wool and a good carbolic soap."

The interfering guest, seated at some distance from the guardian, had overheard part of a conversation in which he complained mildly about my attitude. I could, indeed, be tiresome and difficult. But, in this particular instance, these disagreeable traits were related to the elocution lessons designed to help me acquire the correct local tones. In this context, had the guest troubled to ascertain the details, they were surely not a significant symptom. After ninety minutes with Mme Vaillancourt, a saint might have scowled on hearing:

"Repeat again, making sure every syllable rings out:
Contre qui que ce soit que mon pays m'emploie,
J'accepte aveuglément cette gloire avec joie"[2]

In any event, the guest's main social credential came from being a school friend of the heroic doctor. He could not pass up the opportunity to show the guardian that he could arrange an appointment with Auguste Weygand.

The guardian would eventually fill the role of my adoptive father. In the first years, however, he maintained a dutiful, professional distance from me, and I still knew relatively little about him. He was in his late thirties, conscientious, and rigidly self-disciplined. In repose, his face had a stern aspect, but he could surprise with a smile that would make him look ten years younger. He was fair-haired, of medium height, and still untroubled by any bald patch. I understood that his wife had

---

2 From Corneille's play *Horace* in which the main character prioritizes duty and patriotism over sentiment when he is required to fight his three brothers-in-law to the death.

succumbed to illness some years prior, at which point he moved from Lausanne to Geneva. I never met his family, apparently members of a rigorous sect, from whom he was estranged and who had no tradition of celebrating birthdays.

It took the guardian four days to review the doctor's recommendations. He seemed deeply preoccupied. Finally, he led me into the salon and indicated that I was to sit in one of the large leather armchairs that were normally reserved for visitors.

"Jean-Marc, it will be easier if you make an effort to understand everything before you talk. It is going to be alright if you take it in the proper spirit. Dr Weygand has identified some risks."

I was not encouraged by this opening.

He continued:

"The doctor has found that certain boys develop in such a way that they are more likely to yield to temptations as young men. This is not to say that they are bad. On the contrary, they are often agreeable, but they need to be trained and equipped to overcome the challenges that they will face in the later teens and early twenties. He is convinced that you fall into this category. He has established that you have an identical profile to a valet in Monaco who is currently in deep trouble. His conclusion is based on the scientific study of attitudes and certain physical characteristics, like thin patches in the skull, and appearing young for one's age."

The guardian poured himself a small measure of a medicinal brandy prescribed to prevent infections of the larynx.

"It may be best if I just read the summary recommendations

1. Strikes on the head and games where the cranium could be hit are not advised.

2. Daily exercise, preferably solitary swimming, is required.

3. Two doses of cod liver oil must be taken daily.

4. Body temperature must be charted twice daily. Any fever must be addressed with ice.

5. Youths of his age must be considered potential sources of bad influence and infection. Participation at school or on teams is excluded.

6. The playing of sober and reputable music is encouraged.

7. A rigorous disciplinary regime must be implemented.

"There is something else. He doesn't think you should perform military service. He has mailed a file to Bern. Here, take a look at the dossier. The recommendations are on the first few pages, but he has impressive supporting appendices. There are long quotations from the Greek philosophers, the educationalist Thomas Arnold,[3] Cicero, and many other exceptional minds. It is an excellent compilation. Later, I'll help you find the best passages."

I may not have looked excited at the prospect of an introduction to these distinguished theorists.

"Now go to bed. Over the next few days, I'll explain how we'll implement each suggestion."

Weygand's list represented the type of challenge at which the guardian excelled. I was not yet entirely sure what he did professionally, but everyone affirmed that no one could do it better. I was called into the salon for a review of progress to date. He extracted a few items from paper bags.

"I am spoiling you. Here is a Cary thermometer. Do you see, it has a dial like a watch? I hear they can be recalibrated at the national thermometric institute. The initials refer to M. Lanteigne, the furrier. I don't think he can have used it very much. He ate a pot of pheasant terrine every day for breakfast. Place it like this under your shoulder. You must polish it weekly. This chart paper is used in the best hospitals. You must find me immediately if you

---

3 Dr Arnold, Headmaster of Rugby School, died 1842. He advocated learning classical languages and supported disciplinary intervention to instill 'the simplicity, sobriety and humbleness of mind which are the best ornaments of youth, and offer the best promise of a noble manhood'. Cited in Lytton Strachey *Eminent Victorians*

get a reading outside of the blue lines. Will you take this seriously? I won't accept excuses."

The temperature recommendation, while excessive, would prove to have some merit. I was unused to the Genevan bacteria. When necessary, the guardian, the neighbours and a nurse would watch over me with wet dishcloths, ice, and medicinal pastilles until my fevers subsided.

One of the recommendations was moot, as nobody was given to hitting me around the head.

A bag from one of the city's more exclusive pharmacies contained a bottle:

"It is important to have a good quality cod liver oil. The others don't nourish the brain as effectively. I studied the proceedings of the XIV International Piscatorial Exposition in Stavanger. We can't get the gold medal winner here. It is rarely exported though it did improve the vision of the late Danish queen."

He handed me the silver medallist. The label declared that this potion was administered in the royal nurseries of Scandinavia where it contributed to the 'intelligence, becoming looks, and equitable temperament' of the children. As Weygand had cautioned, I was starting this regimen relatively late. The guardian remained optimistic.

"I am looking forward to seeing it help you grow in so many ways. You must tell me in a couple of weeks when you start to feel stronger and sharper."

The list was not yet complete, but the guardian hinted at exciting possibilities. He would give me more details over the coming days.

2.
Classical Swimming

The consul of a small eastern European country was grateful to the guardian who had assisted him in finding a place for his nation on some prestigious cultural committees. The consul held doctorates from Rome and Cambridge. His published articles on recent archaeological discoveries were well respected. Related to the ruling family, he had funds to organize exhibitions and to erect an imposing consulate with twin croquet lawns and a boathouse. In their early fifties, he and his wife, herself a distinguished classicist, were welcome guests at receptions.

Unfortunately, the expenses of the Genevan mission exceeded those of Bern, Berlin, and Paris combined. The consul's less tactful countrymen enquired whether the national interest had required the couple to build a full-length indoor swimming pool surrounded by arches, each enclosing a mosaic of several hundred thousand pieces. In response, a communiqué sought to dispel the misunderstanding:

> *Geneva should not be compared to the capital city of a mere country. Home to the Red Cross and the League of Nations, it is the capital of global cultural and humanitarian cooperation and aspiration. It is here that we must showcase our nation as a critical component of the new order. The bath area and its art make an indelible positive impression on Genevans and the international community every day.*

This controversy broke out a few days before Weygand recommended swimming as part of my regime.

The guardian met with the consul. It is probable that a great deal was wisely left unsaid for, contrary to the official messaging, no Genevan had ever floated in the pool. This potentially embarrassing issue would lose its sting if I were to practice for two hours early each morning.

The guardian accompanied me on my first visit. After we had registered at the gatehouse, an unsmiling, armed sentry opened a wooden side entrance reinforced with thick steel on the reverse. We proceeded down a long passage to a prison-like door which he unlocked with two separate keys. He then secured it behind us. We climbed a few steps and joined the corridor which presumably led to the consul's private quarters. There was a high-class Belgian carpet and Gobelins tapestries depicting the travels of Saint Paul. When we reached the pool and the changing room, the sentry advised us that he would lock the door. He would return in two hours to escort us back. In an emergency only, we could use a bell pull to request assistance.

I had been well taught in Amphora. The guardian was impressed:

"Very well done! You swim like an otter. I should ask the consul to stock trout for you to chase. I know that you will be well protected here. The exercise will be very beneficial and without the distraction of other teenagers. It is convenient that the treatment is pleasurable, too."

An unshaven, yawning photographer was waiting for me on my third visit. I was told to stand in front of the mosaic of the Sirens in my bathing trunks. This gear had occasioned much debate at the guardian's outfitters. It was finally determined that a full-length male maillot was not required by public decency as my chest was likely to remain innocently hairless for the foreseeable future.

The photographer summoned the energy to set up an ancient camera on a tripod and review the composition from under a cape:

"Don't slouch. Please try to look fit and intelligent. Your image will be featured in our national press. You will project a more dignified appearance with a folded towel draped over your shoulder. There should be a hint of a Roman senator's toga.

Move a little to the left. You are obscuring a Siren's head. Wait while I adjust the lighting."

I grew friendly with the sentry, Ivan. On his country's national day, he offered me a pear and almond sweet with a consistency similar to Turkish Delight. Thereafter he would frequently let his stern official image slip. After about a month, he excitedly showed me the back page of an illustrated news and propaganda magazine. The black and white picture was reproduced with extraordinary clarity. The caption explained:

Mens sana in corpore sano: A grateful swimmer takes advantage of our impressive facilities in Geneva to admire our nation's reinterpretation of classical art and improve his youthful physique.

I was normally alone, but on rare occasions one of the consul's house guests would join me. I needed to be a little cautious in how I described them to the guardian.

I was approaching fifteen when Ivan gave me a brief background on Mme Anastasia, a striking auburn-haired lady in her early thirties. She was known to audiences in Linz and Breslau for her role as Susanna in *The Marriage of Figaro*. She had left the opera on inheriting valuable patents from an uncle who manufactured frost resistant drainage pipes in Cincinnati. The consul's wife had encouraged her distant relative to stay for a few days while she met with private bankers. I eventually realized that Ivan was also trying to tell me something else but was reluctant to engage in gossip about his superior's visitors.

"Jean-Marc, she has been in the pool for about ten minutes. You should be very careful."

"I can stay on the other side and do slow breaststrokes, so I won't splash so much. Is she wearing a bathing cap?"

"That's not really what I meant. I'm sure she's a very nice person, but she may forget that you are still young. I'll ask the steward to come by in a little while."

I had completed a couple of lengths when the lady intercepted me:

"Who is this good-looking boy who swims so elegantly?"

I introduced myself politely.

"You don't have to be so formal. Stand by the side of the pool so I can see you properly."

The lady viewed me closely.

"That's good. Healthy, but nothing too ostentatious. Now turn around. Come back in."

Ivan's warning mixed uneasily with anxiety and the enticing prospect of adventure. But the steward found nothing untoward when he arrived on the pretext of checking how Mme Anastasia would like her morning tea. Perhaps it could be served in the alcove by the mosaic of the demise of Agamemnon? Ivan's fears were well-founded, but I did not quite meet the standard:

"You are delightful, but I shall leave you to the younger generation. You Swiss are so prudish about these things. Do you have noble blood? I shall describe you in exact detail to my niece. My stepsister in Königsberg married an aristocratic Russian *émigré* so the poor girl can't wed just anyone. She is stunningly beautiful with deep brown, poetic eyes. Would you mind a wife who is taller than you? Can you show me your palms?"

I extended my hands. She held my wrists as she turned my palms to catch the light before determining:

"You are stronger than you realize, and you have a tranquil force. Do not talk in a deep voice and go hunting for your girl. She will come to you."

The man had eyebrows, wide, impressive eyebrows. I thought I was alone. I had been practicing dives to recover a scallop shell. These had been successful until the last attempt. Surfacing, I let out a vulgar expression which had crept into my teenage vocabulary.

A voice responded:

"*Quamvis sint sub aqua, sub aqua, maledicere temptant.*"[4]

I turned to see the eyebrows on a tall man in his late thirties.

"Forgive me. But how often do you get the chance to annoy someone in a dead language? It's the only benefit from learning it. Did you recognize the line? From *Metamorphoses*? It's onomatopoeia. You see, it sounds like croaking frogs. Although they are 'under the water, under the water', they try to say bad things. It seems to describe you pretty well. Don't look like that! The steward is bringing coffee and pastries. You must come and let me make amends."

Historians have offered differing interpretations of my breakfast companion. Professor Klemperer of Zwickau asserts:

Facing exposure and arrest, he fled to the Geneva consulate. In this city of hypocritical rectitude, he doubtless deposited the proceeds of his peculations in numbered bank accounts. These funds had been entrusted to his department for the creation of colleges to help extract his fellow citizens from a grinding agricultural poverty.

Dr Schilling of Ann Arbor maintains:

His intelligent and farsighted reforms began to raise literacy and create the cultural and technical base. Their very success was a challenge to the established interests. Made aware of the plots against him, he withdrew to the relative safety of the Geneva consulate where he drafted a persuasive manifesto for liberal education. The facts are uncertain, but he may have ensured that his department's budget was not redeployed. He is said to have done this by the simple expedient of transferring funds to a coded account to which only he had access.

The consul received contradictory cables from the different factions in his home country. A commission would decide in three weeks if his high-ranking but inconvenient guest should be

---

4 Ovid, The *Metamorphoses*

compelled to return under penalty of law. In the meantime, the consul hedged his bets. The man would be kept in a gilded cage. He would be afforded every sign of respect within the compound. But he was not to leave.

I retrieved my shell and joined Stanislas. The tray was set with a silver coffee service and doilies from Bruges. The croissants were superb. Less reassuringly, an unfamiliar armed guard was stationed at each entry to the pool.

By the end of the first week, I had grown fond of Stanislas. In retrospect, he may have enjoyed entertaining me as a brief respite from his political issues. He had an extraordinary knowledge of patisserie, and ensured that there was a fresh selection for me to try each day. He also insisted that we worked our way around the different mosaics. There was one strange requirement.

"I am going to ask you to do something. Don't worry, it is respectable, but you need to keep it to yourself. You must learn, and I mean really learn, the name of the mosaic and a number that I give you. You must know it so that you can recall it without fail if you don't hear from me for twenty-five years. You must never tell anyone."

I was used to instructions whose purpose I did not comprehend.

"Will it be a long number?"

"No, only four digits for each mosaic. I'll explain the story behind each picture, so it sticks more easily in your mind. Today you just need to remember *The Judgement of Paris*—4386. Do you see how uncomfortable Prince Paris looks as he prepares to offer the apple? Based on the ladies' expressions, I'm not sure that I would have chosen Aphrodite."

We did this for five mosaics, and he drilled me on them daily. Finally, the commission announced its decision.

"My trusted friend, I've enjoyed our time together, but I have to return home later today. You can write the numbers down if you want. But they must be in your memory. Unless I tell you anything different, you must go to the Banque des Alpinistes in 1950. There may be something for you. Everything will be locked until that year."

I did go to the bank. It turned out that Stanislas had survived and was living very comfortably. However, a token of appreciation was waiting for me. It would, like the prince's apple, prove a source of discord.

3.
Education

Perhaps I tired the guardian with my questions and conversation as I accompanied him on the boat from Amphora in our first week together. As soon as we arrived at the mainland, he found a stationer's and bought me a fine drawing pad and pencil set. I would need to be quiet while he and his colleagues drafted their report.

Anxious to impress my rescuer, I replicated much of my last drawing class. Working solely from memory, I soon had my twenty leaves, ten flowers, fifteen insects, five fish, and four varieties of pig. The guardian was simultaneously astonished and concerned. Further enquiry soon showed that this knowledge had been acquired at the expense of other subjects. I would sink if I were to go directly into a Genevan school.

The guardian's original plan, before Weygand's intervention, made a great deal of sense. A *cure* across the border in France ran correspondence courses to help the children of expatriate bankers adjust to the Swiss system. This ecclesiastic would teach me remotely for a year while the guardian would coach me in the evenings. In the meantime, the guardian would arrange for me to participate in activities where I could meet children of my own age. All being well, I would make friends who could guide me when school started. The guardian had no illusions about the young. I would doubtless be mocked for my Amphoran accent. I was to have elocution lessons.

The guardian's house had previously been owned by a professor of veterinary science. The dining and drawing rooms had been extended to accommodate lectures and seminars for up to two dozen students. An ugly room had been added off the main hallway destroying what should have been a south-facing view of the garden. The new chamber had no natural light apart from some high transom windows. A steel covered operating table remained in place, as did the strong lamps, sinks, and hoses. Thick leather straps which would have served to lift anaesthetized Saint Bernard dogs hung from the wall. This space was to be my classroom. The guardian was reassuring:

"It looks so much better now. There used to be charts showing diseases of canine jaws. We can decorate it a little, but not with anything distracting. I'll see if I can find my old map of the Roman Empire. The border has dolphins and sea monsters playing among the triremes. It will be nice for you."

We were never sure if the *curé* had been defrocked. He had proposed revisions to a published episcopal sermon which referenced the story of Elisha and the annoying children who were silenced by bears.[5] The bishop did not find the criticism constructive. An acrimonious exchange of pamphlets broke out over theological nuances which had lain dormant since the Middle Ages.

My sympathies lay with the bishop. The *curé* was knowledgeable, in some ways a good teacher, and occasionally showed an unexpected sense of humour. But he did not just correct mistakes. He attacked them. I would mail my output on a regular schedule. It would be returned in a package addressed to the guardian. Errors would be marked in red with a scathing observation that I would have had the correct information had I taken the trouble to study page thirty-two line nine as instructed. A summary page gave scope for a range of adjectives describing my careless and lazy efforts. A score of less than sixteen out of thirty would be marked as a failure. In fairness, we would sometimes be surprised by a line or two of green ink. The guardian had realized that I learned more readily when I accompanied a task with a drawing. He had asked the *curé* to allow me to add illustrations. On rare occasions one of these would earn a compliment.

---

5 2 Kings 2 23-24

The guardian explained that poor work would have consequences. However, he made heroic attempts to help me avoid unfortunate outcomes. He would not directly assist me with my exercises, as he considered that cheating. Instead, he would read the syllabus and, two weeks in advance, would give me an overview of what I was going to learn. He had an unusual aptitude for explaining the context and making the topic seem interesting. This way I had a starting point when confronted by isosceles triangles, Charlemagne, and the geographic features of the Maghreb. If I confessed that I had struggled, he would spend Saturday afternoon helping me redo the assignment. He would then revise the mark when he received the original from the *curé*.

I was in the vet's room attempting to calculate the surface area of a twenty cm diameter tarte normande after Angélique and Marcel had each taken a slice of twenty-two and a half degrees.

"Do you mind if I interrupt you for a few minutes? This may seem a little strange, but it is important."

The guardian placed three little coins on the steel table.

"Do you know what these are?"

Seeing an unfamiliar script, I ventured:

"Are they drachma? Will I have to learn ancient Greek as well?"

"No, not unless you want to. But you are on the right track, though; these are Cyrillic letters. They are Russian kopecks. A delegate left them here when he was recalled to Moscow. Listen, you have a lot of work to do to catch up. Sometimes it may all seem overwhelming and unfair. That is normal. But if things genuinely seem too dismal for you, you must bring me one of these coins. You'll recognize that moment if it ever happens. I promise you I'll take you seriously. I may need a couple of days to make sure that I stand back and see things from a calm perspective. Don't waste them on anything trivial. They are for truly difficult moments. Do you understand?"

Before I could answer, he added:

"It's alright if you don't understand right now. Just make sure you remember this conversation."

I would only redeem one kopeck some years later, and in circumstances that neither of us could have then envisaged.

The guardian was placed in a quandary after Weygand ruled out attendance at school. I would continue with the *curé*, but I would require even greater support as I moved to a slightly more advanced course. I was to have a tutor for two to three hours a day in place of the guardian's coaching. I was unenthusiastic. I did not need anyone else to draw attention to my alleged sloth and ignorance. The guardian had mentioned the name Stéphane Fillion. I had met him once. In his late fifties and with a slightly sarcastic tone, he seemed an unlikely candidate.

"Hello, Jean-Marc, do you like mulberries?"

I looked at the young man who had just come into the vet's room. Dressed in a fashionable striped blazer, he was of athletic build and seemed lively and friendly. But not being sure who he was, I answered carefully:

"I can draw them. There were some trees in the college orchard. The monks must have planted them. But I never ate one. It was not our land."

"That's alright. Do you know Mme Montmagny? One day a year she opens her house for charity and serves the best mulberry ices in Europe. We can talk on the way."

"That is very kind. But the guardian told me I must wait for my new tutor, M Fillion."

"That's me."

I was unconvinced. There was an uncomfortable pause.

"Are you mixing me up with the old fellow with greasy hair and pince-nez? He may be on committees with your guardian. I don't really know him. He's probably very pleasant. We're not related. We just happen to have the same name."

I stood up to get ready. Stéphane came over to straighten my collar and advised me to fasten a button that I had missed. As I did this, he noticed my ink-stained hands:

"What type of pen are you using? The cheap ones from France all leak. Come here. Do you mind if I do it? This stuff can be hard to remove."

He held my hands under the tap and scrubbed vigorously with a nail brush and pumice.

"That's better. It's not your fault. Ink gets everywhere."

He shepherded me out into the sunshine.

I felt very small next to the confident and personable Stéphane. He was telling me a long and seemingly irrelevant story about his favourite uncle who used to install chocolate processing equipment. He had accompanied a shipment to Lourenço Marques in Mozambique. As he disembarked, he learned that his employer had gone bankrupt and could not pay his return passage. He headed to the Swiss mission. The representative and his wife were bedridden with malaria while their seven children ran riot. The resourceful uncle promptly set up a classroom. Within a few months he was operating a school for French-speaking expatriates or anyone who wished to learn the language.

The nephew missed his uncle and decorated his room with his postcards. He wrote and asked if he could join him in this land which seemed more interesting than Geneva in February. To humour the boy, the uncle set four conditions:

He must have his parents' permission regardless of his age.

He must learn fluent Portuguese.

The uncle would pay for his passage to Mozambique, but the boy must always have enough funds to return to Switzerland.

He must prove over four years that he is a good teacher at all secondary levels.

The determined Stéphane found a summer job at a Portuguese importer of textiles. He made friends, was introduced into the Portuguese community, and would soon correspond with his uncle in the language of the Lusiad. He also worked alongside his father to build up the necessary funds.

The guardian had shared the *curé*'s assessments with Stéphane, who in turn had mailed copies to Africa along with the outline of my entire secondary level syllabus. In addition to the regular Swiss certificate exams, I was to take tests set by the uncle. If I passed, Stéphane would have met the criteria for a good teacher. He refrained from adding that he might need to be a very good one given such an unpromising scholar. More immediately, I seemed to need some elementary advice:

"Do you want to stop and do up your left lace? It will come untied again if you don't make sure both sides are of equal length and pulled tight."

Stéphane was equally comfortable talking to dukes and carpenters. He met both through his father's business which involved the specialist restoration of ancient features in castles and cathedrals across Europe. He felt no need to prepare me before we entered the Montmagny residence. Our hostess was clearly at the summit of Genevan society. We were surrounded by pink Sèvres urns which eventually gave way to cabinets of Meissen milkmaids and shepherdesses. Smartly dressed ladies with furs, diamonds, and pearls filled the salons. The occasional ailing husband could be glimpsed perching on a Chippendale chair.

"Stéphane, I am thrilled to see you! I was hoping you would come. It is so good of you to support us every year. I still remember how well-behaved you were when your dear mother first brought you. I do so enjoy her contributions at committee meetings. Sometimes I think she is the only person in town who knows what is really going on. She does such inspiring work with those poor youths."

I was a few steps behind Stéphane, overwhelmed and acutely conscious that I was the worst-dressed guest in the mansion. To add to my embarrassment, my other lace was coming undone. Catching sight of me, Mme Montmagny lowered her voice slightly:

"You are so kind to bring him on an outing."

Stéphane explained lightly that he was simply my tutor. Mme Montmagny did not seem to find this entirely probable. Nonetheless, she extended an elegantly gloved hand. I responded, thankful that no ink remained on my fingers to sully the white kid leather.

"Jean-Marc, what a pleasure! We are always looking for young supporters. Would you boys like your mulberries in the summerhouse instead of with all of us old biddies? If I see anyone under ninety, I'll send them your way. I'll have the servants bring out good sized portions."

My year consisted of three terms of sixteen weeks. At Easter, the *curé*, who suffered from bursitis, would pause our instruction to take an extended trip to Lourdes, Lisieux, or Compostela from whence he would send warm letters of benediction. For twelve of the sixteen weeks, Stéphane would enthusiastically explain equations, warring kings, and Latin syntax, and answer my muddled questions with the patience of Job.

"No. The one with six wives was called Henry, but he died years before and had nothing to do with the War of the Three Henrys in France. Get out your squared paper, and I'll help you make a timeline to get it clearer."

But he would yield to stress as he awaited the test papers from the uncle.

"Didn't I tell you to revise those verbs last Wednesday? Didn't I? I'm not jeopardizing Africa and everything I'm working for because you are dead idle. I'm setting an extra test for tomorrow, and you had better get it right!"

I did not fully appreciate Stéphane's skill until, years later, I realized that five separate teachers were struggling to impart roughly the same syllabus to my eldest son. The guardian recognized Stéphane's talent and would invite him to dinner when early evening storms threatened to make the roads unsafe for his little motorcycle. I would listen uncomprehendingly as they discussed current topics:

"Did you see that Jean Baptiste Perrin won this year's Nobel prize in physics for the sedimentation equilibrium? I'm not sure that I understood the graphs in the paper."

My final sessions with Stéphane did not end on the right note. The exams had been in an unfamiliar format and much harder than either of us expected. We were both tense, exhausted, and irritable. I was growing up and, on one occasion, no longer unquestioningly respectful. Why did I have to start preparing for a retake, including on Saturdays, before it was confirmed I had failed?

It would be weeks before we received the results from Mozambique. We learned later that my papers were routed via Lisbon where a helpful censor expanded on my answers referencing Vasco da Gama and Prince Henry the Navigator.

The guardian made no comment as he handed me the postcard. On the side with the address, crosses in the pre-printed columns showed algebra and classical translation as Unsatisfactory. The Excellent and Very Good columns were untouched. Most of the entries reposed in the Adequate column with a couple under Good. The other side of the card, where one might normally expect to find a sepia image of the Beaux Arts railway station, constituted the certificate itself. An asterisk in indelible ink affirmed that I had scraped by, albeit at 'Pass—Inferior level'. My tutor had scored his first *baccalauréat* from the Independent Francophone School of Portuguese East Africa. The serial number 00001 suggested that this was the uncle's inaugural venture into formal accreditations.

Stéphane happened to mention his leaving date and train in a note to the guardian as they adjusted a minor discrepancy in the tuition invoices. At the station, family and friends surrounded him.

None of them knew me, and I stood discreetly by a pillar. I felt very guilty. I should never have answered back to an adult, particularly one who had helped me so much over the last years. Isolated from children of my own age, I could not gauge how abnormal this behaviour might be. Perhaps it was an early symptom of the problems foretold by Weygand. Stéphane saw me and had his brother bring me forward.

"Jean-Marc, I'm so glad you are here! I'll send you my address. Promise you'll write? Luc, show Jean-Marc where your workshop is. Look after my friend if he ever needs anything. I'm going to miss him. I don't think I could have survived being stuck in that vet's room with anyone else."

My preparatory sessions with Stéphane meant that I had a sporting chance of passing the increasingly rigorous assignments from the *cure*. The summary pages began to contain less red ink. As I neared the end of the syllabus and prepared to go to design school, I was surprised to receive an invitation to lunch. I accepted out of curiosity. It was too late for him to hurt me. Perhaps he wanted to apologize.

We had never met. Shamefully, I had pictured the *cure* in an unflattering caricature. He was doubtless old and flabby with a choleric red face which would crease as he found the exact phrase to embroil me in ever deeper trouble.

The restaurant happened to be full of middle-aged men waiting for spouses or business associates. The waiter did not recognize his name. I checked with a few gentlemen who seemed to match the profile. I eliminated a trim figure with a well wrapped package. He must surely be a father with his daughter's birthday present. He saw me but did not react. There was no one with clerical attire. I returned to the reception area.

The *cure* must have formed his own image of me as a big-boned oaf.

"Jean-Marc, I'm so sorry. You passed me, but I was anticipating someone taller. Entirely my fault. Very foolish of me."

"*Benedictus benedicat, per Jesum Christum Dominum nostrum.*"

Grace was said, and we could sample the pea soup *Saint-Germain*. The *curé* was a good conversationalist. He made me laugh as he recounted a picaresque excursion to the Sanctuary of Fatima with a parishioner who proved to be less rehabilitated than the prison chaplain had believed.

As the meal ended, he opened the package.

"Jean-Marc, I was left this by a congregant."

The extensively illustrated volume recounted a morality tale. A farmer of flax and rhubarb married a seamstress. They had a son who was slightly deaf. The father consulted a sorcerer who sold him a hearing trumpet. Unknown to the parents, this magical device would let the son hear not only what he was told but also the full story. The father had committed various sins of omission in describing his past. These were not particularly serious in themselves, but they eroded the son's trust. He became cold towards the father who fell on bad times as apothecaries made less use of rhubarb in their medicines. The final winter scene showed the son watching indifferently as the father was forced to auction his remaining coat to pay his debts.

The *curé* continued:

"I think you would probably come out well if anyone listened to you through the magic hearing trumpet. In any event, you would be a better custodian of the engravings. You don't know how much pleasure I derived from your illustrations. You are very talented."

I thanked the *curé* profusely. I would, however, fail the hearing trumpet test as a parent and all because of Weygand.

4.
The Industrial Chapel

A small sign, placed low on the wall in a grimy industrial area, carried the message 'Enter. All are welcome.' The rust and faded paint suggested that this was not a particularly pressing invitation. The guardian steered me through the entrance and down a long underground corridor. Locked doors led to Assembly, Industrial Valves, Military Timers, and Supervisors Only. We finally surfaced to find ourselves in a misty walled courtyard with a substantial chapel.

I had hoped to get a guitar as part of Weygand's recommendation that music should form part of my renovation. The guardian had dismissed this idea. Too many inappropriate compositions existed for that instrument.

"But don't worry. I just need to finalize the arrangements. I think I can get you access to something more uplifting. I'm not bringing you up to perform in shady bars across the border."

The chapel was surrounded by a factory which made timers and gauges. The business had been established originally by a Yorkshire magnate who planned to combine British engineering with Swiss horological expertise. The facility had a large English-speaking staff until the first world war. The chapel catered to their spiritual needs but had an ulterior purpose. Employees were encouraged to attend short French language services between shifts. A well-trained choir sang to the accompaniment of a magnificent Casavant organ from Quebec. The gentle harmonies of Purcell, Handel, and Tallis were to entice the local workers to the religion of the parent company in Sheffield.

The choir was now disbanded. The vicar had retired to the salubrious south coast of England. The assemblers had appreciated the anthems while politely declining to convert from their more austere practices. The organ stood unused except for a few lessons for employees' children. A frail, elderly director of music was in charge. He opened the chapel door and gestured for us to come in from the persistent drizzle.

The chapel was built in the Victorian gothic style, complete with replicas of sepulchres of ancient knights. The factory blocked most of the natural light. There was no heating. The few electric lights would dim to orange when current was diverted to certain manufacturing processes. The director led us to an organ loft positioned so that the player could see almost nothing of the nave. Our guide had a pleasant manner, and I paid close attention as he demonstrated the features of the instrument.

The guardian knew that my mother was musical and had taught me on the only organ on the island.

"Jean-Marc, can you play *Le Noel des petits oiseaux* for us?"

"I'm sorry. I don't know it. Is it a carol? Do you mind if I play *For unto us a child is born* or *Rejoice greatly, O daughter of Zion*?"

I could play competently within my narrow repertoire. The director would attempt to widen it. However, he was often ill, and I would be alone. I could feel a little uncomfortable in the gloomy surroundings of the chapel. On occasion the factory's primitive production lines would stop, freeing the employees to form an unscheduled audience. I would enjoy their company until the supervisor announced that manufacturing was about to resume.

The chapel and organ were listed as attractions in *The Organist's Guide to Christian Europe,* published in German and English. I had only the most rudimentary grasp of these languages. This was unfortunate. The visitors, who mostly communicated in polished French, made offers which I could not pursue:

"Sorry, we did not mean to startle you. Are you alright? We did enjoy that last piece! The toccata in D by Samuel Scheidt, am I correct? May we inspect your Casavant? It is wonderful to see such an instrument in Europe."

The speaker, a man in his late forties, examined the keys, stops, pipes, and pedals with infectious interest. He civilly asked my permission to play some Mozart. He would have been an excellent mentor, for his arrangements from *The Magic Flute* made my renderings seem colourless in comparison.

He continued.

"This is truly a strange setting. It reminds me of the prison chapel where I lead the Epiphany concerts. One of the inmates is a remarkable tenor. He's taller, but otherwise you are so alike that you could be his younger brother. He's well-read and very cooperative in rehearsals. He worked in the export department of a wine merchant where he switched labels on a good blended wine for an expensive one. The deception passed unnoticed for over a year. The growers ensured that he got a long sentence. He should have had such a different life. But I am sure that you can marshal greater moral resources. This is my wife, Lotte. I'm Heinrich de Ritter, head of the Berliner Terpsichorean Academy of Music. *Sprichst du Deutsch?* No? What a shame! I'd have submitted your name to our scholarship committee."

5.
The Last Recommendation

The last recommendation posed a problem for the guardian. Weygand's text strongly implied that he was referring to the type of discipline routinely administered in schools and institutions of the period. Although the guardian could be strict and was often perplexed by my behaviour, his native humanity held him back from unwarranted severity. He would have expected an occasional misadventure at school or with a tutor, but Weygand's prescription, while not unheard of at the time, was of a different order.

He decided to ask the advice of three qualified acquaintances. I was not told who these middle-aged men were, or why they were interviewing me, but to be truthful and unafraid.

At the first interview, a tall man with a heavy physique met me in the vet's room and gently asked me about my friends. I had none, but I told him about Paul. We were born two days apart and grew up almost as brothers. We learned to swim in a natural shallow seawater pool and had our adventures as we explored the island together. Paul was fair-haired and taller. He was certainly smarter, for I would often ask him to explain our lessons. Then he started to get a little breathless. At first, I would help carry his satchel to school. Within a year he would be too tired to continue in the afternoon, so I would escort him home at lunchtimes before running back to class. We had a last birthday when he rallied, and we swam a few strokes in the pool while our parents watched anxiously. He died shortly before the earthquake. I was too young to attend his funeral but, following the local custom, I gathered herbs from the monastery hill to accompany him. I had never spoken of this in Geneva, and suddenly self-conscious and tearful, felt myself turning red as I apologized:

"I am so sorry. I did not mean to..."

My interviewer was reassuring as he interrupted:

"Not at all, not at all. I think Paul must have been very lucky to have had you as his friend. Thank you for talking with me."

He put a comforting hand on my shoulder before saying that he would be in touch with the guardian.

The tall man was the Inspector of Jails and Prisons. The guardian knew him from a rehabilitation foundation. While modestly hesitating to disagree with Weygand, he dismissed the physician's suggestion. If I misbehaved, I should be treated like any other boy. But he saw no justification for imposing a severe regime. I was adapting to radically different circumstances, and it was natural that I might occasionally be a little difficult. I was, he believed, "fundamentally of sound character".

The second interviewer was only in Geneva for a few days and was obliged to fit me in relatively late in the evening. I was tired, for I had been up early to go swimming. I had worked hard on an assignment from the *curé* only to panic minutes after I had mailed it in case I had written Hannibal when I meant Hasdrubal. I then endured a particularly difficult session with Mme Vaillancourt whose voice grew louder and louder as she demonstrated a pronunciation which I disliked and could not satisfactorily reproduce.

I must have been close to falling asleep, for I was taken by surprise when an important-looking man strode into the room.

"*Qui ambulat in tenebris nescit quo vadat.* "[6]

I looked vacant.

"He who walks in darkness does not know where he is going. The illumination in the hall is wholly inadequate. I nearly tripped on the Tabriz rug."

Rising to my feet, I unconsciously greeted him in my natural Amphoran accent. He winced at my Franco-Italian vowels.

---

6 John 12:35

Attempting to remedy the situation, I switched to the enunciation of my elocution lessons. He must have thought that I was mocking his polished diction, for he glowered venomously.

He peppered me with questions about my education and was appalled that I could not discuss the origins of the Helvetic Confederation or correctly name the palace of Louis XIV.

"Are you ignorant or being deliberately obtuse? Let's try Mediterranean history then. Please tell me the significance of the battle of Lepanto."[7]

I attempted to explain that I was from Amphora, where we had an entirely different syllabus. But this overbearing adult would not accept that subjects other than literature, history, and the classics might be worthy of study. I noted that Amphorans could not only identify the plants and insects, but we could draw them exactly and distinguish pest from pollinator. He interjected:

"Yes, you told me already about the nature rambles. But I am interested in real education. Can you give me the story line of a single work by Voltaire or Molière?"

He had unintentionally insulted the memory of Father who sometimes taught agricultural botany to the older classes. Speaking quietly as I tried to control my anger, I replied that I was familiar with Voltaire's *Candide* and its conclusion, "*Faut cultiver notre jardin*". Then, with unwonted insolence, I added:

"When our house was destroyed by the earthquake and Mother was ill, it was more useful to know for real how to manage the hives and the orchard."

He shrugged and left.

The guardian read me extracts of the report. Written in elegant prose, they depicted me as rude, ignorant, idle, and in urgent need of improvement. As I had guessed, its author was the principal of one of Switzerland's most exclusive academies. His signature was accompanied by qualifications from the Sorbonne, Prague, and Zurich.

---

7 Lepanto, 1571, Catholic vessels defeated the Ottoman ships

The final interviewer greeted me amiably and confessed that he had never seen the Mediterranean.

"You must tell me all about Amphora. It is so good to meet someone from a different background. My wife and I always attend the talks by explorers at the Geography Institute. You should go. The next one is about finding rare rhododendrons in the Himalayas. They have a very fine magic lantern."

I could not compete with this apparatus, but he nodded encouragingly as I embarked on the history and geography of the island. The great powers at the Congress of Koblenz had declared the Island of Amphora "not a state, but a rock without deep anchorage or significance". But therein lay the secret of the island's independence. Remote and difficult to access by larger ships, it was largely left to its own devices. It was settled by monks who devoted themselves to prayer and beekeeping. They sent the amphora of honey as tribute to rulers on the mainland who otherwise left them alone. The monastery incorporated a form of agricultural college for the lesser nobility of France and Italy. They would study Virgil's *Georgics* and learn how to develop their fields and fruit trees. The last monk died in the late nineteenth century, and a wealthy Franco-Dutch family took over the college. They expanded the arable area with dikes, and improved irrigation. The island was vulnerable to droughts, and the roofs on the houses were all designed to capture water in large barrels. Our long-term sustainability was always in doubt. Parents would fret that so many young men left for the mainland where they could have motorized bicycles and meet girls. But in better years, we had some of Europe's finest fruit, honey, nuts, and fish. We spoke French but borrowed heavily from Italian. The college had a concert level organ, which Mother was encouraged to play after the previous organist passed. Father was an assistant to the Franco-Dutch family, but he also had teaching responsibilities and managed our small orchards.

In 1923 the earthquake struck. The dikes gave way, and a major spring now rose uselessly under the sea. Our house and much of the college collapsed. We never found Father. Mother contracted tuberculosis and did not survive six months. The island's independence counted against us, for not a single naval vessel steamed to our rescue. After almost a year the only organization to take action was a charitable committee in Geneva. Its initiative nearly failed when two key members fell sick the day before they were meant to leave. Although not his normal role, the guardian volunteered to take one of the places.

My interviewer listened courteously to my lengthy monologue and asked a few questions after I finished:

"Let me see if I have this right. You were eleven at the time of the earthquake and just turning thirteen as you arrived in Switzerland?"

"Aside from the TB, have you or anyone in your family had any significant physical or mental illness?"

I shook my head.

"Very good. Stay where you are. I just need to examine your hands and cranial contours."

I am not sure what he imagined he felt under my hair, but he muttered to himself:

"Very subtle, but it is definitely there. Good thing Weygand found it."

The doctor served with the guardian on a committee for the assistance of undernourished juveniles and was a noted specialist on adolescence. His assessment directly contradicted the principal's, for he found me to be polite, knowledgeable, and friendly. However, he was clearly in awe of Weygand and stated that the physical indicators supported the diagnosis and consequently the prescribed treatment.

The guardian mailed gracious letters to each interviewer thanking them for their time. He commented to me in an unguarded aside that he might as well have consulted the oracle at Delphi. He deliberated for a few days as he attempted to reconcile the varying opinions. Finally, he called me into his study.

He had to accord most weight to the opinions of the principal and the doctor as they had the better professional qualifications. However, the good character reviews of the doctor and inspector of prisons would be allowed to count heavily in my favour. I needed to understand that there were forms of discipline which were very effective but purely mental. Every week he would assign me a text to be learned and recited back to him exactly. This would take place in the vet's room. If I performed as required, there would be no need for more severe consequences. However, I should consider myself on probation. I could be put on the full program as recommended by Weygand at any time if my behaviour were unsatisfactory.

As a young man, the guardian had been an accomplished amateur actor. In particular, he had played the title role in Corneille's *Horace* and could still, nearly twenty years later, deliver his lines with pleasure and without hesitation. In the first week of my new regime, I was confronted with an interminable text, a translated extract of Cicero's *De Senectute*, the treatise on old age. He heard me gasp when I saw how long it was:

"Don't be silly. Just break it down one section at a time, and you'll be fine. But first study it so you find the meaning and the interest. Then it will be easy. I have selected passages that have been enjoyed for two thousand years. I was not surprised that Dr Weygand included this one in his appendix."

Despite genuine efforts, and a frustrated rage in which I threw the book across the room, I could not master more than the first few lines, which I recited slowly and painfully.

"*O admirable service of old age, if indeed it takes from us what in youth is more harmful than all things else! For I would have you hear, young men, an ancient discourse of Archytas of Tarentum, a man of great distinction and celebrity... "Man has received from nature," said he, "no more fatal scourge than bodily pleasure, by which the passions in their eagerness for gratification are made reckless and are released from all restraint. Hence spring treasons against one's country; hence, overthrows of states; hence, clandestine plots with enemies. In fine, there is no form of guilt, no atrocity of evil, to the accomplishment of which men are not driven by lust for pleasure. Debaucheries, adulteries, and all enormities of that kind have no other inducing cause than*[8]... I'm sorry. I'm really trying, but it's too hard."

Thankfully, it was evident that my failure was due to incompetence rather than poor attitude. I was let off with a stern warning. The guardian then switched to giving me Latin phrases and the maxims of La Rochefoucauld. These were much easier. I would insert them, sometimes appropriately, into compositions for the *curé*.

Thus, the guardian and I came to a *modus vivendi* which endured for some months until I ruined everything on the day of the raincoat incident.

The guardian had protected me as far as he could by stretching the definition of discipline into something which Weygand had certainly not intended. I repaid this by blundering into a situation where I would undermine his resolve with persistent half-truths and evasive answers. The raincoat incident would undoubtedly have been disagreeable, but it would never have convinced the guardian to change his strategy if the ground had not been prepared.

The improbable source of my temptation was a stern baker in her mid-seventies.

I was on my escape route from Mme Vaillancourt's elocution lessons. The Peugeots and Alfa Romeos, the bankers in business dress, and the department stores with elevators were all different from Amphora and absorbing. But today the only sound seemed

---

8 From Andrew Peabody's translation of 1884

to come from the penetrating voices of a couple who followed a few paces behind me.

"Could you do laundry for Dorothée next week? Her wrist looked really swollen."

"Are you joking? She has a better washtub than we do, and a wringer. It's not my fault if she uses them for crushing elderflowers and nasturtium seeds."

I was uninterested in Dorothée's unorthodox domestic pursuits. The accents grated on me. The man spoke in affected Parisian tones as if attempting to ingratiate himself with Mme Vaillancourt. His lady friend had a whining delivery.

Although I couldn't help noting their manner of speech, I had had enough of elocution and voices for one day. I just wished to be alone in a world without words. I wanted to stand by the beach, as I did in Amphora when I needed time to think about Paul and if he would ever get better. I felt tired though I was not ill. Too much had changed in my life in scarcely three months. I could not absorb it all.

I slowed down so that the couple would pass me. They wore unusual sandals, suede with soles which made an irritating double clack as they passed, first a wooden sound, then a metallic chink.

It would have been around four in the afternoon when I caught the familiar aroma of herbed bread. Bakeries would not normally fire the ovens this late in the day. But Amphoran rolls would be baked now and kept warm in crocks to enhance the flavour before the evening meal. The loaves in the window were all of the same shape with one end raised in a peak to represent monastery hill. The wicker baskets had the little blue cross symbol of Amphora. A faded sign announced that this was the *Boulangerie Beaulac.*

As I looked in the window, I reflected that no one on the island at that time would be looking at such a display. The Amphoran harvest had failed. Any bread there would be the 'Starvation Loaf', a grey lump from flour designed to minimize milling waste. The guardian kept a well-stocked larder, carefully introducing me to new tastes, like *pâté* with Armagnac and blue cheeses. His bread, however, was plentiful but bland. It lacked the character of Amphoran loaves where one broke the crust and the aroma of sage, or thyme, or a combination of herbs and spices would spread across the table. The bread, carefully flavoured to complement the main course, was always served warm with Amphoran butter with its hint of sea salt. Mother's specialty was a dill loaf sprinkled with crushed almonds that she would serve with fish.

The guardian was a principled man who would get up at four-thirty am to prepare his material so that he could coach me accurately and with conviction when he returned from work. And, while I had never been really deprived, I had been through enough poor seasons back home to be truly grateful that he ensured that my plate was full. When he first took me in, I had offered to work for him and expected to eat in the kitchen, but he insisted that I dine with him and his visitors as though I were family. I did not want to disappoint him. This sentiment, however, conflicted with other feelings that were less admirable.

I don't recall if the term 'total immersion' existed in those days. The guardian, however, had grasped the concept. He had a concern, which I thought excessive, that I would be teased and hurt if I did not fully conform to Genevan habits. Now, I give him more credit, for I will never forget the incident many years later when I found my Lebanese neighbour's son bullied and crying behind our fence. In any event, the guardian explained his position to me:

"You must understand that this is for your own benefit. I would never forgive myself if I saw you surrounded by mocking youths or sneering colleagues. You must forget your Amphoran accent, vocabulary, and habits for at least two years while you throw yourself into Swiss life. By then, you will be as Genevan as anyone can be. I know this is hard, but I telephoned Prof Ulrich of the Helvetic Otorhinolingual Institute who speaks six languages and goes to conferences in Seville. He insists it is the only way. Promise you can do this for me?"

I had promised. But, like an addict, I was drawn powerfully towards the aroma of bread and the memory of home. I feared Mme Beaulac would surely reintroduce me to the forbidden accent, vocabulary, and habits. The mental struggle was brief and painful. Temptation emerged victorious.

I entered the austerely decorated establishment. I had no money and no intention of buying anything. This realization dawned on me after I had gained Mme Beaulac's attention. She held up her hand:

"Young man, I'll be right with you. I just need to check this order for the Congress of Reformed Theologians. Ginette is out delivering our new spiced greengage tarts. Choose what you need, or are you picking up an order?"

"I'm so sorry. I just wanted to see someone else from Amphora. I don't want anything. I'll get out of your way."

She responded that I was not to go anywhere. I stood uncomfortably just inside the entrance while two or three other customers were served. A calendar with small engravings of milling machines was on the wall behind the counter. A clean but much scratched steel counter ran the length of the galley-shaped premises. Two worn armchairs looked as if they had accommodated buyers since the last century: Mme Beaulac's customers did not just order a half dozen croissants, they waited patiently for a consultation on which flavours of bread might best accompany their menus. Except in the window, there was no display. Mme Beaulac supplied the finest hotels and restaurants who bought from her published bill of wares. Competent retail customers were tolerated.

Mme Beaulac wore black under a white baker's apron. Her lace bonnet was black and old-fashioned as though she might be a widow. Her face was deceptive. It was without remarkable features, but it somehow transmitted a peculiar force. If her look indicated that a customer should sit, he sat. If she gave a sign of approval, the customer would beam like a praised school child.

Ginette returned, dressed in a pillbox hat and a smart jacket, as though signalling that her pink and red cake boxes could bypass the tradesman's entrance. Mme Beaulac examined me closely:

"Why are you here? Did Massimo send you? Tell me the truth."

My explanation took in the earthquake, the guardian, elocution lessons, and my new waxed jacket in a single sentence. Its incoherence and obvious lack of preparation seemed to reassure her that I had no malign intent.

"Comb your hair and straighten your collar. You have to look at least vaguely respectable to come to this side of the counter. I've just got time for a cup of herbal tea. Where did you live?"

Mme Beaulac had a remarkable memory:

"*Casa des Huîtres*, that was opposite the field where the Dutch farmer planted those absurd willow trees? They just dry out the soil. I used to pass the house every day. I did not know the family, but I saw the husband training espalier pear trees on the garden wall. There was a sweet little girl who would wave at me. Would she have been your mother?"

We derived most pleasure from reminiscing about terms which would be obscure to anyone who had not visited the island.

"This is the recipe I used to confuse the choco-gendarmes", for example, referred to an ill-fated attempt by the Dutch family to tax imported cocoa. The residents responded by colouring all their baking deep brown to perplex the inspectors. A younger Mme Beaulac seemed to have been the originator of many anecdotes which had been passed down as folklore. They typically ended on the lines such as this:

"So, we let the inspectors find the tins in the barn. When they opened them, they were full of old fish heads."

These stories would terminate abruptly if anyone else came in earshot. Mme Beaulac had an image to maintain.

Otherwise, our conversations were mundane but important to me. I would tell her that my assignments from *the* curé were impossible. She would respond that I should stop complaining. I was lucky to have an education that would lead to a polished desk, maybe even one with a leather blotter and writing set. Would I like to sample a sage duck *vol-au-vent?*

Guilt at breaking my promise to the guardian turned insidiously into pride in my subterfuge. My time with Mme Beaulac gave me my dose of Amphora, and it became hard to contemplate breaking the habit.

So long as I had my lessons with Mme Vaillancourt, I could easily spend ten or fifteen minutes in the bakery without anyone noticing. But then my accent improved, I suspect more from conversing with the guardian than from my pronunciation training. One evening he informed me:

"I won't renew your elocution course. The sessions are expensive. I don't think anyone reasonable would bully you now just because of your accent. Your language is not too bad, though it would do you no harm to think through your subordinate clauses."

"I won't be able to see Mme Vaillancourt anymore? I was getting better. This week she let me sit on the sofa next to her bichon. She has a photo of Maurice Chevalier[9] in the same spot with the bichon's grandmother."

"You whined about every lesson. I was very disappointed in your attitude. I don't understand you. You finish on Friday."

With hindsight, I clearly mishandled the situation. The guardian was not unreasonable. Once my accent improved, he would almost certainly have granted permission for me to pay an occasional visit to the bakery. Notwithstanding his important excursions to Seville, the obscure Prof Ulrich's opinion was not a

---

9 Maurice Chevalier 1888-1972, popular singer

semi-divine pronouncement like Weygand's. The guardian could have overwritten it. Mme Beaulac had been in Geneva so long that her voice, while distinctive, was unlikely to undo my progress. But I was determined to keep my visits a secret. This was difficult as I had no reason to be in that slightly dull part of town once my lessons ended.

The guardian did not understand how difficult it was for me to abandon what I knew in order to conform to his standards. His success came from an uncanny ability to have his committees perform their appointed missions. He was puzzled that I had trouble enacting changes that were surely in my best interest.

His table was set differently from my parents', and I was firmly admonished when I placed the forks and spoons in the way I had been taught. My handwriting, while neat, was not in the right style. I used pencil when ink was appropriate. I did not follow the proper conventions for buttoning the top of my shirts or lacing boots.

"I don't see why you are making such a fuss. I am not asking you to do anything difficult. It is for your own good or you will be picked on for doing things differently. Now go and change. Nobody wears that type of sweater with shorts."

My clandestine moments with Mme Beaulac became a respite from the guardian's well-intentioned but suffocating guidance. I obstinately refused to give him any chance to interfere.

The guardian began to notice discrepancies in my accounts of how I had spent the day. I tried to avoid outright lies, but my narrative was often misleading. I was not helped by our many retired neighbours who would mention to the guardian when they had seen me and from which direction I was coming.

"That does not make sense. If you finished the organ practice at four pm why did M Lebel see you coming down rue Rimouski at five-thirty when he gave you the artichokes from his garden?

Were you buying cigarettes? I will need to be much stricter if I can't trust you."

I had not been smoking but, as everyone else did waiting for the trams, I may have smelled of tobacco. In those days it was almost expected that boys would experiment with cigarettes. I left the impression that this was my venial sin. A slightly disreputable shop near the bakery sold single Gauloise cigarettes, and no one cared about my age. With suspect ethical logic, this allowed me to admit reluctantly, but truthfully, that I had smoked: the guardian would mark that as my error. He would ask no more dangerous questions about where I had been, and I did not have a lie on my conscience. Happily, I had no difficulty in giving up the habit a few years later.

The smoking cover story meant that I was cast awkwardly in the role of a mischievous rascal. This was not to my advantage when other failings came to light.

6.
The Raincoat Incident

The guardian could not have been clearer:

"You won't forget, will you? It is very important. And you must come prepared for heavy rain. Apparently, the storm may come our way. It caused massive flooding in Milan. And don't be late."

We were to meet in the bookshop and buy the exact editions required for the next part of the *curé*'s syllabus. He would instruct me, for example, to attempt a précis of lines three to twenty-five on page thirty-two. The guardian had carefully listed out the books on a blue sheet of paper that I was to bring. Immediately after our appointment he had a meeting with a family charity which might release several hundred thousand francs for the relief of injured workers. He had a week like this maybe once a quarter when he would need me to manage myself properly for a few days.

The bookshop was, in fact, a large publishing enterprise occupying an entire city block and, being built on a hillside, had a surprising number of floors descending at the back. The levels on the main street housed the general bookshop with several specialist departments for the nearby theological and medical institutes. There was a section dealing in high value manuscripts and first editions, and a general second-hand bookstore. There was an educational supply room for items such as exercise books and geometry sets. I was also to discover that some strange societies were housed in the building. The lower levels contained presses known for the quality of their engraved documents and illustrations. Authors and professors would spend hours with the proprietor choosing their fonts, inks, papers, and binding. The guardian was a frequent customer as his foundations published papers on areas of concern. He knew the proprietor very well and collaborated with him on the Suisse Romande literacy movement.

The building had a confusing layout. One would be in a broad, well-lit aisle surrounded by luxury editions. A few steps away, there would be a gloomy, narrow passage blocked by a theologian who suffered from a back injury. He would ask for help to access volumes on the lower shelves and would press one to accept pungent throat lozenges in gratitude. On one visit an elderly political theorist mistook me for a valet. He ordered me to pack up the complete plays of Racine and carry them to his home.

"I'm very sorry, sir. I don't work here. I'm looking for a book for my correspondence course."

His voice carried.

"Then your reward will be celestial for your kindness to a stranger. Make sure they are in alphabetical order."

He had been a customer for over sixty years before his faculties began to fail. An assistant with a heavy ledger who had been taking inventory gently guided him to the periodicals section while another reassured me that he intended no harm. She would give me a free magazine comparing French and Italian motorcars.

I checked the weather from the upper windows before I left for the bookstore. There was no sign of a cloud, and it was hot. I did not want to be carrying a raincoat. I was sure I would not be gone too long and could return before any potential rain. I stuffed a blue paper into my back pocket and set off. In the tram I reflected that the guardian was not particularly impressed with my performance. I was not yet inured to the *curé*'s biting comments. These had disheartened me, and my results were deteriorating. The guardian had, understandably, snapped at me: having ignored his advice to put my ink bottle in a safer place, I knocked the full contents onto the floor. Once he was less busy, maybe I could do one of those drawings that he liked so much. Perhaps the Parthian horsemen or William Tell would be good subjects. Thus preoccupied, I did not notice the sky turning a sinister greenish black as a storm approached.

I was to meet the guardian in the educational supplies section as I needed a particular type of quadrille paper for geometry and algebra. It was hard to find what one required as products seemed to be almost randomly held behind the counter rather than on open shelves. The assistants were friendly in the other sections, but here enquiries were liable to be met with a response on the lines of:

"You can't just ask for an eraser! What make and hardness do you need? Why don't you come back tomorrow with a written specification from an adult?"

I avoided contact with M Cartier on the main counter. He always wore a tight waistcoat which made him look even thinner and would consult his fob watch as though impatient to undertake a more important task. He seemed to relish challenging me.

"Are you sure you picked the right exercise book? Normally we sell these ones to older students. The ones over there have multiplication tables on the back cover. They would be more at your level."

Mme Hortense did not work every day, but she was much more agreeable. She said my deep brown eyes reminded her of a violinist she had once known. She would adjust her half-moon glasses as she wondered if I were familiar with the Bach partitas which had moved her as a younger woman.

I arrived exactly on time and greeted the guardian with the fact that I was punctual. He was not pleased and took me to the window:

"Where is your raincoat? Don't you see the storm? You can't go home as you are. You are a nuisance. Don't you understand how much is riding on my meeting tonight? Can't you do anything right? Give me the book list."

I pulled out the blue paper. It was the correct colour but the wrong list. Instead of textbooks it enumerated the garments which I needed to replace those which I had outgrown.

The dam broke. He did not raise his voice, but it would have been obvious to any passerby, including M Cartier and the proprietor, that he was furious. I was ungrateful, self-centred, thoughtless, disobedient, and lazy. He had been very patient with me. I had abused his trust. He barked at me to find the quadrille paper if I were capable of doing so.

I did not hurry back and saw that he was in conversation with the proprietor. The latter pressed a bell, and soon an individual in his mid-twenties joined them only to cross the room and return with a rod from a display with a range of instruments of instruction. To my relief he put it back and came a few minutes later with a pamphlet. Summoning up my courage, I slowly approached the group.

They were studying the cover. The proprietor was in mid-conversation:

"Isn't it fine work? It was really just a trial for young Étienne, our new engraver. We won't get too many orders for the pamphlet itself, but I showed it to some bankers. They admired the style, and I am very hopeful that we will print their illustrated cheques in the future. Étienne manages to get so much detail into a small space that he could design postage stamps."

The engraving was indeed impressive. To the left, two superbly surly youths represented Indolence and Miscreance. On the right-hand side, well-groomed figures with self-congratulatory smiles shook hands as Obedience and Diligence. In the middle of the design was an open book as an unsubtle hint that appropriate literature could achieve the inspiring transformation from one side to the other. Nonetheless, I thought I detected a sly suggestion that the designer did not take this proposition too seriously. Regardless, engraving was a skill that I would like to learn. I would be interested to meet this Étienne. I was less taken with the pamphlet's title: *The Society for the Amelioration of Youth through Literature: A Compelling Manifesto.*

The guardian needed to leave for his meeting. He briefly introduced me to Laurent, who turned out to be the proprietor's nephew. He had been a classics teacher at the Collège de Genève until the month before but had been asked to do his part in the family business. He projected the image of an efficient young manager, tidy and ready to assist any customer. It was hard to determine what lay behind his official mask and whether a warmer character would emerge in private life.

As the guardian left, he added:

"Listen. You must stay here with Laurent. He has very kindly agreed to take you home later as he needs to deliver confidential exam papers to a professor in our street. You must give him your book list, and he will have it filled and delivered. Do you see how much extra work you have caused? I don't have time to explain, but he'll deal with you and lay out your new arrangements. We'll talk in the morning."

Laurent led me through a door and down a level. There were long ramps rather than stairs so that supply carts could move between floors. I saw an entry marked 'Étienne' and asked if I might meet him. I missed my drawing classes from Amphora. In Geneva, I had found no one with whom I could discuss my drawing of an earwig with its pincers on the guardian's buddleia. Étienne's studio had frosted glass in the door, like detective agencies in the American films, and internal windows displaying the crests of the different cantons. A small 'E' at the lower right suggested that this was his own work. I liked Étienne instantly. He was slightly younger than Laurent with a studious air which quickly gave way to a ready smile. With mildly tousled hair and less formal than his colleague, he seemed more approachable. He enthusiastically showed me his current projects.

"I've been very lucky this month. Sometimes I have boring assignments, like illustrating a guide to mortgage calculations. This one is for a strange work, a story about confused woodland birds banding together to protect their nests from predators. It is great for me. I had fun drawing this hawk in a sinister dark oak with gnarled branches. Do you like it, or is it overdone? I had a full moon in my first sketch, but I think the crescent is more effective. Which do you think is better?"

Laurent watched a little impatiently and left to check on an order saying that I must be ready in fifteen minutes. By the time he returned I had promised to show Étienne, who was also working on an outline for the Suisse Roma tanneries, a drawing I had made of a Roman soldier with shield and sandals.

We descended more ramps. On some levels there was a throbbing vibration from the presses and the smell of oil and ink. The walls were an industrial grey with a lime green stripe which must have added some cheer when fresh. Now dirty and chipped, it achieved the opposite effect. We left the bottom ramp to the accompaniment of sinister mechanical and roaring noises from the building's furnaces and pumps. Laurent showed me into a basement room with a pressed earth floor:

"Be very careful not to damage the soil. Do you see those red chips? They are from Roman bricks. They date from around fifty BC when this may have been a guardhouse. Anyway, sit down. I hear that you are in deep trouble."

The windowless room had grimy white walls decorated only with a small display of artifacts, presumably from an earlier excavation of the floor. The collection consisted of a coin corroded to the point of illegibility, a broken iron nail, half a brick, and a brass piece labelled as a 'man's buckle or wealthy matron's head ornament'. There were two uncomfortable wooden chairs, a solid writing desk with burn marks that seemed to date from the days of candlelight, and a bookshelf. The latter held volumes with unrelentingly tedious titles, such as *The Mental Adventure of Classical Philology.*

I was a little afraid of Laurent as a former teacher. I understood that schoolmasters in Geneva could be strict. He seemed business-like and was not returning my glances. He continued:

"We'll come to what happens to you today. But before then, I need you to understand the plan going forward. Your doctor recommended substantial discipline, and apparently you have proved that you need it."

He paused to study my reaction.

I wanted to say how I hated Weygand and that stupid, interfering dinner guest. This was all their fault. Before they got involved, I could always work things out with the guardian. He would growl, but his anger would soon subside. It seemed wiser to stay silent.

Laurent continued.

"There is a new educational theory, Intensive Improvement by Literature. You'll learn all about it in the coming weeks. Essentially, it says that everything a youth needs to know in order to be a worthy citizen already exists in a printed text. The challenge is to translate the message and transfer it into his brain while it is still forming. The concept is promoted by the Society for Amelioration, the ones with the pamphlet. The proprietor lets them use this room while they get funding for other premises. They like the atmosphere here which they describe as spartan and authentic. Following their program will count as approved discipline. But don't think it is a soft option."

He stopped again to see if I had any comments. I stayed mute.

"We don't know how big a movement this will be. Think of all the printing if just ten percent of parents use the program. I've been made a business partner from our side. I'll have sessions with you twice a week. I need to be fully familiar with the material for when it gets adopted across Europe. I won't stand for any nonsense from you. But maybe it won't be too bad. It will be an exciting project if you approach it in the right spirit. You've been very quiet. Any questions?"

I had no intelligent queries on how the program might work or how I should prepare. I enquired:

"If I try hard, will you look after me?"

I had stumbled on a satisfactory response. His face softened.

"Yes, I will. But you must take this seriously, or you will be punished."

It turned out that Laurent, although he could make it very clear that I was taxing the limits of his patience, would demonstrate commendable restraint. I was to be safer with him than I would have been in most schools of the period. However, this realization lay in the future, and I was afraid.

Silent, I followed Laurent up the ramps until he deposited me in a room full of books from an estate:

"Look through the piles on the left for first editions or anything special like a signed copy. You don't have to, you understand? But it is better than feeling sorry for yourself. It will be about an hour before I can lock up the offices."

My mind focused angrily on Weygand. Why did everyone listen to him, just because he had sprayed a few mosquitos in some territory that no one could find on the map? Why had the interfering guest picked on me? There had been a fair-haired boy of roughly my age at the dinner. He had a silk shirt and had not left his mother's side for a minute. Why was he not referred to Weygand too?

Ashamed of my snide thoughts about Silk Shirt, I managed to calm down a little and reviewed my surroundings. In other circumstances, I might have been intrigued by the bookcases with their leaded glass and rare volumes. There was a large, ornate parchment map of the Mediterranean world from about the fifteenth century. It did not show Amphora. I refused to inspect the rest of it.

Eventually, I found a fine leather-bound copy of Ferdinand Buisson's *Sébastien Castellion*[10]. I knew nothing of Genevan history but was reassured that someone had protested burning at the stake. Perhaps other practices would change in the coming centuries. This banal train of thought was cut short when an agitated figure burst into the room and shouted:

"The storm, it's flooding the storage in the old stables. Come and move boxes. Now!"

The rain was still falling, and reddish-brown water covered the walkway between the stables and the dock. I had light shoes which squelched, and the back of my shirt was soaked. The heavy boxes contained reams of bond paper and lacquered Italian fountain pens. I had managed to carry almost all of them to safety when I heard Laurent:

"They just cleared the drain on the road. The water should start to go down now. Has anyone seen a little dark-haired chap?"

I could not catch the reply, but Laurent continued:

"Yves, we're not meant to use the customers as forced labour."

I saw Laurent as he rounded the corner by the stables and looked in.

"Jean-Marc, did you clear all that yourself? Really? You did a magnificent job. I'm proud of you. I'm so sorry. Étienne is still here, as his tram route has lost power. Ask him to show you where we keep the lemon biscuits."

As he had promised the guardian, Laurent, joined by Étienne, took me home in the company van. This was an elegant vehicle with a polished brass grill and gold and black livery on the side. There were few motors in Amphora, and the guardian did not drive. This was only the seventh vehicle that I had ever been in. Mysterious levers and switches protruded from the dashboard.

---

10 Buisson won the 1927 Nobel peace prize. His biography of Castellio deals with the resistance to Protestant religious intolerance.

"Alright, Jean-Marc, listen to the engine. Very slowly and carefully push the white rod on the left until it runs smoothly. That's the choke. You are adjusting the mixture of fuel and air as the motor warms up."

The power had failed in much of the city. We delivered the exam papers to a bearded professor of mathematics who double checked the complex problems slowly by candlelight. There was no electricity at the guardian's house.

"We can't abandon you alone here in the dark. We'll wait with you until the guardian gets back."

"That is kind, but I'm used to paraffin lamps from Amphora. I don't need electricity. I'll be fine."

"No. We feel responsible for you. It would not be right for us to leave."

I lit the lamp from the guardian's front porch and found the correct blue paper with the book list. I handed Étienne my picture of the Roman soldier. I was unsure what I was supposed to do with my chaperones. They installed themselves in the kitchen and attempted conversation.

"This is an interesting booklist. Jean-Marc, have you decided what you want to be when you are older?"

I really wanted to be an orchard keeper but feared that this might not have been considered an appropriately ambitious response. I murmured something about wanting to work with aeroplanes.

I offered to make tea. The kettle warmed even more slowly than usual on the coke range. A stoker, who attended to all the boilers and ranges on the street, would remove the ashes and replenish it very early in the morning. I would sometimes hear his horses as they pulled the cart with the coke and ashbin. But at this time of night, the plates emitted little heat.

"Jean-Marc, are you sure you did not put in too much water? Does it normally take this long to boil?"

I finally succeeded as a host. Laurent, sitting upright, was still as formally dressed as if he were in the store. Étienne had taken off his jacket, rolled up his sleeves, and was languidly inspecting the ornate tongs that we used with the sugar cubes:

"Jean-Marc, I think this depicts a canoe on the Demerara River. Come and look."

They were on their second cups when a taxi pulled up. Laurent briefly updated the guardian, finishing with:

"He put in a Herculean effort clearing that inventory from the stable. He has inner strength. I'm sure we can work well together."

At last, they left, and I could retreat upstairs alone.

7.
Amelioration through Literature

I had once advanced an idea to build a hive on a flat section of a roof immediately outside my bedroom window. I could save the guardian his modest expenditure on honey while ensuring that the garden was properly pollinated. Horrified at the prospect of swarms penetrating the apertures of his house, the guardian had chosen his words less carefully than usual.

"The problem with ideas, particularly well-intentioned ones, is that they are so frequently wrong."

The new arrangements with Laurent and the Society made perfect sense to the guardian. The benefits would come from modern and appropriate methods. The Society for the Amelioration of Youth through Literature seemed an eminently fitting vehicle.

Many years later, I was helping my youngest daughter with her course work when I came across a passage:

In Geneva the zeitgeist of the 1920s favoured initiatives which would now seem quixotic. Members of the League of Nations tried repeatedly to establish Esperanto as an official language. They came close to succeeding, only to be blocked by French resistance.[11] A few streets away, the Society for the Amelioration of Youth through Literature was formed.

The Society's Compelling Manifesto optimistically sought to improve the lot of youth by packaging the world's accumulated wisdom in one Master Volume. The new generation would avoid the mistakes that led to full prisons, degradation, Solferino,[12] and the Great War. They would become obedient and diligent citizens. Indolence and

---

11 There was a proposal to teach Esperanto in schools in the League's member states. France exercised its veto.

12 Henri Dunant's revulsion over the suffering at the battle of Solferino in 1859 contributed to the foundation of the Red Cross.

miscreance would be the failings of the past. The passages in the Master Volume were all instructive, with questions and exercises designed to reinforce understanding. With proper sponsorship, members believed, the program could exceed even the Red Cross in its contribution to peace and tolerance.

The members of the Society had an almost fanatical belief in the power of their texts. They could not comprehend that an adolescent might not be inspired to action by their favourite extracts from Socrates or Milton. They could not picture the bored teenagers drearily rote learning a passage and then floundering through questions. Utopia was not attained. And yet, to their subsequent embarrassment, many well-known thinkers subscribed to the Society's methods and publicly anticipated a renaissance of the human character.

The guardian and I did not dwell on the raincoat incident. I vented my feelings in an unpleasant adolescent drawing of an avenging angel using a heavy club to drive Weygand and the interfering guest over a cliff. But then it was time to move forward. The Society's aims were the subject of glowing editorials. Perhaps I had a future as part of this exciting new movement.

The global president of the Society for Amelioration, Mme Therrien, was delighted that Laurent would be working with me on my program. He would surely soon see the benefits, and the printing presses in the bookstore would become the point from which the Society's message might be propagated to all Europe, maybe even America. Mme Therrien was of Franco-British descent. As a goddaughter of the Bishop of Bath and Wells, she was noted for her charitable work with inebriate spinsters. She had married a Swiss philosopher and now sought new methods to divert weaker brethren from their ill-chosen paths. She was in her early fifties, tall, and of striking appearance accentuated by silver brooches depicting shepherds and sheep dogs.

My first session with the Society took place in an atmosphere of celebration. Mme Therrien produced the oat-based confections which had given such pleasure at Bible study sessions with her Scottish cousins. Speaking in the mahogany-panelled boardroom above the bookstore, she announced that:

"Jean-Marc and Laurent represent a new dawn. We look forward to tracking their progress as our great enterprise moves forward. I eagerly await monthly reports as Jean-Marc develops into the type of young man that will be a credit to the new vision of society. Laurent will be our standard bearer in the world of publishing. We all have limitless confidence in both their abilities."

Mme Therrien did not reveal the basis for her confidence.

Our rise to the heights was to be chronicled by her niece, Renée. She would join our sessions periodically. My first, mistaken, impression of Renée was of a pleasant, soft-spoken, woman in her mid-thirties. She was smartly dressed, but in soft colours as though she were politely declining the limelight.

The proprietor and Laurent seemed a little taken aback at the president's outpourings. Nonetheless, they managed polite and appropriate responses. A photograph was taken of the group. I was positioned cross-legged on the floor in front of the seated adults. Then Laurent and I were posed together. The ceremony ended when Mme Therrien presented me with signed copies of the manifesto and the Master Volume. I also received a leaflet published by the Scotia Oat Company with simple recipes. The products would promote healthy digestion and lucid thinking.

The speeches had consumed much of the first hour. On our way down the ramps to the guardhouse room, Laurent was intercepted by an overwrought printer. Prof Valois, an early champion of Bauhaus typography, was known for his idiosyncratic opposition to typefaces with serifs. But his contribution to a festschrift would be in an edition set with the offending ornamentation. This convenient crisis absorbed a good twenty minutes.

We finally reached our bleak quarters, where Roman guards had sheltered from irascible Helvetic tribesmen. It would have been much more convenient to work out of Laurent's office, but symbolism trumped practicality. The president had been clear that we would work out of the Society's premises.

Almost at the end of our scheduled time, Laurent and I studied each other. He was obviously senior, but we were both starting something unfamiliar under excessive expectations. A faint smile hinted that we might get on better than I had feared.

"Jean-Marc, what have you got us into? I keep looking for a halo as you transform into the 'credit to the new vision'."

Laurent could be a little formal, sometimes addressing me as if speaking to a school assembly. Nonetheless, he had a good teaching style, and we made it safely through the four introductory sessions consisting of classical and modern visions of the model citizen. Renée listed me in the welcome section of the Society's newsletter. I was presented with a card indicating that I was a junior member. Foolishly, I believed that we had found an easy option to meet Weygand's disciplinary recommendation.

A chair with arms was brought into the guardhouse room for Renée to join us as we tackled the more substantive texts. Thus enthroned, she would ask the questions that I could not answer. The pleasant person that we had originally met would now fix us with a cold stare as if she had caught us defacing historic manuscripts. Her voice would remain calm as she observed:

"Laurent, I am disappointed. That was not a difficult chapter. It is one of the best translations of Shakespeare that I have seen. Why can't Jean-Marc manage better commentary on the advice of Polonius to Laertes?"

An almost incomprehensible treatise by a Danish theorist included the quotation from Tennyson:

And slowly answer'd Arthur from the barge:

"The old order changeth, yielding place to new,
And God fulfils Himself in many ways,
Lest one good custom should corrupt the world."

Laurent and I looked helplessly at each other as we were asked to explain why the corrupting custom would be described as good rather than bad.

On occasion Renée would add:

"Victor, Tomas, Magdalena, and Gudrun only speak French as a second language, but they are making much better progress. It is a matter of effort and dedication to the cause."

I understood these annoying paragons to be the children of representatives at the League of Nations.

If she was very disappointed, she would preface her remarks:

"Laurent, please ask Jean-Marc to stand outside with the door closed. We need to discuss his difficulties."

She would address a pleasantry to me at the start of the session, but otherwise she would not communicate directly with a junior member. We could not accuse her of hypocrisy. She knew the entire oeuvre fluently. It was a mystery to her that any motivated individual could not achieve the same understanding.

I was handed two thick dossiers labelled "Jean-Marc Correspondence" after the guardian's death many years later. I had been unaware of the following exchanges:

Renée opened the discussion on watermarked writing paper the colour of a robin's egg:

"We are concerned that Jean-Marc is not achieving the results of which he is capable. We suggest disciplinary incentives to raise his level of effort. It should be noted that Laurent tenders excuses on his behalf instead of compelling him to greater heights."

The guardian sent a sensitively worded query, recorded in carbon copy, to Laurent who responded in an old-fashioned copperplate script:

"In contrast to Mlle Renée Therrien, I have been a teacher. I have reacted sharply on the rare occasions when I felt Jean-Marc was indolent. For the rest, I believe he sincerely tries his best. It is not given to everyone to master an encyclopedic knowledge of the world's deepest thinkers. Undue pressure would simply result in frustration and disillusionment."

With unfortunate timing, Weygand sent a note the same week seeking a follow-up appointment. This request was typewritten, a vulgarity which the guardian considered suitable only for invoices and communications from municipal officials.

"I was delighted that you made such satisfactory arrangements for Jean-Marc's swimming and music. But your letter from many months ago did not answer all my recommendations. Does he have an appropriately rigorous disciplinary structure? Could you arrange for the patient to see me within the next three months? This is a critical time in his development."

The guardian underlined incoming mail and made notes in the margins. He had not been brought up on Corneille for nothing; he would do his duty, however uncomfortable it might be for him or me. And some of the euphemistically worded suggestions, if implemented, could have been very uncomfortable indeed.

The guardian kept his internal struggles to himself. Doubtless his humanitarian instincts would have led him to follow Laurent's advice. On the other hand, a fear of adopting an easier but cowardly path instead of following the wisdom of qualified experts, would have inclined him to take the harder road proposed by Weygand and Renée. It is, perhaps, no coincidence that his ulcer should have flared up around this time. One of the recipes in the oat leaflet claimed to be 'a known and trusted cure' for that condition. I presented the guardian with the results of my amateurish baking.

"Jean-Marc, you have such a good heart! But I knew that already from how you looked after your mother. This is so very kind of you."

I had made my gesture with no ulterior motive and was ignorant of all the correspondence that had crossed the guardian's desk. But my good deed may have been rewarded. The file contained a pencil draft of a response to Laurent. It accepted his argument about undue pressure but suggested further sanctions to be administered at his discretion. This last clause was now crossed out.

The guardian convalesced quickly, which he generously credited to the oats while tactfully conveying that another batch would not be necessary. He responded separately to Renée and Laurent.

"Jean-Marc has a good and gentle nature. We must respect his limitations without applying excessive pressure. He is already challenged by his correspondence course. He should continue with the Society's program. I expect Laurent to insist on high standards, but we must not set expectations that exceed the boy's capacity. I see every indication that he can be formed into a kind and admirable citizen."

Renée replied by return of post on a sheet of white bond paper bordered with a blue line so dark that it resembled mourning stationery.

"I will respect your decision, although it occasions the Society considerable anguish. The president and I had hoped that Jean-Marc would be pushed to elevate himself to his highest attainable level. The next newsletter will reflect that he has transferred from Junior Member to Junior Associate Member. Nonetheless, we wish him well."

The indignity of demotion was compensated by Renée's absence from the guardroom. The sessions became almost tolerable, and Laurent quietly excused me from committing the more sententious paragraphs to memory. Unfortunately, the interfering guest received the newsletter as a donor to the Society. He took the incriminating page about my changed status when he next met Dr Weygand for badminton and brandy.

My appointment with the doctor took place several weeks later in a villa by the lake. The residence might have been delightful in summer, but rain mixed with sleet had been falling for two days. The damp air penetrated the space unchallenged by any heating, and the grey waters of the lake were scarcely visible across the sodden lawn. I waited in my underwear in a cold, white-tiled room until Weygand arrived, warmly dressed in tweeds and sporting a sandalwood cologne. He inspected my lip, calves, and forearms before noting correctly that more hair would normally be evident on a boy of my age. He then asked me how things were going.

"I like my tutor, Stéphane. He wants to go to Africa and has a bicycle with a little motor on the front wheel. We once had mulberry ices with Mme Montmagny. This week we are starting the *Aeneid.*"

"You are in the program for the Society for the Amelioration of Youth through Literature?"

"I'm only a junior associate member now. Some of the texts are very heavy going. I think even Laurent must be bored by some of them, but he is too professional to show it."

"I see. Is anyone very severe with you?"

"Not really, or at least not often. I get lectured sternly if my work is not good, or the guardian thinks I have been smoking."

Weygand led me to an even more frigid corridor lined with plaster craniums of differing characteristics. Drafts entered through the French doors and sash windows of an adjoining salon. I sat on a low metal stool facing his closed door for maybe an hour until he called me in. I admired the new electric radiator behind his desk. I had not seen one before with two elements, let alone one adorned with a chrome Prometheus trying to fend off the eagle. I had hoped to warm myself in front of it, but the doctor gestured me away, perhaps concerned that I might come close enough to read his observations.

"You must prepare yourself for a much more rigorous regime. Moral and mental training will help you face the challenges which nature will soon send your way. Mlle Ronsard will type the notes that I have just made and send them to your guardian."

He must have been referring to the sentences below:

"The youth who sits outside my office retains all the indicators of potential delinquency that I first observed. He will experience a delayed and dangerous transition to maturity, as amply evidenced by the fate of others with his mental and physical characteristics. It would be unconscionable not to reinforce his mitigated disciplinary regime, which seems milder than that practiced in many schools. I am particularly distressed that his instructors, Stéphane and Laurent, do not adopt a more commanding posture. The fact that Jean-Marc appears a pleasant individual does not absolve us from applying the treatments that his condition requires. Many a young man has been lost to debasement and ignominy because his doctors, or his guardians, have had their objectivity clouded by an ersatz parental affection. We already see Jean-Marc's decline in his shameful demotion within the Society for Amelioration. This shocking development was common gossip in my club."

This poisonous missive was not filed along with the other correspondence in the dossier and would surface separately in later life.

The guardian never showed me the letter but asked:

"What did you say to Dr Weygand? Did you make any flippant remarks that he might have misunderstood? Did you discuss the Society for Amelioration?"

Deeply troubled, the guardian scarcely spoke for three days. He had made his earlier decision based on his better judgement and on Laurent's advice. But what if he had taken the wrong course? He was decisive and confident, but he was not arrogant. Who was he to oppose the greatest doctor of the age? Weygand's text left no room for ambiguity. Was the guardian like his colleague who hesitated over his doctor's urgent advice to approve an amputation for his child? By the time the parents were persuaded, a fatal gangrene had taken hold. Was my humiliatingly public demotion really a first symptom?

Laurent and I were wrestling with a convoluted metaphorical passage by a deeply obscure Italian mystic. It was, by far, the most challenging one we encountered. If we had understood it, we might apparently have acquired the virtues of patience and self-abnegation. I was working my way through the questions on this text when the guardian came into the vet's room.

"Can you show me what you have been doing for the Society? You know that your demotion is being mocked throughout the city? Weygand sees it as the start of your moral deterioration."

I pointed to the text and the questions. He read them carefully.

"Jean-Marc, can you take a recess? Leave your exercise book and the Master Volume here. Come back in an hour."

I went into the garden for some fresh air. I hated the Society; I hated Weygand and Renée. What was going to happen? Would Laurent get new instructions to be severe with me? Why was the wretched garden so overgrown? You could not take two steps without brushing against a twig or a web. If I had been allowed, I could have made it into a working orchard. The meagre crop lasted only until mid-December when we switched to tins of excessively sweetened white currants from Jutland.

The guardian had arrived at a conclusion. He waved me back into the vet's room.

"Perhaps Dr Weygand was a little hard on you. I'm not sure I could do everything that the Society asks. Some texts are very good, but I've never heard of this mystic and wouldn't expect you to have all the answers. Just promise me that you will really apply yourself. I'll check with Laurent from time to time when I'm in the bookstore."

Displeased at the guardian's failure to follow his advice, Weygand never summoned me for another follow-up. My problems were not over, but the most dangerous implications of Weygand's last recommendation were safely averted. His diagnosis was to resurface many years later with damaging effect.

8.
The Juvenile House

Paradoxically, it was when the guardian was at his most exasperated that he would sometimes be at his most understanding. With Weygand's influence in brief remission, he would try gentler approaches.

I was anticipating the worst as he recited my transgressions. By now I had learned to gauge his level of irritation. A stern voice and a slight reddening of the face indicated the annoyance of a provoked, but not unreasonable, mentor. If this was supplemented by a bulging vein on the forehead, I knew that he was really angry. The highest level was the vein and an ominous pounding of the fist. So far, I had never merited the last stage which I had only witnessed when some bureaucratic mishap resulted in a returned shipment of desperately needed humanitarian supplies. Today the vein was prominent, as I had defied his repeated request to rewrite an essay which, the *curé* complained, simply copied paragraphs from the textbook. Having ensured that I knew what I deserved, his tone changed:

"Listen, I know that things can be difficult for you. It is easy to become discouraged and for the mind to become stale. I've arranged a surprise for tomorrow. I'll get you up very early and Henri will be waiting for you by the back door. It will be a long day so I have packed a bag with things you may need. Remember it is very chilly early in the morning. The farmers are worried about frost on their strawberries."

My expectations were restrained. The guardian had previously arranged a treat for me, and I appreciated the spirit in which it was intended. I had enjoyed the break from the routine, and some hot chestnuts from a street vendor. My destination proved to be a sparsely-attended afternoon concert of Handel's

Israel in Egypt performed by a visiting choir which thundered its way through the Red Sea in discordant British accents.

I did not know Henri particularly well. He was an energetic gardener and handyman in his late thirties. He was employed by a widow in one of the grander houses up the street. The guardian paid some fraction of his salary and would have his services one or two days a month. He had always been pleasant to me if somewhat distant. Unfortunately, I had a disturbing image in my mind. I had enjoyed playing with the widow's Belgian Shepherd. Sadly, Réal began to suffer from various ailments. As was the custom in those days, Henri had 'taken care of it' in the coal shed before burying the dog in a corner of the garden where he planted red currant bushes.

Henri, in a heavy sweater, met me promptly at three-thirty am. It was too early for the trams, and he explained that we had about an hour's walk ahead of us. He carried my bag and we exchanged a few remarks as we marched briskly down deserted roads towards a more industrial part of town by the lake. I was very intrigued, for I could not imagine what might be awaiting us. We passed through unfamiliar streets until I recognized the outline of a large, former factory, then known popularly as the House of Juvenile Death.

Everyone in the city knew the story of this establishment which had been rehearsed on front pages for years. Some thirty years prior, a wealthy banker had a chef whose wife passed away, leaving him with a young son. The sympathetic banker encouraged his own children to include the boy in their games and, later, in their sessions with a tutor. When the child was about ten, his father became aggressive to the staff. He was dismissed and evicted. Five years later, the boy was incarcerated for repeatedly stealing loaves of bread. He caught an infection. When the pastor came to see him, his last wish was that his only possession, an inscribed Bible from the banker, be returned to its donor with his sincere thanks. Much moved, the banker resolved that no youth who committed crimes from desperation rather than malice should incur the same fate.

The banker's institutions were revolutionary and attracted attention from Tsarist Russia to Dublin. Youths in the prison system and guilty of only crimes resulting from destitution were subjected to a series of interviews. If they had the right attitude and motivation, they were conditionally admitted to one of the institutions. The separate boys' and girls' colleges operated on the same principles. Instead of cutting the residents off from the city, they brought the citizens to them. Four nights a week, the residents would be assigned specific seats in the dining room. One day they would find themselves conversing with students from the local colleges, on another to volunteers from the churches or the teaching professions. Similar groups would teach them craft skills, sports, or board games. In the morning, they would learn basic literacy and sufficient practical arithmetic to run a small business. In the afternoons, they would practice technical skills in well-funded workshops. The results were spectacular, though different in the separate colleges.

Mme Chaléat of the smaller girls' college seemingly knew everyone in Geneva. It was said that if a resident admired a flower, the next day she would be on a tour of the city greenhouses with the head botanist. A girl who expressed an interest in astronomy would find herself on a nocturnal picnic with a professor and his family to study a meteor shower. The most talented women in the city were called on to offer individual tuition and guidance. Her alumni ignored the prejudices of the age and progressed in fields as diverse as physics, millinery, zoology, horticulture, and horology. Critics complained that the best way for a girl to receive a good education in Geneva was to be caught stealing a cake.

The boys could not match the girls in individual achievement. Their probation focused on teamwork and good manners. Any resident who would not look out for all his team members was promptly returned to the penal system. The graduates were renowned as polite motor mechanics. A Swiss chief steward on a Mediterranean steamer explained the effect of this culture:

"I employed four young men from the college. They followed instruction and performed adequately enough. I then contracted appendicitis and had to leave them to their own devices. When I recovered, I was showered with compliments from the captain and passengers. It was no good managing them as individual employees. I would just give the tasks to the team and they would work out who could do them best, what touches they could add, and where they should support each other."

The Contessa di Monte San Rosario recorded an encounter with the boys in her published memoirs:

I was secretary of the Association for Italian Swiss Cultural Advancement. I had taken Mme Laval de BonChemin to present an award to an Italian composer living outside Geneva. She was well into her eighties and dressed in a formal style that fell from fashion in the previous century. We endured an interminable violin sonata, but she was in great spirits and held the group captive with her award speech. She had a way of relating to everyone from shy young watercolourists to wealthy patrons of the arts.

As I drove back, she became tired and imperiously directed me to take a short cut. We were soon lost in a commercial area near the lake. Then steam rose from the front of the car and we stopped. A dozen youths appeared from nowhere in athletic gear. They had strong accents, and I had some difficulty understanding them. They volunteered to push us to a garage. I could see no public telephones, and there was no alternative. I was worried as dusk fell and they rolled us through the gates of what seemed to be an old factory. Two boys ran ahead and opened the doors to the cleanest workshop that one could imagine. One of the older youths escorted us to an office overlooking the floor. He explained that my radiator had sprung a leak, spraying water over the electrics. However, they had a car identical to mine which they used for training. They would transfer its radiator and later repair mine for their own use. The switch would take a little time as his team could only work safely once the engine had cooled. As he explained this, I watched fascinated as the other young men emerged in spotless overalls and, as though with choreography, divided into teams to polish my car and to remove the part from the training vehicle. The two boys who had opened the gates appeared with tea and biscotti, which they had somehow conjured up. Thus revived, my elderly companion requested to use the facilities, and they led her down a corridor.

The older boy had resolutely refused to accept any payment, insisting that we were doing the team a favour by letting them gain experience on a real-life breakdown. In my briefcase I carried spare award certificates in case a recipient ever found an error. I took one of these and made it out for mechanical services to the Association. I began to have second thoughts as I reviewed the document. In the left margin Jubal, Miriam, and Saint Cecilia looked out from between garlands of roses and peonies. On the right, Orpheus, Eurydice, and some obscure, artistically-inclined saint contended with carnations and chrysanthemums. The crests of the ancient universities which supported the society adorned the top and bottom margins. This affected style might well seem risible to mechanically-inclined adolescents. These reflections were interrupted as I realized that my companion had been gone for a long time. Worried, I set out to check on her.

The corridor was lined with the residents' drawings, and my companion had returned to her most admirable form with an impromptu art appreciation class:

"I particularly like the way that the background tells a story that reinforces what one sees in the foreground. That shaft of sunlight and the rising flock of birds adds so much interest without distracting from the central theme. Is this one of yours? You should feel very proud. Perhaps I could arrange for a group of you to join me in the gallery one day? I would love to show you around."

The boys listened enraptured.

The older youth came to tell us that the repair was completed. Loïdic and Didier would lead us on bicycles back to the main road.

I collected my things from the office and presented the certificate to the group. At first, I thought my worst fears had been realized. They said nothing. Eventually one of them whispered to the older boy who diffidently apologized:

"Please excuse us. We are so overcome by the award that we don't know how to thank you. We have never received anything like this."

He paused nervously:

"Would it be alright to ask you a question?"

"Of course, please."

"Is the lady a member of the Italian royal family?"

I was immeasurably grieved to hear of the disasters which befell them.

The Contessa was not exaggerating when she spoke of disaster. After years of successful operation, the College's boys began to fall ill. They died in such numbers that a playing field shrank as sections were reserved for graves. Undignified disputes broke out between the administrators, the doctors, and the police as to who was responsible. The papers engaged in unwholesome speculation about the boys' diet and hygiene.

A Czech speaking electrician eventually found the reason. The factory had used some highly toxic substances imported from Prague. When the business went bankrupt, a case had been concealed in an alcove above what became the linen cupboard. The chemicals eventually corroded the packaging. As the youths bounded up the adjacent stairs, a little poison would sprinkle onto their pillow cases. The source was found too late. The best staff had left. The institution was placed under a Committee for Juvenile Reformation, which was exempted from the inspections of the prison authorities. The training was cynically replaced by masonry arts, a euphemism for having the inmates fashion Corinthian columns in a quarry. The boys continued to die, but in smaller batches and of the accepted causes of exhaustion and exposure.

I was struck by an uncomfortable thought. Perhaps Henri was to 'take care of me' by enrolling me in the House of Juvenile Death. This would solve many headaches for the guardian and might explain the bag with my clothes. It was still dark, and it would be easy to push me through an entrance. We turned into what seemed to be a walled cul-de-sac in front of the building. In this exigent my focus turned obtusely to the most trivial consideration. My watch had been gaining time, and the guardian had lent me one of his on the strict understanding that it was to be returned in the same condition that I received it. I took it off and asked Henri if he would look after it. He seemed mildly surprised but put the timepiece safely in an inner pocket. We passed the main gate and proceeded to a narrow passage at the back of the building. I could discern no exit, but there were several basement-level entrances. No one would see or hear anything. We continued on until, finally, Henri opened a heavy door which led from the passage to the street.

"That shortcut saved us a good ten minutes. Otherwise, you have to do two sides of a triangle and come back up the hill again. A long time ago I would come here with some lads from the church, and we would show the kids how to hurdle. They were a little herd-like but their team did well in relay events."

We entered a tenebrous warehouse on the docks. Its pitted cement floors covered with dirty crates seemed a most improbable starting point for anything agreeable.

"Camille, this is Jean-Marc. He's the one I told you about."

"Hello Jean-Marc. Don't look so worried! I'm not old and cantankerous like Henri."

"Jean-Marc, don't mind Camille. My young cousin hasn't made a sensible remark in his twenty-two years. He flashes that annoying smile and gets away with murder."

I did not know how to respond to this banter.

It emerged that I would spend the day on one of the last delivery boats to ply the lake. There had once been a small fleet, but it had been unable to compete with the trains and trucks.

There was a chill over the water, and I appreciated the winter sweater from the bag. But the sunrise was truly glorious as the red light caught the mountains and reflected on the still morning water. We docked at a pig farm where we unloaded large cans of paraffin. The next call was at an isolation sanatorium where we placed hampers of food and medicine on a jetty without meeting anyone. A few stops later, we tied up next to a millionaire's elegant but stranded motor vessel and transferred a heavy component to a waiting mechanic. The bored but talkative owner in plus fours engaged us in a long conversation about defective marine motors. He seemed amused to see me and instructed Camille:

"Your little brother will never make it to able seaman unless you feed him properly."

He nodded to a steward who came out with a plate of quails' eggs and caviar-laden canapés.

"This was meant for the party we missed when the engine gave out. Keep the plate. My wife has gone off Spode. She finds it *démodé*. We have commissioned a dinner service from Limoges, some geometric art deco thing that will be in fashion for about a week."

We landed supplies at a series of grand residences. Camille and Henri let me help with the lighter cargo and made me feel useful and appreciated.

Our last stop was to pick up a large shipment of *Fromages du Lac*. The farmer had the nicest daughters who insisted that we sample their product in generously cut sandwiches. It was comfortably warm by now, and we sat outside at a massive table overlooking the wild flowers in the fields and the bay. Their attentions were mainly focused on the good-looking Camille, but the younger one, Mireille, who was maybe fifteen or sixteen, took my hand and said I must have a tour of the dairy.

I was allowed to steer for part of the way back.

The guardian had achieved his objective. I returned excited and refreshed. As I went upstairs, I could hear him thanking Henri, who responded:

"We enjoyed his company. He's quiet, but a good kid."

Then after a pause:

"I nearly forgot. He asked me to look after your watch."

"That was very responsible of him. It is better that it did not get splashed."

"He handed it to me when we took that shortcut by the Juvenile College. He couldn't have thought...? No, surely not?"

"I don't know what goes on in his mind sometimes. But he is good about taking his cod liver oil. They say that it works wonders in brain formation."

9.
Friends

The other treatments imposed as a result of Weygand were deeply annoying, but the most damaging was the isolation from people of my own age. I missed Paul and my other friends. The guardian was an upright man but relentlessly grown up and sensible. He had a fine, dry sense of humour, but he would never descend into levity.

Surprisingly, it was the bookstore which provided some measure of friendship even if those with whom I interacted most closely were about a decade older than I was. The old proprietor was an extraordinary businessman. He recruited his employees based on their enthusiasm for their subjects and would encourage them to attend any talk or exhibition that was remotely germane to their field. The upper levels had rooms that could seat up to fifty people, and programs could include anything from the use of cobalt in specialist inks, to the art of paper marbling, or the detection of fake first editions. This approach resulted in a highly engaged staff who would willingly discuss all aspects of their craft. Their presses had a reputation throughout the French speaking countries and won contracts for lucrative high-quality editions.

The proprietor was partly responsible for my visits to the Society, but he bore me no animosity. His suggestions had been made purely to help out his old acquaintance whom I had so distressed. Encountering me in the corridor, he enquired:

"How are you doing? Have you made many friends since you arrived in Geneva?"

I struggled to answer this simple question. Weygand had put an end to attending school or joining any team where I might be corrupted.

"Not really. But Étienne is alright. I wish I could learn to draw like him."

On my next visit, Laurent instructed me that we must go to the proprietor's office, which was large and intimidating with oppressive green wallpapers, a massive ormolu clock supported by Neptune and Salacia's chariot, and uncomfortable antique chairs:

"Don't look so nervous! You're not trembling, are you? I've told Étienne to go to the exhibition of illustrations by Gustave Doré, John Tenniel, and Thomas Bewick. You know, purgatory, the poem with the dead albatross, Alice, rural dogs, and suchlike. It may give him some ideas.

I've written a note to your guardian to ask his permission if you would like to go."

We spent a good four hours at the Institute. I had anticipated rows of dreary pictures in a dusty gallery, but Étienne brought the engravings alive by explaining the technical features almost as though I were his junior colleague. The well-informed staff appeared delighted to help their only visitors under sixty and encouraged us to ask questions.

"Sorry, which story is this? Why are these heads emerging from a frozen lake?"

"Yes, isn't that a dreadful punishment? It is the *Inferno*. Dante and Virgil are standing on the ice trying to avoid trampling on the heads of traitors who have been condemned to freeze in Lake Cocytus. Compare the simple background here to this one of the giant Antaeus gently lowering Dante and Virgil into the Last Circle of Hell."

It was an inspiring afternoon, and I enjoyed experimenting with the different styles. To my surprise, I was relatively good at depicting gloom and foreboding. The ability to represent felicity convincingly eluded me. Later I would try to improve the illustrations for a child's story for a deaf girl whom I was helping as a volunteer. Hitting the right note was much harder than it looked.

A few weeks later, I had time to fill before meeting Laurent and headed to the engraving department. As I approached Étienne's door, I heard a wonderful laugh, feminine and infectious. I entered to see him chatting with a girl about three years older than me. I found her utterly amazing. She had long blonde hair, lively blue eyes, and projected the cheerful confidence of a film star. I would not forget her.

"I am so sorry. Am I interrupting?"

"Not at all. Jean-Marc, meet my cousin Céline. She came by because we will be illustrating a pamphlet for the International Society of Christian Organists. Her mother is on the Committee. Céline, Jean-Marc is the friend who came to the exhibition with me."

My confidence rose on hearing myself described as a friend.

Céline looked as if she might be about to leave, but Étienne stopped her:

"I know what is wrong. The picture they gave us is of someone far too old. The plan is to get younger people from across the whole French-speaking world interested in organ music, right? Our neighbour, Mme Gingras, is a bookkeeper at that strange factory with the English chapel. She mentioned something about a young prodigy who plays the organ there a couple of days a week. Maybe if we ask her, we could use him, if he is not too weedy."

This was my moment:

"You mean the chapel on rue de Villeneuve? She may be referring to someone else, but I do play there on Tuesdays and Thursdays."

Étienne inspected me critically:

"Alright, it is decided. We can use Renaissance man here as the model. When is a good day for me to come with you? But don't expect too much. The organ is one of those stupid instruments where you have your back turned to everyone."

Despite the challenges of the positioning, Étienne created an intriguing image. He permitted himself a certain artistic license, the better to capture the imagination of musical youth from Indochina to Montreal. It was well over a year before I met Céline again, but I had banked some important points as Étienne's friend. And I would need many points and much luck if I were to be allowed into her family.

A few months later I was to add a bar to Étienne's status. I was heading down the ramp with Laurent when he ambushed us:

"This will only take five minutes. I have the keys."

I was beginning to know the plant fairly well but was lost as we headed through several corridors into a room with a safe-like door. Étienne manipulated the keys and a combination lock before finally we entered accompanied by a lugubrious guard in a creased uniform. The vault was full of financial documents, share certificates, promissory notes, mortgage releases, and bonds, all with finely engraved designs and lettering.

Étienne handed me a large sheet of high-quality paper:

"Look closely. What do you see in the design? I was not allowed to show you this before, but the debenture issue was officially announced last night for the Suisse Roma Tanneries."

He had taken the drawing of the Roman soldier which I had given him on the night of the raincoat incident and, with deft perspective, used it as the view through a window of a merchant's villa.

"See here. The initials of some J-M character along with mine. When the proprietor showed this to the client, apparently, they ignored all my intricate artwork to discuss the soldier's leather belt and what sort of curing process was used in those days. Come to my office afterwards. I'll give you a copy, but you understand that it has to be marked specimen and have a corner cut off?"

The guardian and I had been navigating turbulent waters. But he was delighted when I showed him the debenture and my initials.

"What extraordinary talent! I know you'll end up channelling it properly."

And like a proud parent, he had me show it to every visitor for the next few weeks.

He had congratulated me on the picture at the organ but never mentioned it afterwards. I was not sure if he did not care for the design, or was uneasy about me being a model even in such a respectable publication.

I remained cautious of Laurent, but I was partially reassured when Étienne explained the significance of the lemon biscuit that I had been given after carrying the boxes from the stables on that first night. These expensive delicacies with limoncello filling were imported from Perugia and only offered to the most favoured customers. The staff were expected to take the arrowroot alternatives. Laurent could be a little formal, but he did not look down on me. I regretted that Étienne did not give me his insight until it was too late to share my biscuit with him.

My sessions with the Society were scheduled for the afternoon after my organ practice. The proprietor and the guardian could not have agreed on a more inconvenient time of day for Laurent to attend to me in the ancient guardhouse. He was charged with verifying progress on the day's activities and preparing a report for management before locking up. The layout of the ramps meant that one travelled the length of roughly five blocks one way to get from the management offices to the Society's office in the basement. The only means to accomplish his assigned tasks was to combine the journeys with his reviews, first for the functions by the North ramps and, on the way up, for the ones on the South. The process could sometimes take an hour and a half until we returned to Laurent's office where he would give me a serially numbered note to the guardian confirming my attendance.

At first, I would stand bored and sullen behind Laurent. But he would drop Étienne's name into his questions:

"Can I show that run for the Léman Yachting Club Annual as complete with one thousand copies? The one with Étienne's engraving of the sloop and the gaff-rigged fishing boats?"

I would edge nearer to take a look. And gradually I would start to develop an interest as I began to follow the process from conception to the final product.

Laurent missed teaching. He had only joined the bookstore because an uncle had died suddenly, leaving him as next in line. His own father was exempt having entered the church. He would distract me from my apprehensive meditations as we walked on the ramps by explaining the business. The conversations about blurred serifs, inks, papers, and pressures began to make sense. His focus was always on quality. He set high standards and was generous when they were attained:

"Raoul, this is fantastic! Jean-Marc, do you see the pink on the flamingo in the frontispiece? It is such a difficult colour to get right. We imported a special ink from Lebanon. It is partially derived from molluscs. The monks used the same substances in illuminated manuscripts. Next week we must have a copy in the front window display."

When eventually Laurent was promoted and Hervé would often take over, I received different but equally useful insights. Hervé's background was in cost accounting. Short, in his late twenties, and with wiry hair, he would hunt for waste with the enthusiasm of a terrier on the trail of a rodent. As we rummaged through scrap bins, he would comment on the lines of:

"Look at this! We'll never make money on these technical manuals. All this because the diagram of the valve on page six is upside down. And it is on expensive, heavy-duty paper."

My elderly organ teacher had registered me in a low-key local competition. I had not the remotest chance of winning as it called for a much wider repertoire than I could manage. However, my baroque fugues were well received and included in the final recital. I was alone. The teacher was ill again. The guardian did not particularly enjoy classical music and was, in any case, tied up in one of those weeks where he had to prioritize work. But I had left him a written schedule, or I thought I had. The other competitors received little silver cups as had been previously announced. Everyone was ready to leave when I heard my name called. I advanced nervously towards the lectern.

"Young man, you did not merit a prize. Listen to me!"

The speaker, a professor emeritus with a loud but slow delivery, launched into an analogy comparing my playing to an apple tart that his sister-in-law had made in the little town of Saint-Saphorin. The tart had uneven thickness in the pastry, and the apple slices were crudely cut. I started to turn red. He cannot have been very well, for he continued even more slowly stopping to catch his breath every other sentence. Her dessert was quite unlike the exquisite patisserie of the Café Laurentien. My embarrassment fermented while he wandered off on a digression about the lost orchards of Geneva and the Vaud. Finally, he came to my rescue with the word "but". It was his sister-in-law's tart that he would want on his deathbed. It was original, unique, and represented the true aromas of the best, old varieties. My playing was the same. He had heard Handel's fugue in E^{13} a thousand times, but my interpretation (really Mother's, which I reproduced faithfully) gave him the same thrill as if he were listening for the first time. I needed to broaden my repertoire, but that should not stop me from applying to the Conservatoire.

"Maybe this will help." He handed me a framed letter of recommendation with magnificent calligraphy. And with that, he closed the proceedings. The seating and lighting were such that I had not really seen the audience. In any case, I was not expecting to find anyone that I knew. I slipped quietly out of a side entrance.

"There he is. Catch him before he gets on the tram!"

I was cornered in the bus shelter. I could see Laurent, Hervé, and Renaud, the storekeeper, in their best clothes, accompanied, strangely, by Mme Béatrice Labeaume from scores and libretti and now dripping with amethysts. They were all rushing towards

---

13 HWV 612

me as though in a nightmare. My mind was still spinning from the professor's address. My immediate thought was that I must have forgotten to leave the schedule for the guardian. And now there would be retribution. With hindsight, there was no real reason, apart from my age, for this sudden angst, but it was very real.

"You are quivering all over. Are you alright? Do you need a doctor? Sit down here. Should we get you some water from the tobacconist?"

"We didn't mean to frighten you. We wanted to see if you would like a little celebration with us. Then Laurent and Béatrice can take you home in the van."

I belatedly began to piece the obvious clues together and asked Hervé:

"Were you in the concert?"

"Yes, of course. Your stuff was much better than those dreary pieces at the beginning."

"Who were you there for?"

"For you, idiot! Guillaume thought he recognized your name when he proofed the program."

It came as a surprise that the competition organizers could have afforded our quality printing.

"Anyway, Bertrand mentioned it to the proprietor, and he wanted us to come. You are our mascot now. Nurse sent Étienne home with a temperature this morning, or he would have joined us."

"Do you feel up to a croque monsieur at that place by the fountain? It will do you good to eat something."

I was very appreciative of the meal and touched by the truly generous comments of my companions. But, once alone, I was profoundly ashamed of my moment of panic. If I were a soldier, would I be the one that would be shot for being too frightened to advance? Perhaps I really was a nobody who needed to be toughened up. I hid the recommendation flat on a high shelf and never mentioned it. It would resurface years later at an awkward moment.

I had, it turned out, left the schedule in exactly the right place. The guardian, who was away at a late meeting, had written a note wishing me good luck.

10.
A Critical Lunch

I was lightly dressed in my new white and blue sweater. In the post office, a lady with a feather boa had remarked that it made me look dapper. I had not anticipated being outside for more than a couple of minutes at each end of my trip. This plan went awry when a burst sewer stopped the trams, causing me to divert through an unfamiliar residential area to find another line.

There were two figures across the empty road, both bundled up against a bitter wind with their features concealed by hats and scarves.

"Jean-Louis, is that you?"

"Sorry, I mean 'Jean-Marc'. Remember me?"

It was Céline, Étienne's cousin, accompanied by her mother, Mme Jodoin.

"Maman, Jean-Marc is Étienne's friend. He was the organist in the brochure."

"Then we must invite him to lunch. Besides, he'll turn into a pillar of ice if we don't get him inside. Jean-Marc, can you join us?"

We headed into a nearby house whose heavy wrought iron gates and solid wooden door seemed to imply that casual visitors were not expected. The oak-panelled corridor walls were covered with prints of Swiss mercenaries in battle along with a couple of executions. The latter were tasteful and not too graphic given the subject matter. The fraught glances between the presiding officials and the relatives were well captured, and the ladies all wore mantillas for the occasion. Céline saw that they had caught my attention:

"Don't worry! We've pretty much given that up. The little figure with the blue tricorne, notebook, and quill is my French great-grandfather. He kept the judicial records somewhere in the

Camargue around the time of the Revolution. It's best not to bring the subject up with Papa, or he'll insist on showing you the collection. Great-grandad took a button as a souvenir from each executed client, labelled them, and arranged them in a display cabinet in the bedroom. Great-grandmother was very annoyed. In fairness, some of the buttons are quite beautiful with crests and ivory and amber."

It was too early to eat. Céline and her mother needed to finish the cooking. I was dispatched across a frozen vegetable garden to the old stables to meet her brothers, Honoré and Euzèbe. They were older than her, in the very late teens or early twenties. I knocked gently on the door. Nothing happened. I knocked a little louder. I heard an expletive. One of three giants opened the door and glared at me. He was untidy, dark-haired, and perspiring through his tennis shirt.

"I didn't mean to disturb you. Mme Jodoin wanted me to meet Céline's brothers."

The stables had been transformed into a games room and gymnasium. The brothers were deep in a table tennis match which they were not going to interrupt for some uninvited boy. They were both fair-haired and looked to be frequent users of the pommel horse, medicine balls, and weights which littered the other side of the room. The unkempt man who had admitted me took his leave though it was not clear if either brother heard him:

"I'm going before your father gets home. Tomorrow I'll bring a discus."

The room was undecorated except for a small corner over a table. There was a framed photograph of Céline and her brothers. But something did not seem right. On closer inspection of the photograph, the background wallpaper and the slope of the back of the sofa were not correctly aligned. It looked as if a vertical section had been cut out, and I surmised that someone had been excised from the scene.

Honoré finally emerged victorious over his sweat-drenched sibling.

"Sorry about that. We have to keep putting Euzèbe back in his place. I let him win once a month, or he gets all morose. So, who are you?"

I gave a quick introduction, adding that I was invited to lunch. This last information caused an exchange of glances.

"Was it Mother who invited you?"

"Yes, I suppose so. She and Céline were together."

One giant observed to the other:

"Réjean is banned, but he's allowed in?"

My way was blocked by my hosts.

"Our friend of eighteen years can't eat with us anymore because he used an uncouth word in front of Papa. It's not your fault, but we'll be watching you."

As we walked back to the house, Euzèbe threw a pebble at a pigeon which was investigating some scrawny brussels sprouts. He missed by an inch and shrugged as the bird headed over the fence into the neighbour's garden.

Saturday lunch was no casual affair. The dining room was large and dark. Severe family portraits looked down from the ancient walls. The cutlery was immaculately polished, but the effect was lost in the dismal light that filtered through a north facing window. M Jodoin worked in the morning, but by one-fifteen pm he would be ready to preside. I had hoped to be seated next to Céline. The house convention dictated that I should be placed on the bench between the two brothers. Neither had washed after their exertions. Initially they ignored me, reaching over for the condiments as if I did not exist. A reproving glance from the head of the long table encouraged them to attempt conversation:

"Jean-Marc, where do you go skiing? Have you tried the new wax? It knocked several seconds off our last descents."

"I've never tried winter sports. It was too warm in Amphora. But I swim for two hours every day."

"What are your times? Does someone record you with a chronometer, or do you just paddle around?"

"I swim lengths. I could never afford it, but maybe if I had one of those new waterproof watches, I could time myself. I think they are called Oysters?"

Céline gave me a supportive look as she tried to turn the conversation to more comfortable subjects:

"Isn't an English girl, I think she's called Miss Gleitze,[14] planning to swim the Channel wearing one of those watches?"

The brothers ignored this conversational opening and gave me one last chance to demonstrate that I could provide more satisfactory answers.

"What teams are you on? Do you row? You are not too heavy. You might make an acceptable coxswain."

The Jodoins were in their late forties. Mme Jodoin was calm and hospitable with dark hair that was beginning to grey. She spent much of her week in charitable works. I liked her, but thought I detected a note of sadness behind her naturally friendly nature. She introduced me to her husband:

"Étienne always has such nice friends. Céline met Jean-Marc in his office. That's how Jean-Marc ended up in the Organist's pamphlet. He is a talented musician. We ran into him in the street just now."

M Jodoin, balding, heavyset, and with a handlebar moustache, was an intimidating figure who worked in the magistrate's office. He offered a welcome before returning to his theme:

"Jean-Marc, have you been following the Quirion case? It is absurd. The crook is obviously guilty of stealing the car. Yet, he gets away with a warning after some story about a

---

14 In 1927 Mercedes Gleitze, who was British but of German ancestry, swam the English Channel. She wore a Rolex Oyster watch.

misunderstanding with the garage owner. If he misunderstands right and wrong, he should be in a different type of institution! I'd have recommended at least fifteen years. If this is allowed to go on, they'll have to start fitting all motor cars with starter locks. Can you imagine? But Jean-Marc, tell us a little about yourself. Which school do you go to? It is a little early, but have you thought about your military service?"

This was not the moment to reveal that, as a potential delinquent, my life was now governed by Weygand's diagnosis.

"I was originally meant to take a correspondence course and then join the Swiss school system. But I have a very talented tutor. If I pass the right exams, Stéphane will become a teacher in Lourenço Marques."

"I'm sorry, do you mean he'll go to Africa?"

The conversation diverted to the enterprising Stéphane. And then a leg of lamb took priority.

I was not completely safe. M Jodoin returned to the subject of my education. Fortunately, he seemed to have grown accustomed to the idea of a tutor by the time he reached the *crème brûlée.*

"Maybe I should have considered that for my two boys. If we had locked them in the cellar with a tutor for four years, perhaps they would be able to talk about something other than sports. At least they would not confuse Patagonia with Paphlagonia. If it is not too late, I should hire this Stéphane."

The brothers shot me looks which suggested they were ready to push me back out into the cold. One of them asked:

"Jean-Marc, how do you think you will handle your military training? In my intake three recruits fainted on the first day and another cried."

Mme Jodoin put a halt to this line of questioning.

"That's enough! It is far too early to be discussing his service. I'm sure he'll be fine. I'm more interested in knowing where he learned to play the organ."

The brothers left for an important-sounding tournament. M Jodoin focused on his Saturday cigar. I explained that my mother played the island organ. I would do my homework in the little assembly hall before sitting next to her and learning to reproduce the same music. Mme Jodoin listened attentively and asked if she could come to the chapel one day when I would be playing. Céline did not seem to share her mother's musical inclinations, but she paid close attention. Although I was still young, she was making a deep impression on me. She had a heavy winter pullover with a diamond pattern when we arrived but had switched to a shapely yellow cardigan before the meal. Her eyes were an unusually deep blue.

The Jodoins were expecting a visitor. I thanked them and, with a diagram and clear instructions on how to get to the nearest tram, set off into the frigid street. As I did so, the guest's car pulled up. I could not see the driver clearly, but I thought I saw his hand lift off the wheel in a discreet gesture of recognition.

Étienne and Céline were related through the maternal branch and did not share the same surname. As I returned home, I thought I had read something related to the Jodoin family. It had meant nothing at the time. The guardian gave me his copies of an illustrated monthly magazine. Ignoring my overdue assignment from Stéphane, I searched through these until I came upon the article.

> *We commend Albert Jodoin for taking the difficult and heart-breaking decision to place justice and honesty ahead of family ties. One can only imagine the grief of an uncle who must report his adopted nephew to the authorities. Yet, one would expect no less of an official in the magistracy. Happily, the resolution of this case seems to be in the interests of both the nephew and society.*

The text indicated that the nephew, Philippe, aged fifteen of medium height, was in possession of a bicycle. He freely admitted that it did not belong to him. Its owner, according to Philippe, was a notorious bully who had hurt his friend. He left anonymous notes for the alleged thug saying that the bicycle would be returned only after his victims had received an apology. M Jodoin discovered the unusually coloured bicycle concealed under towels in his old stable. He interrogated his nephew and informed the police.

Collège Ste Agathe did not have a bad reputation. It offered year-round education high in the mountains for the inconvenient offspring of businessmen and politicians. In term time, the pupils would follow a conventional syllabus. Instead of vacations, they would practice the basics of geology and agriculture. These skills, together with weak family ties, allowed the vice-principal to operate a form of placement system. Graduating students were quietly persuaded to sign contracts for mining and farming jobs overseas. One intrepid new employee observed to a fellow passenger, who happened to be a reporter, that, of his three predecessors, one died of malaria, one of cholera, and another was injured by rebels.

The court agreed that there were mitigating circumstances and Philippe could attend Ste Agathe. His embarrassed cousins removed him from the family photograph.

11.
Édith

The guardian employed a couple who would cater dinner parties roughly every two weeks. We had a large dining room. It had been extended by the previous owner for his seminars and retained a fine frieze of pigs, boars, and root vegetables above the wainscotting. Less agreeably, it had large, ill-fitting windows. In winter, guests would stifle sneezes as they were assailed by drafts. In summer, they would perspire as if in a greenhouse. Unless the meal was strictly a dinner meeting, I would be present on the condition that I courteously said goodnight before retiring immediately after the dessert.

The guardian liked for members of any newly-formed committee to get to know each other socially before they settled down to work. The guests were often international, worthy, devoted to good causes, and heavy going. My fork would be raised with an appetizing piece of schnitzel when a middle-aged fellow diner would turn to me and say something similar to:

"Of course, it is your generation which will have to fix the mess which we have made. Are you familiar with the plight of agricultural orphans in Westphalia?"

I would make my best attempt at polite conversation until my interlocutor would relieve me with:

"But I have talked too much. Our plates are getting cold."

The dinners improved after Mme Poulenc passed away, and the guardian could ask her daughter, Édith, to join the group. To meet the standards of decorum of our conservative neighbours, another older lady would always be invited to accompany her.

Édith was elegant and in her early forties. She worked at the university, ostensibly as the departmental librarian, though it was rumoured that much of the biology department's output contained her insights published under the names of the male professors.

She was unmarried, having looked after her infirm mother for many years. Or at least that was the superficial explanation. Many years later, she would confide to my daughter that her father had moved the family to Paris and Vienna as part of his job with an insurance company. On her return to Geneva in her early twenties, she had found the city dull and provincial. She missed Mozart and Rossini at the Staatsoper, and the relaxed parties given by her friends. It had been some ten years since she left Geneva. Her former school companions found that she was now unlike them. She overheard conversations suggesting that she had succumbed to dangerous influences while abroad. Her taste in dress and her use of crystal glassware for cocktails was cited as evidence that she had embraced frivolous aspects of Viennese culture.

Édith then found a position in Munich with a friend who published a series of popular botanical guides. Here she became engaged, but tragically her fiancé was an early casualty of the Great War. Her father passed while she was in Germany, and she felt it her duty to return and look after her austere mother.

I noticed that at first Édith would only attend the dinners occasionally, but after about six months it was as though she were jointly hosting them with the guardian. Certainly, they made an excellent team. Édith carried her culture lightly, but she could charm an Italian naturalist with an apposite quotation from Dante, appreciate a German silviculturist's reference to Goethe, and comment on the mildew-resistant properties of new varieties of wheat. The dinner topics became more interesting, quieter guests were drawn into the discussion, and there was laughter. Heavy lined curtains helped subdue the drafts. Both the guardian and Édith seemed to dress a little more sharply as time went on. Indeed, the guardian's silver tie pin seemed to have the same discreet William Tell apple and arrow motif as Édith's earrings, tasteful but restrained.

I liked Édith even though I was initially a little intimidated by her brisk professional demeanour. One evening the guests were from a famine relief society. The conversation turned to two very similar looking moths. The caterpillar of one would devastate a crop, the other was largely harmless and the moth was an excellent pollinator. We had been taught about both species in Amphora. I slipped out between courses and fortunately remembered these lepidoptera well enough to draw a quick but passable sketch highlighting the differences. I passed this to Édith who, deep in deliberation, responded with, "Yes, of course" as though every sentient youth would be expected to know these things. She used the drawing in her discussion with the guests over pest control methods. Eventually the conversation moved on. I saw Édith look again at the sketch and then at me. She gave me a nod of acknowledgement which meant more than words.

One evening, instead of calling me down, the guardian came up to my room on the third floor. The space had previously been used to store veterinary specimens and did not have a door but, being approachable only by the back stairs, this was not a real problem. The floorboards creaked in the corridor, and I always had plenty of advance notice. The guardian himself slept on the second floor which was always off-limits to me, for reasons which he would not explain until much later. He knocked on the wall and asked permission to enter and sit on the bed.

Our dinner guests were prone to making casual suggestions about my future. Lately one had returned from America where he had seen a crop-dusting biplane. He believed that these machines would sharply reduce famine and represented the ideal career. Another diner was the uncle of an Olympic swimmer in Lausanne who ran training sessions on breaststroke sprints. Hearing of my visits to the consul's pool, he speculated that his nephew could have me ready to compete in the 1928 Olympics in Amsterdam, although I should not expect a medal until the next one in

America. The guardian might have pursued one of these proposals. I waited anxiously.

"Jean-Marc, you don't realize how much progress you are making. Do you remember how untidy your room used to be? You even have the bedcover folded with a proper hospital corner. "

He could not have come to my room simply to comment on my bed-making. I prepared for a more significant announcement.

"The next time Henri goes on the roof to fix a tile, I'll ask him to clean the windows in your gable. I once slept up here when the other floors were being painted. I saw Orion's Belt and Venus. Do you get pleasure from the constellations? You should enjoy them now. They will be harder to see if the road switches from gas to bright electric street lamps."

We talked for a few more minutes about astronomy. The guardian opened the windows and turned off the light. There were passing clouds, but we could still make out Sirius and part of Cassiopeia. I felt unusually close to him and remembered my father taking me out on an exceptionally clear night to view a very faint speck, which was Jupiter. The guardian turned the lamp back on, took a breath, and sat down again.

"Listen, Jean-Marc, you know that you mean everything to me? I realize that message can sometimes get obscured when we are contending with Weygand and the *curé* and so forth. That happens at your age. Anyway, I need to tell you something, but it's not going to change how I feel for you. Do you understand?"

I was not sure that I did, but I responded affirmatively.

"Édith and I have become engaged. We will be married at the end of next month, and she will come to live with us."

The guardian looked at me anxiously.

"Congratulations! She is a nice lady. I'm very happy for you." He smiled.

"Good. Do you have any questions?"

"When she is here and there are no other guests, should I go to my room immediately after dessert? If I need new socks, will I still come to you?"

I would be allowed to join the guardian and Édith in the drawing room for thirty minutes after dinner. This meant a great deal to me. Unless I had done something really wrong, this was the time when the guardian would be relaxed. I could ask for his help on anything from earache to whether it would be proper for me to address Laurent's assistant by her first name. My socks and person would remain the guardian's concern. Édith did not plan to intervene in our existing arrangements.

The guardian and Édith were planning to travel after the wedding. It was unclear who would look after me in their absence until we received an unexpected suggestion. Shortly before I met Édith, the guardian had held a dinner with one of the more difficult groups. The members were developing a scheme to provide migrant workers with a form of insurance against injuries at work. This committee had not reached consensus on their charter for achieving this laudable goal. The disappointed members were taciturn. Finland and Portugal were not on speaking terms. Belgium and Bulgaria could not look at each other. In desperation, the guardian sent me from the dinner table to fetch a publication which might interest them. This document grimly detailed accidents caused by insobriety and careless merriment.

As it happened, the paper had a quotation on its cover:

For pleasure thwarts good counsel, is the enemy of reason, and, if I may so speak, blindfolds the eyes of the mind, nor has it anything in common with virtue.

Denmark turned to me:

"Do you know where this is from?"

"I think it is Cicero.[15] My guardian made me learn it"

---

15 *De Senectute.* Translation by Andrew Peabody 1884.

Impressed, he enquired about other texts that I was made to study. The committee unanimously commended the guardian on my upbringing:

"So many youths today are spoiled and spineless. One wonders whether they will have the moral framework to make the right decisions if there is another war. It is wonderfully refreshing that you are training this one to be well-mannered and industrious. He will thank you for it in the future."

They then reminisced jovially about their own youthful learnings.

The dinner party apparently made a deep impression on the team. A few weeks later they sent a fine Easter egg with a card addressed to both the guardian and myself. Later, on learning of the impending matrimony, Romania suggested that his brother's family should look after me while the guardian and Édith enjoyed a three-week honeymoon on the Nile. His nieces and nephews needed to practice their French. The guardian made me promise to continue with the cod liver oil, the temperature checks, and the avoidance of any violent sports. My other restrictions were temporarily suspended.

I made it to Bucharest by appearing nervous and so clearly incompetent that kindly passengers in fur hats steered me to the right connecting trains and answered questions for me at the borders. I was very grateful for this last service. My Amphora papers consisted of an amiable letter from my friend Paul's godmother. She explained that all the official stamps had been lost in the earthquake. The registrar had died but, as his assistant, she could vouch for me. Had I heard that the breakwater might be rebuilt?

My Swiss status was lost in a sea of bureaucracy. My father was missing but not officially confirmed dead, so Forms in the A series did not apply. I was not the guardian's legally adopted son, so we could not use Form B. Switzerland did not recognize

Amphora as a country, which ruled out most of the remaining alphabet.

The children in Bucharest had been brought up with French nannies and tutors. Their vocabulary was probably richer than mine. I was able to provide a little help with the occasional oddity in their grammar, but above all I got to enjoy companionship with three girls and two boys of my generation.

On the first morning, I took my temperature and swallowed my cod liver oil a little furtively in case they might tease me for these unorthodox practices.

"Jean-Marc, what are you taking? Can we see the bottle?"

They read the effusive claims on the label. Ileana, the oldest girl, remarked:

"So, this is why your eyes are so full of life! I thought you looked different from the boys around here. Would you mind if Alex and I tried some, just until Wednesday? We need to look good for the concert. And maybe it will help make Alex a little smarter too."

Her brother, who was admiring the thermometer, added:

"You Swiss really know how to make instruments."

My new friends cheerfully showed me around their city, Carol Park, the Patriarchal Cathedral, and the coffee houses, as I revelled in my vacation from the *curé* and Weygand. I loved them, and we exchanged letters for years afterwards.

The family was well-connected. My host was concerned about my lack of proper documents and feared that I might be refused entry at one of the several borders between Romania and Switzerland. Alexandru, the eldest son, earned a little pocket money as a page at the Royal Palace. Strings were pulled, and I was appointed to the same position and lent a uniform. My duties consisted of mirroring Alex as he bowed and opened the other side of the double doors. I tried to imitate his effortless action as I pulled against the weight of the thick, solid wood, over three meters high, and adorned with eagles, cherubs, and heavy metal crests. The doors led to a chamber where meritorious citizens would receive titles and honours.

When it was time for me to return, my host presented me with a magnificent vellum credential informing all to whom it might concern that I was a page courier on official business for King Ferdinand. He gave me some sealed letters for his brother in a leather pouch embossed with royal insignia. This was to remain tied to me throughout the journey. In the event, the border guards were more interested in the older passengers, and I did not need to establish my diplomatic status. The guardian was a little shocked by my host's ruse. But, relaxed and cheerful after his honeymoon, he allowed me a few francs to frame this strange certificate.

Édith left my management in the guardian's hands, but occasionally she would make an exception to support me:

"Édouard, of course Jean-Marc can't find shirts with those collars. No one his age has worn that style for the last twenty years. You should let him go to Bovet Suisse. They will have something appropriate."

She quietly arranged an increase in my allowance and, to the guardian's surprise, encouraged me to spend it on some popular magazines.

"You can't only read those old texts from the Society. I'm sure they are very good for you, but you also need to know what is happening in this century. There is a prize of a picnic hamper and accordion if you can write the winning lyrics for the competition in *The Swiss Adventurer.*"

Soon after moving in with us, Édith invited a distant and slightly humourless cousin to dinner. Our guest was of delicate disposition, and I had been forewarned that no seasonings or oils would be used in any of the recipes. I was not paying much attention to the conversation, which concerned a politician who set policy based on astrological advice. Then suddenly I heard Édith's voice:

"Jean-Marc, what star sign are you? When is your birthday?"

I looked up from my boiled chicken with semolina.

"I'm not sure about the sign. My birthday was last Tuesday."

She responded:

"Are you joking? Édouard, did you know that? Why did you not tell us? What did you do?"

I was not sure how to answer these questions but volunteered the following:

"It's alright. I made three cards, like I used to get. Father always drew a car or an aeroplane, Mother would do an animal or a plant, and my friend Paul would sketch me doing something made up. This year I drew one of those Ford Trimotor aeroplanes, a chameleon, and me swimming with a walrus in front of the consul's murals, the one with Ariadne and the bull. I'm using them as bookmarks now. Sometimes, if I have a better report from the *curé*, the guardian will give me one of those candied almonds that he has on his desk. I kept three for my birthday."

I had never seen Édith look so upset.

"But why did you keep it to yourself? We'd have been happy to celebrate with you."

I fell back on my standard adolescent answers:

"I don't know. It's hard to explain."

Then making a little more effort, I managed:

"I know it does not make any sense, but for a day I have my old life back again and I'm with my friend Paul and my parents. His birthday was just before mine."

Édith looked slightly relieved:

"No, that does make sense. We don't want to intrude on your memories. But you must also have a Genevan birthday. I remember that the Michaelmas daisies were flowering when Édouard first pointed you out to me. You wore that naturally-dyed linen shirt which matched them. You had just arrived that week and were exploring the garden. We can use September twenty-ninth.[16]

Édouard, we must absolutely organize a proper celebration. How long has Jean-Marc been here?"

During Édith's first years, Weygand's treatment plan would have seemed non-negotiable. The guardian had already mitigated it as far as his sense of duty would allow. Nonetheless, without in any way undermining the guardian's authority, Édith quietly helped keep my challenges in perspective. We were having coffee in a sheltered corner of the patio when she asked:

"Édouard, this is the first warm day we've had all spring. Would it be so terrible if Jean-Marc took the afternoon off? He could take that new steamer on the lake and deliver my mother's psalter to Cousin Amédée in Nyon."

Before the guardian could ask if I was already late with my assignments, she added:

"There is a dusty Roman museum in the castle there. You could explain to the *curé* that he needed an educational trip to learn about Julius Caesar."

She clearly saw that it was unhealthy to be separated from people of my own age. At one lunch she interrupted the guardian and me with:

"I feel like I'm listening to two aged coachmen. I'm not sure my graduate students would even know those old terms for a car!"

Biding her time, she laid the groundwork with the guardian for my transition into the world of my contemporaries. I am sure that it is due to her that I could spend my final teenage years in design college with several months in student lodgings.

---

16 Michaelmas day is September twenty-ninth for many denominations.

12.
The Institute of the Deaf

One of the guardian's dinner guests was an enthusiastic young sanitation engineer from Amsterdam. Over the minestrone this stocky individual engaged Édith in an earnest discussion of algae in city reservoirs and how high concentrations impacted the purification process. She gamely pursued this topic until serving the cod *meunière* required her attention. The other guests were safely occupied in other conversations, and he turned his gold-rimmed glasses in my direction.

"Jean-Marc, have you ever visited Amsterdam?"

He described the well-engineered bridges, sluice-gates, and canals in his neighbourhood and explained why there was no flooding even in the worst storms. The teenagers were equally noteworthy. Every evening these youths would load up their bicycles with unsold loaves from the bakeries and take them to the soup kitchens.

"Jean-Marc, I'm sure you must make a similar contribution. Tell us some of the places where you volunteer."

The other voices had become quiet as the diners picked up Édith's elegant fish knives to tackle the cod. Everyone seemed to be looking at me.

There was a pause before I emitted an embarrassed stammer.

The guardian seemed unsure whether to intervene. He picked up his silver napkin ring, turned it around, and put it down. He cleared his throat as it became clear that I needed rescue:

"Jean-Marc, Bernhard has described an excellent example for you to follow. You are nearly fifteen and old enough now. We'll help you find an appropriate cause."

I hoped that the guardian had forgotten. He rarely forgot anything, but I clung to the notion that a comment thrown out at a dinner might not constitute a firm commitment. However, some three weeks later he returned from a walk and informed me before even taking his coat off:

"Édith and I have arranged for you to assist at the Institute for the Deaf on weekend afternoons. It will do you good to help others. Mme Langlois, the director, is expecting you at one-twenty pm. They maintain high standards for the residents, so make sure that your shoes are polished and your hair is tidy."

I resigned myself sulkily to this assignment. I had enjoyed Saturdays and Sundays exploring the woods and fields which were then easily accessible from the city. I would return with leaves and insects which I would draw and attempt to identify. The guardian had tolerated this pastime but considered it a little childish. I was to put this rustic pursuit behind me and learn the value of service.

The institute was a large edifice at the top of a steep hill. The front grounds, with rose beds and tidy herbaceous borders, were pleasant. The building, decorated with asymmetrical turrets and disfigured with unsympathetic extensions, was not. I found the director's office, a bright room with curved windows and painted a pale pink. The furniture was upholstered with scenes of willow trees and troubadours with lutes. Mme Langlois was in her sixties, dressed in a matching pearl grey skirt and blazer, and initially had the manner of a severe headmistress. She fitted me with white armbands bearing two red trumpets in the shape of the cross while assessing my skills.

"So, Jean-Marc, do you know any of the versions of sign language?"

"I'm sorry, no."

She handed me a list of books in the Institute's library. They all seemed to be by obscure authors of whom I had never heard.

"Would you be able to recommend any of these if a resident wanted to read something with travel and romance?"

"I'm sorry, no."

"I see."

A knock on the door halted the questions temporarily. The secretary had brought us tea. The cups and saucers were small, delicate, and eggshell-thin. The pattern showed a figure by a river against the background of a mountain range. I studied the cup and handle carefully. The bottom of the handle had an ornate curve, and I vaguely remembered that there was some rule of etiquette about how a teacup of this type should be held with the little finger correctly positioned. I hoped Mme Langlois would drink first. She would certainly notice if I made an error.

My host jumped to a conclusion:

"I am impressed that you are interested in the design. It is based on the Psalm: *I will lift up mine eyes unto the hills: from whence cometh my help.*"

She gestured towards the view of the Jura mountains and continued:

"In difficult times, I have often drawn inspiration from this tea set. It was a wedding present from a great-uncle who founded a school of Christian ceramics in Pondicherry. I only use it with the better blends of tea. But, please, drink before it gets cold."

I politely declined the offer of a Marie biscuit. They looked dry, and any crumbs would have stood out accusingly against the polished wood surface of the table. I finished my tea without committing any major *faux pas*. Mme Langlois retrieved my cup and saucer and placed them safely across the room.

The interview resumed. I was too young to be entrusted with a scalding urn for the residents' morning coffee. However, the institute was not able to replace the junior gardener in this budget year. Perhaps I could help with the weeding? I would need to return tomorrow in more appropriate clothes.

Sensing my disappointment at the weeding option, Mme Langlois continued in a gentler tone:

"Walking through the garden is very important therapy for the residents. Your contribution will be significant and appreciated. But first let me take you on a tour of the building. In bad weather you'll be able to give a hand to the domestic staff. We keep the institute so clean that you will find very few bacteria here."

We set off down a long dark corridor. The spotless cement floor had a strong odour of disinfectant. Mme Langlois explained that the brass rail on the side would be a candidate for polishing on wet days. We came to a hallway where an imposing oil painting depicted an ill-clad Sisyphus dismally rolling his rock up the hill in Hades.

"Isn't this quite magnificent? We had it appraised last year. We are told it dates from 1560 and is by a follower of Titian. Other residents have left us pictures of gambolling lambs and the deportation of the Acadians."

We passed the refectory where a bust of Socrates looked down from a large mantelpiece. The rooms had strange pictures and ornaments, but they were not excessive in number, well-displayed, and helped to create an ambience that more closely resembled a slightly eccentric hotel in a sleepy resort than a medical institution.

We inspected a bleach-scented laundry room where I might one day graduate to folding towels. We passed through a slightly stuffy day room with the oil painting of the lambs. A few somnolent residents below it made faint gestures of greeting as we made our way to an outside patio. To access the French door, we had to negotiate an elderly couple presiding over a cart with the tea urn and a plate of minute apricot jam sandwiches cut into triangles. The front garden was well-tended and laid out in clean geometric shapes, but, at the rear, eight large beds were overcome with bindweed, dandelions, and groundsel. A former head gardener had been inspired by the British horticulturist, Gertrude Jekyll. The rear beds nearest the house were to be planted in a cottage garden style with a carefully selected profusion of colours and shapes. The plots a little further away would grow herbs and vegetables interspersed with delphiniums and nicotiana. This ambitious project won awards for several years before the head gardener died. It proved unsustainable, and now fuchsias and lupins competed with the weeds while potatoes and lavender shared space with self-seeded forget-me-nots and violas. Mme Langlois reassured me:

"It is not as bad as it looks. Just tackle half a bed on each visit. The former director's wife spent time in America and had this hedge apple fence planted to screen the compost heap. Later in the year it will be covered in inedible fruit, like tennis balls but green. Be careful, it is thorny. She was a strange lady. She once collected the fruit for a most peculiar party on All Hallow's Eve."

My efforts may not have been very effective from a horticultural perspective, but my presence seemed to please the residents. They would watch for me as one might look out for a fawn which only appears in the garden at certain times of day. They would wave and helpfully point out areas which I had missed with my trowel. Two ladies would smuggle out sandwiches for me in their purses. I appreciated this kind gesture, although my hands were often rather muddy for eating.

The green balls had formed some months later when I was accosted by the burly driver of a small delivery vehicle. He strode over in immaculately pressed working clothes and peered at me.

"I'm Davide Carter. Mme Langlois said you would be able to give us a hand. It should not take too long. Are you the only person here today? No offence, I was expecting someone stronger. You should practice your press-ups before you do your turn in the army."

He untied the pickup's canvas cover to reveal a Louis XVI dresser which had been converted to house electrical equipment.

"We must be very careful. One jolt could damage the valves. They are expensive and imported from Leipzig. M de Saint Hilaire will be here in a minute to supervise."

I enquired:

"Is it a radio receiver?"

"No! Haven't you heard? Really? It was in all the papers. De Saint Hilaire has designed a machine that will louden voices so that partially deaf people can hear them. You can change the pitch if the patients hear men better than women or vice-versa. It is a Swiss invention. You should feel very privileged to be part of this."

In truth, I was dirty, perspiring, and hoping for a glass of water after rooting out dandelions.

The well-groomed and energetic M de Saint Hilaire walked out from the building. He wore a white cable sweater and a boater with a silk band. He must have been in his forties and had an excited verbal delivery as though he were encouraging Davide and me to win a tennis doubles final:

"Come on, boys, this is one of the most important things that you will ever do. You look like you might have just enough muscle between you to handle it. Edge the dresser towards the back of the truck. Then the gardener must steady it while Davide takes the left side, and he takes the right. Do you understand?"

Before we could reply, a large hawk swooped over us before disappearing into the compost heap and re-emerging with something between its claws.

De Saint Hilaire watched it and observed:

"Aren't hawks meant to be a good omen? What are those things like green oranges?"

I seemed to win credit by explaining that the American settlers had used *maclura pomifera* for edging their homesteads.

As Davide and I struggled across the courtyard with the heavy cabinet, de Saint Hilaire kept telling me about the plans for his businesses.

"I'll need someone after I build my factory in Plan-les-Ouates. You can plant those American things round the perimeter. We'll have dill and sunflowers by the boardroom window. They will represent vigorous growth. I don't want little things like snowdrops. Did Davide tell you he used to train recruits? He'd be able to get you running up mountains with a rifle and a fifty-pound transmitter in your backpack. Do you know morse code? You'll need it if you want to be an apprentice tester on one of my other inventions. My Théophile was fluent in it when he was eleven. He was only allowed cake and pastries if he spelled them out in Morse. Now he occupies an important post at the foreign ministry in Bern. He starts at two am and decodes urgent signals from our *chargés d'affaires* in Montevideo, Bogota, and..."

He did not finish the thought and barked at me:

"Pay attention, will you? You need to keep the machine level! Concentrate as if you were a waiter with a tray of hot drinks! Hopeless, utterly hopeless."

I felt a retrospective sympathy for the young Théophile as he attempted to spell out *'profiterole'* in morse.

The equipment was heavy, and I was in some discomfort by the time we lowered it delicately in one of the ground floor rooms.

"Gardener, don't leave us now. You must stay while we test it and show it to the staff and volunteers."

I managed to escape to have some water and telephone the guardian to say I might be late.

On my return to the room with the equipment, de Saint Hilaire continued:

"Now watch while I set it up. We only need to use these two switches on the left at first. Once the valves warm up and you hear a faint hum, turn these three dials to the right. It is so simple. Now, Davide, speak quietly into the microphone. Whatever your name is, hold this to your ear while I adjust the dial."

Davide's voice sounded loud and changed from bass to a strange falsetto as de Saint Hilaire adjusted the dials.

"Excellent. Now, gardener, try working the dials. That's good. You have the hang of it."

I had a few minutes to rinse my face and tidy up before Mme Langlois and the volunteer team arrived. The women were in cardigans and sensible shoes while the few elderly men looked exhausted and ready to return home. After some flowery preamble, de Saint Hilaire explained:

"During the first months, one of my technicians will operate the voice magnifier for you during the week. He will make notes that we can show to prospective investors. But on the weekend, one of the volunteer team members must manage it. It is very easy, as even your juvenile gardener can now demonstrate. Meanwhile I will describe the process."

De Saint Hilaire expounded incomprehensibly about rheostats, capacitors, and thermionic diodes. I flicked the two switches, waited for the hum, and turned the three dials. The other volunteers were at least forty years older than I was, confused by the presentation, and suspicious of the electric machine. As a result, it was decided that I should be recalled from my weeding duties. I was to be the weekend operator in charge of one of Europe's most innovative devices. During the day I was to ensure that no liquids came near it and that nothing was ever placed on the cabinet or the vent holes. At dusk I was to unplug it and wait seven minutes for the valves to cool before carefully unfolding a dust cover embroidered with the national flag and the verse from Isaiah:

"Then shall the eyes of the blind be opened and the ears of the deaf unstopped."

On Saturdays, I would set up the machine so that visitors could communicate with their relatives without shouting. I would offer the male residents an earpiece mounted on an uncomfortable but effective heavy metal frame which could be adjusted for head size by turning a large butterfly nut. The ladies preferred to hold the speaker on a tortoise shell stick. This meant that I did not interfere with their coiffure or offend propriety by standing too close.

On Sunday afternoons, the chaplain for the Institute would take fifteen minutes with members of his flock who had at least some hearing ability. He was a gaunt, serious man in his forties with a recent doctorate in divinity and a somewhat sombre countenance. I would adjust the machine, ensure that the congregant was comfortable, and discreetly withdraw.

I wore my best shirt with cufflinks and attempted to project a professional image as befitted my new position. But perhaps I came over as a little self-important. The chaplain never warmed to me. When the last resident had left, he would lead me in prayer. We would request strength to resist pride, arrogance, and vanity.

One of the doors from the room with the voice magnifier opened onto the cobbled courtyard. I was waiting in the autumn sunshine for the pastor to finish with a resident when a sweet, dark-haired girl of around seven sat by me on the bench and gestured shyly at a picture book. I knew that she was Julie, the sole survivor of a tragic gas explosion which had killed her family. The doctors were uncertain whether her loss of hearing and speech was permanent, or even whether it was physical or a result of the psychological trauma. I was roughly the age of her eldest brother. The older staff and volunteers were good, kind people, but maybe rather brisk and intimidating to this young child in her pretty blue and yellow dress.

Happily, Julie could read, and I scrawled "Back in two minutes" in my exercise book when the chaplain tapped impatiently on the window to indicate that I needed to set up the next patient. Returning, I ran my finger along the text in her book, reading it aloud in case this might help her hearing. When we came to the pictures, I would react with exaggerated facial expressions which amused her, and suddenly she hugged me.

Mme Langlois must have observed us from one of the many windows which overlooked the courtyard. I was putting the cover on the machine when I received a message that she needed to see me in her office immediately.

"I'm sorry. Did I do something wrong? The girl came and seemed to want to share the book with me."

"No. On the contrary. I have not seen Julie look so happy. Listen, I know it is asking a lot, but can you come back every day for three weeks to read with her for an hour? If her issue is in her mind, she may open up to you. If not, the company will still do her good. The last report was encouraging, and the doctors don't see any irreversible physical damage that would prevent her from hearing again. It is alright if you dress less formally."

"I'd enjoy helping her. Would you mind writing a note to my guardian? Otherwise, he'll suspect I'm off playing baccarat at Thonon."

I was not prepared for her reply:

"Benoît, my late husband, was remarkably skilled at the tables. We had wonderful times in Thonon when we were younger. But don't tell that to the residents! I'll have my secretary deliver the note tomorrow."

The few children's books at the Institute, published by a local Guild for Moral Advancement, were edifying rather than entertaining. On my next visit to the bookstore, I asked Étienne for recommendations. He gave me his *Alice au pays des merveilles*. He would use an English copy to reference the engraving technique.

One of the more energetic residents was M Boudillet, a tall, semi-retired journalist with a taste for boldly-coloured cravats. He had lost his hearing during the Great War from the percussion of a nearby shell. The other residents did not entirely approve of him: he had recently acquired a Leica with an amazingly fast shutter and had embraced the trend towards candid photography. His output included promenaders wrestling with frilly parasols in a summer breeze, and an executive under an umbrella nonchalantly watching his drenched chauffeur repair a pneumatic tire. One irate subscriber complained in a letter to the editor:

"M Boudillet should understand that the camera is properly deployed to show mankind at its best: tidy, smiling,

courageous, and respectable. He demeans his craft with images of the quotidian and the undignified."

For my part, I rather liked this unconventional septuagenarian who, every few weeks, would change his beard or moustache. He let me examine his precious Leica and would gently tease the chaplain by looking to me as though I were the one running his Sunday session.

Julie adored *Alice.* Her morale had definitely improved, but her hearing had not returned. In a few days, a decision would have to be made about her longer-term care. The afternoons were still warm enough for us to sit outside in the sheltered courtyard, and I resumed my reading. When I came to one of the pictures, I stopped for a sip of water and said:

"I've been doing all the hard work. Can you tell me who this is?"

"*C'est le Chat du Cheshire. Tu le sais bien.*"

"Very good! My throat is dry. Can you read the rest of the page?"

Julie stumbled over a couple of the longer adverbs, but her voice was clear with only the smallest suggestion that her hearing might be damaged. I heard the click of a camera shutter.

Boudillet had the timing of a great correspondent. The photo caught the moment perfectly. Julie was clearly happy, and yet there was a hint of her underlying bravery. I happened to be relatively presentable with sleeves neatly rolled, and my arm bands on the right way up. The article was published the next day as follow up to an earlier account of the gas explosion.

Julie recovered her speech and almost all her hearing. She was able to leave the Institute to join an excellent foster family. She made me promise to keep in touch. Without knowing it, she and her picture were to render me a great service.

13.
Below the Roller Coaster

I was slowly becoming independent and had just started to spend most weeknights in a student lodging near the design college. I was a little more confident and had been delighted when the elderly salesman in boys' hosiery and shirts at the guardian's tailor handed me over to his colleague with the words:

"Take good care of him. He can now wear the smaller sizes in the menswear section."

My elevation to menswear was not necessarily matched on other levels of maturity. I did not yet need to shave regularly, and my voice did not take on the bolder timbre of some of my friends. Nonetheless, I was making progress towards adulthood in the company of friends at the college. They did not hesitate to remark that I was a little different, but they liked having me participate in their social activities and their teasing was gentle and good-natured.

I was about to leave the guardian's after a Sunday visit when the telephone rang. The guardian called me over and whispered, "Julie's family". I had seen her a few times in the months after she was adopted, but now our interaction at the Institute for the Deaf seemed far in the past.

It was her foster mother:

"Jean-Marc, I have no right to ask. We promised Julie a trip to the fair next week, but we are all in quarantine with measles. Julie had it long ago. Do you have immunity? Would you be able to take her?"

Julie must have been nearly eleven now. My moment of responsibility had arrived. I had sometimes looked after the neighbour's dog, but, in Geneva, I had never been entrusted with taking anyone anywhere.

My preparations were sufficiently thorough that they could have passed military inspection. I had researched the buses and trams. I had an alternate plan in case any road was closed. I had walked the route so I knew exactly where the fair would be and where we could stop for a break or shelter from rain.

I was normally at pains to project a more mature student image. To please Julie, however, I would wear a scarf with a pattern of steam trains which she had made for me years ago in one of her rehabilitation classes. My hair would not be fashionably greased. She had often commented on my dishevelled locks, which brought back fond memories of her brother.

The doctors remained cautious despite Julie's remarkable recovery. Her foster parents were quite clear. On no account were we to go on the roller coaster where the abrupt changes in air pressure could damage her hearing. Bumper cars, a new invention which I had never seen, were out of the question. We would enjoy the fairground organ, candy floss, and the many stalls.

Julie seemed to be flourishing. No longer frail and shy, she was ready to explore all the attractions:

"Jean-Marc, can we watch the dancers from Omsk? At the end they run into the crowd and give the girls white roses."

The fair, while doubtless modest by the standards of Berlin or Paris, seemed enormous to Julie and me. It stretched over several fields and included a python with a sinister large lump in its middle, Italian clowns, speed knitters who could produce a sweater in three minutes, and a Silk Road with a Bactrian camel, exotic fabrics, spices, and trinkets. We had foregone the forbidden rides despite the tempting squeals emanating from the rumbling roller coaster, and fate had rewarded us with luck at the stalls. Julie had thrown a quoit over an upright spear earning an approving murmur from the spectators.

"Come, Jean-Marc. Help me choose my prize. I like the pen, but look at the jewellery."

She had finally selected a small bracelet of semi-precious stones. A little later, I managed to aim a horseshoe into the mouth of the painted devil. For my prize, I selected a china elephant painted with red hearts in a folk-art style. The ornament was for Julie.

Julie's foster mother had given her a few francs to buy me a present from one of the food vendors. She handed me the bracelet and the elephant while I reserved our place at an outside table.

"Jean-Marc, can you put the bracelet around my elephant? He'll look like he belongs to a maharajah with his jewelled harness. He is so cute!"

She took a few steps, stooped, and returned with two little white daisies.

"These are for him, too."

The fair was getting a little crowded, and I kept a careful eye on Julie as she stood in a queue to buy 'the best wurst outside of Regensburg'. Reassuringly, she happened to be next to a Swiss German lady who we knew faintly, as she had sometimes cooked at the Institute for the Deaf.

I sat alone with my scarf, dressing an elephant in a bracelet and flowers. A voice said softly, "Hello Jean-Marc, I see you have new toys." before calling out, "Céline, it's that kid, the one who came to lunch a couple of years ago."

I reddened and turned to see Céline's older brother, Honoré. He leaned over me with an expression that left me unable to determine if this was just the same banter that he exchanged with his brother. I did not know how to reply, and he did not offer any remark on the lines of 'I'm only teasing'. Behind him was Céline, enjoying the company of a handsome, tall, blond friend in an expensive Italian jacket and a leather cap. He put his hand on her back as he guided her past a marshy patch. They had come with Étienne and his fiancée, who waved from a stall, the Walls of Jericho, where they were competing for a sealed tureen of carrot and ginger soup. The contestants needed to stamp on the floor and blow the horns with sufficient vigour to make an artificial wall collapse. I wished they had been closer, for Étienne would surely have found the right words to put me at ease.

Céline greeted me:

"Hello, Jean-Marc, this is my friend, Olaf. His family moved here from Norway. He skis with my brothers, or at least he's teaching them how to slalom. He won a medal last year."

We all professed to be pleased to meet each other. I was still concerned about Julie and watched as the wurst line came to a halt, ready for the next batches from the grill and boil pan. The vendors' adult son, in lederhosen, entertained the waiting customers with a spirited rendition of *Ein Jäger aus Kurpfalz*. The cook seemed to be explaining this folk song to Julie who was not looking in my direction.

Olaf could not resist:

"So, Jean-Marc, that is a very fine elephant?"

"It's not for me. It's a present for my friend Julie. She is buying us sausages."

"That's nice. But when you get older, you should remember that it is normally the boy who pays."

I could see that Céline was uncomfortable with the conversation. She broke in:

"Have you been on the roller coaster yet? They say that it is almost like the Russian Mountain in Copenhagen. Do you want to come with us? I'd be happy to get you tickets."

"I'm sorry, I can't. Julie is not allowed because of the pressures in her ears. I promised I'd watch her."

"Which one is she?"

"The one in the white skirt and the embroidered yellow blouse."

Julie was now deep in conversation with the cook as they studied the chalkboard menu. There was little indication that she had any connection with me. The party offered unpersuasive goodbyes and, rejoining Étienne and Marie-Pierre, headed past a wax Napoleon Bonaparte towards the roller coaster. I gloomily reflected that I stood no chance against Olaf. Even if I had been dressed smartly, I could not have competed against this cosmopolitan skiing champion. I should try to put Céline out of my mind, at least for now. Julie came back, smiling and with three different varieties of sausage that she had carefully selected on advice from the cook.

"Sorry it took so long. But it looked as if you were with some friends?"

"Yes, I suppose they were friends. But tell me about the types of sausage."

I forced myself to look cheerful and focused on making sure that Julie had only good memories of the day.

Two months later, I was surprised to receive an invitation to accompany Céline to an exhibition of works by Lucas Cranach the Elder[17] on the unlikely grounds that I was the only friend sufficiently artistic to enjoy them. Cupid was playing a deep hand which would not be explained to me until years later.

---

17 Lucas Cranach the Elder died 1553, and his son are known for portraits of German Protestant reformers including Martin Luther and Philip Melanchthon.

14.
A Rumour and an Interview

Unusually that week, the texts which I needed to study for the Society were not in the Master Volume, but spread across four particularly heavy tomes which I had taken home. I was now struggling to board the crowded tram with them on my way back to the bookstore. One of the older print room mechanics saw me:

"Jean-Marc, come here. Take my seat. You can't carry those old books all the way. Are they as dreary as they look?"

He was of a kind disposition, with a slight limp, apparently the result of being kicked by the irritable horse which was eventually replaced by the bookstore's motorized van. I knew him relatively well from Laurent's tours. He would explain at length how some improper adjustment had been detected only to concede that it had been fixed in two minutes with no material loss to production.

When we arrived at our destination, he insisted, to my mild embarrassment, on helping me by carrying two of the books into the building. I accompanied him like a child being escorted into school by an overprotective parent. As it happened, a meeting on the revised shift schedules had just ended, and we were greeted in the corridor by almost the entire production crew.

I appreciated small courtesies such as these, but I also sensed a certain deference as I grew older. I could not understand this, and it made me feel faintly uncomfortable. Doors were held open politely, if unnecessarily, and the cruder terms for some of the mechanical breakdowns were no longer employed in my presence. The new apprentices determinedly addressed me as 'Monsieur', though I would have much preferred 'Jean-Marc' or 'J-M'.

I was on one of my last visits to the bookstore with Hervé, who increasingly stood in for Laurent who was on a trip to a paper vendor. Hervé seemed to enjoy the occasional session with me as a break from his duties as an operations accountant. He was less formal than Laurent, certainly well-read, and had no problem guiding me through the texts from the Society. Following Laurent's practice, he would take the opportunity to check on the operations for the daily report as we went to and from the basement. He and Herménégilde, the production supervisor, had just determined that a much-anticipated treatise on Pauline theology would have to be reworked over the weekend. The extensive Hebrew and Greek quotations had been incorrectly set and were drastically out of proportion to the other fonts. Hervé and Herménégilde explained to the setter:

"There is no choice. We committed that the volume would be ready for the international symposium. Professors are travelling from Edinburgh and Johannesburg to discuss the new interpretation. The author met his deadlines."

There was an uncomfortable silence broken only by the rumbling of the presses through the thin partition of the supervisor's office. The employee, a pencil-thin new father, looked broken:

"My parents are only here until the midday train on Sunday. They came specially to see their grandson and spend time with me. They can't afford another trip from Nantes this year."

Herménégilde replied gently:

"I'm really sorry, but you are the only person here who knows the languages and foreign character sets well enough. Listen, I'll see if Luc can work some overtime. He used to speak Greek with his grandmother. Come in on Sunday afternoon as soon as you have seen your parents off. I'll be here, and we'll work all night if we have to."

After thanking the supervisor, the distressed employee noticed me and flushed.

"Jean-Marc, I'm so sorry. It won't ever happen again."

Mystified, I murmured something trite to the effect that we all make mistakes.

As we went down the ramp to the basement, I gave Hervé a questioning look. By now it was clear that I would soon be released from my obligations at the Society, and he felt comfortable talking freely to me.

"It's alright. Everyone knows you outrank Herménégilde and me."

I stared blankly at him until he continued:

"There is a rumour that you are related to the proprietor's family. Look, there is a certain logic even if it is completely wrong. Why else would Laurent take you on his reviews and expose you to every aspect of the business? Why does the proprietor suddenly ask us how you are doing in the middle of a meeting on ink wastage? Didn't he ask Étienne to take you to an exhibition? Laurent's aunt, or maybe she was a second cousin, worked here. Then she disappeared to Italy for a rest cure of nine months before settling in Corsica. Apparently, the timing would have been just right for you to be her son. You're not, are you?"

He paused.

"But seriously, you've picked up more knowledge than you realize. You've reminded me more than once when I forgot to check something important. You remember, when we nearly bound the Italian edition of *Reflections of an Antiquarian from Lausanne* with the French cover, or when they were about to scrap the good version of *A Guide to Hydraulic Pumps*. You're alright."

As Hervé noted correctly, I had been given a privileged view of the business, and there was a tacit assumption that I would work in the bookstore. This option was not out of the question, but my history there had included inglorious elements. I had hated most of the boring texts from the wretched Society and struggled to memorize their interminable sentences. I had been frustrated and even petulant in front of Laurent and Hervé. As I walked home past the Reformation Wall and the statues of Calvin and Knox, I reflected that it might be better to find my own way. Towards the end of my time at the design college, I saw an advertisement for a junior position at the local office of a Swedish manufacturer of printing presses.

The guardian was delighted that I had secured an interview. While cautioning me not to raise my hopes unreasonably, he attempted to make me successful. He took me into his study where he had set up a tray with peach nectar, candied orange slices, and a pad of paper for me to take notes. Here I was fully briefed on the company, its capitalization, its markets, and the unpronounceable names of the board members. I had a new shirt and fresh laces.

"Everyone would understand if you were struck by lightning on the way to an interview. But if you turn up with untied shoes or a missing button, it is a clear sign that you cannot be trusted with the company's assets. I've arranged an appointment for you at Baudet just before the interview. He is one of the best barbers in the city. I've told him to send me the bill, so follow his recommendations."

The Salon Baudet aimed for discretion. Each customer was taken to their own small room. I would not be able to see if the manager of the neighbouring bank had his nails filed, or if his hair owed its lustre to a bottle from Germany. I was assigned a chair in a cell with a small, frosted glass window, and decorated with hunting scenes, a post horn, and the mounted heads of a fox and a mountain goat. My session was under the personal direction of Baudet's pallid grandson, who must have been in his mid-twenties. He did not cut hair himself but issued a stream of instructions to a longsuffering assistant nearly three times his age:

"The gentleman's future career could depend on this. Make sure to use a very close razor and apply a strong aftershave. It is alright if it burns a little. He needs to look vigorous with healthy skin. Don't use one of the older pomades. We don't want him to give off the scents of the last century."

I was unaware of the disastrous result until I returned home some hours later. I was nearly nineteen, though I was routinely mistaken for sixteen. With rosy cheeks, fresh shave, and a schoolboy haircut, I now resembled a fourteen-year-old who had been tidied up to attend a family wedding.

Mlle Lebel, the receptionist at the printing company, greeted me amicably in a polished Parisian accent. Before I had the chance to give my name, she guided me into the office of the chief accountant. Balding and with heavy glasses, he immediately pushed an open ledger aside, beamed, and then looked confused.

"Mlle Lebel, this person is not my nephew."

He smiled again and turned to me.

"Are you Marc-André's friend from the rowing club? You will be very welcome to join us for a late lunch."

I explained that I had come for the interview.

Mlle Lebel apologized to the chief accountant:

"You can see how I thought he might be your young nephew. I'm so sorry."

She led me to a seat in the reception area and cast irritated glances in my direction until the chimes of a grandfather clock in the hallway confirmed that it was time for the interview. We ascended an elegant, curved staircase before she thrust me into the oak-panelled meeting room with its chandelier, discoloured by cigarette smoke, and sepia portraits of the company's unsmiling founders:

"Here is the candidate. I already told him that you don't have much time."

The managers, one from sales and one from operations, offered a sufficiently professional welcome. Sales looked tired and kept polishing his glasses. Operations had a trace of a Swedish accent and seemed taken with his new mechanical pencil. He disassembled and reassembled it while outlining the responsibilities of the position. I could see that it was a fine instrument in nickel and with a replaceable built-in eraser and a compartment for spare leads. After a few standard opening queries, he asked the question that was designed to expose my unsuitability and let us all head home:

"The Superna-365 is one of our main competitors. What do you know of its strengths and weaknesses?"

Laurent loved the Superna-365. The print quality was impeccable, illustrations were clear, and it could handle a wide variety of specialist grade papers. Hervé would fume about the set-up time, the slow run speed, the additional operator, and the exorbitant cost of maintenance. I had nothing to lose. I had examples and anecdotes. The words came and I delivered a tolerably articulate presentation in industry terminology. By the end the interested interviewers were asking questions:

"You said that you ran the *Histoire sincère des pêcheurs* on the Superna-365? That must have been a big run. Would the Dura-32 have been an option?"

It was a close decision, but fortunately Laurent had explained to me how the many footnotes and engravings would be better reproduced on the Superna-365.

The interview ended with warm handshakes. There were other candidates. I would receive a letter if I were successful.

I did not obtain the position. However, four months later an envelope arrived from Stockholm with a stamp in the image of King Gustaf V. The guardian, who otherwise expressed little interest in Nordic affairs, could not stand him.

"Let him go and play tennis! Either the man should have a proper coronation and wear his crown, or he should abdicate."[18]

The company was to launch a revolutionary new product. It would be versatile enough to allow small to medium volume

---

18 The King, who reigned from 1907 to 1950, played competitive tennis for Sweden under an alias. He broke with the tradition of a coronation as Sweden adjusted to a new political model.

printers to run with one machine where before they would have needed several. Would I be interested in joining a new Swiss subsidiary helping to sell, install, and maintain this? I would need to include my exact measurements in my reply. I would be provided with a wool suit to provide technical support at sales meetings and two sets of overalls for setting up the machinery. Training would be provided in Gothenburg where I would meet my counterparts from Paris and Marseille.

I showed the letter to the guardian and Édith. They both congratulated me enthusiastically before turning to other details. Édith assured me:

"You will do very well. But we can't let you go to Sweden without proper cashmere-lined gloves. One of our biologists went there to study lichens. The Swedes on the team were all fine, but he got frostbite. His thesis was not well-received, but he composed some enchanting poems about decaying branches in a frozen forest. What is your hand size?"

The guardian excused himself for a few minutes before returning with a little red box. He explained:

"Jean-Marc, I'd like you to have this. But it is not very Genevan, so I'll understand if you prefer not to accept. It is from a different culture. It would be to keep you safe as you travel to your different projects."

The box contained a substantial Saint Christopher medallion in sterling silver and protected in a felt pouch. Such images were not common in the city of Calvin. And this was of a quality that placed it far above anything that one might normally encounter. Turning it over, I saw that it was engraved with 'J-M' and the year of my birth. I was moved and put it around my neck before finding my words:

"Thank you. This means so much to me. I never expected anything like this."

As I returned to my lodgings, I was puzzled. The medallion, while very much appreciated, did not seem to fit with the guardian's taste. And when would he have purchased it and had it engraved? I was curious, but it seemed inappropriate to probe. The guardian would have told me the background if he wanted me to know.

I also shared the exciting news about my job with Mme Beaulac. It affected her more than I anticipated.

"I am so proud of you. Will you have a big desk? You must send me a postcard from Gothenburg. Come here, Massimo."

She held me in an embrace. Then, embarrassed, she pulled away. "I mean 'Jean-Marc.'" Her tone did not invite a follow-up. Massimo was to remain a mystery for several months.

15.
The Chinese Gooseberry

I had enjoyed my afternoon with Céline at the Lucas Cranach exhibition but was still uncertain how serious she might be. She clearly seemed to like my company and enjoyed joking with me. But she was three years older, more experienced, and perhaps merely looking for an agreeable companion until a more suitable permanent candidate might emerge. For my part, I was smitten but, lacking confidence, was unsure why she should have selected someone whose attributes seemed so far below hers on any worldly ranking. Shy and unused to such a dilemma, I wrestled with my best course of action. I could just afford to take her once to a restaurant that she had mentioned in passing. Maybe I could improve my wardrobe so I would look older and more fashionable like Olaf.

My friend Xavier from the design college seemed a good source of advice. Lively and with curly dark locks and soulful eyes, he was popular with the girls and could banter with an audacity which would have earned anyone else a cold stare. We met in a rundown café where he was entitled to half-price salami sandwiches in exchange for playing the guitar on Friday nights. He listened intently as I outlined my situation before responding amicably:

"You are a total idiot! Now I know why you always lose at cards. You are playing in the wrong suit. It will be a disaster if you try to imitate Olaf and end up taking Céline to a restaurant where you can only afford the goulash. Look, people seem to like you, though heaven knows why. But you come over as genuine. Think of it this way. If she is with Olaf, she'd expect the best pineapple. If she is with you, she'd be more impressed with a couple of small wild strawberries so long as you'd gone to the trouble of finding them for her."

I was not entirely reassured by this insight. The daughter of M Jodoin might be intrigued for a month or two by wild strawberries. In the longer term, an Olaf who could run to a menu with a choice of peach melba or *bananes flambées* might be a more prudent choice. Nonetheless, Xavier was right that I should be true to myself and not put on airs.

It was a warm autumn, and I suggested to Céline that we might take a bus on the weekend and go for a walk in the country.

Céline contemplated my recommendation:

"What a lovely idea! Maybe we can go by the river. Or how about a picnic at the Apothecary's Arboretum? It has all sorts of strange plants that were thought to be medicinal. Couples from the colleges go there on weekends."

I knew a little of the history of the arboretum. It was some thirty kilometres out of the city. Its perimeter enclosed a dozen large walled gardens where, over many centuries, pharmacists had cultivated roots and leaves for their cures. It had been rigorously closed to the public until relatively recently when it had been taken over by a government research institute. The property was termed an arboretum in reference to the medicinal trees which shielded it from the road and village of St. Pantaléon des Remèdes, but the apothecaries had experimented with all flora from the smallest fungi to the bark of the largest redwood.

I mentioned my proposed trip to Édith and the guardian. They approved with such enthusiasm that I was momentarily afraid that they thought I was inviting them.

"How exciting! We've been meaning to go. I'll fetch the *Botanic Explorer,* which has a long article on it. You should absolutely see the sassafras from North America. It must be a truly magical tree with its three different types of leaf. But you should be very careful what you touch. Some of the plants have very powerful effects. Make sure you wear long trousers and gloves."

Édith added:

"M and Mme Prévost from the horticultural society were quite overcome by the mystical ambience. They had to be escorted back to the village for chamomile tea, but the experience has inspired them to represent the walled gardens in a tapestry. I have given them the Persian threads from my mother's embroidery case."

Céline and I decided to make the trip despite the unusual humidity and chance of thunder. I sported a carefully-pressed pair of hiking shorts and my best long socks. Céline had an attractive primrose skirt and a small knapsack. The middle-aged driver of the ancient Post Bus gave us a strange, slightly leering look as we boarded and told him our destination. The only other passengers were an elderly lady in a bonnet who grimaced with every jolt of the bus, and two couples who took over the back seats and giggled throughout the journey.

We disembarked along with the two couples who, familiar with the layout, disappeared like deer down an ill-defined track into the wood. Céline and I stayed on the main path, though even this was overgrown and dark with unfamiliar trees and creepers. An occasional scarcely legible plaque under the gnarled trees would advise that the bark could be boiled and used to treat indigestion or choler. Some dismal twigs in the undergrowth were marked as 'Toxic to rabbits. Cures gout and migraines.' We were several weeks ahead of the main leaf fall, but sufficient dry leaves had dropped to ensure that any movement resulted in a loud rustling.

"Jean-Marc, watch out!"

Céline pointed to a little clearing by the side of the path. She held my arm and continued:

"Something moved. I think it was a weasel."

I had just caught some motion out of the corner of my eye. I would have described it as a slithering action, but I had not seen enough to say that it might have been a reptile. I responded:

"I'd love to see a weasel up close. Though this wood is eerie enough that there could also be a wyvern or a gryphon lurking behind the giant nettles."

Céline replied teasingly:

"You really must start reading stories for grownups, but I know what you mean. I don't think anything has changed since the ancient apothecaries were poking around looking for therapeutic roots."

We continued for some twenty minutes passing the sassafras. I carefully picked a couple of its leaves off the ground for Édith, making sure that my exposed knees did not brush against unknown flora. I was fascinated by this botanical oddity, though Céline was less impressed:

"It doesn't look very special. I think I prefer plants and people that don't try to be too many different things at once."

We crossed a small ridge, and suddenly the wood gave way to a view looking down over the brick walled gardens, each the size of two tennis courts, on a gentle south facing slope. Little irrigation channels led off a stream that seemed to rise from a spring at the edge of the wood. We paused for a hardboiled egg and a *cornichon* from Céline's knapsack before heading down the path.

When we reached the gardens, we could see that the brick walls were just high enough to prevent anyone from looking over them. Each plot was accessed through solid wood doors and the rusting remains of jail-size locks suggested that the apothecaries had kept their recipes and rare, imported plants a close secret from their rivals. The first few beds were pleasant but not dramatically different from commercial herb gardens with basil, dill, marjoram, thyme, and lavender. Only a few strange plants gave unfamiliar scents as we gingerly crushed a sample leaf.

An earnest man, lean, in his mid-thirties, bearded and with thick glasses, gestured for us to enter the next garden. He greeted us with:

"I have waited fourteen years for this moment! My first trial with *Actinidia* failed. After seven years I discovered that all the plants were male pollinators and not fruit-bearing. A missionary friend in China sent more seeds and now I have fruit. He tried shipping root stock, but it did not survive the passage of the Arabian Sea."

He excitedly led us to a series of stout wooden pergolas covered with runners and pointed to some hives:

"You don't know how difficult this is. I have to protect the plants against our climate and the flowers don't have nectar, only pollen, and the bees aren't particularly attracted to them. You have to saturate the garden with bees to get any result."

Céline and I had never seen the fruit before. Some of it was a golden yellow, but most of the vines carried a yellow-green object which our host referred to as a Chinese gooseberry. He urged us:

"You must try these. You are a little old, but they have properties that help children grow. They may be the first ones ever cultivated and sampled in this country. I am cooling a Sauternes in the stream to accompany them"

Céline and I exchanged glances while our new acquaintance, Narcisse, stepped away to extract glasses, plates, and knives from a battered wicker picnic basket. While he was out of earshot Céline observed:

"I'm sure it's safe, but we'll let him take the first bite."

She extracted some walnuts and lemon cake from her satchel to share.

The fruit was excellent with a unique and unfamiliar taste. Céline urged me:

"Jean-Marc, have another. I want to see if it can add an inch to your height."

Many years later we realized that we had eaten from a variety distantly related to the kiwifruit, a plant not generally known in Europe until we were well into our sixties.

Narcisse proved to be the seventh son of a wealthy manufacturer of patent medicines. His brothers ran the business while he followed a different inclination:

"My philosophy is that most of what we need has already been given to us in nature. We just need to learn how to extract and cultivate it. I'm sure we could replace one of our pharmaceutical factories with a field of plants with purgative roots."

On learning that I was in the printing trade, he took us to an adjacent garden and showed us several dull-looking perennials:

"We have gone backwards. Our ancestors used these for printing dyes. Much healthier than the concoctions they use today."

I noticed Céline glancing at her watch, although there was plenty of time before the bus. Narcisse and I were discussing the use of grease bands to control winter moths on fruit trees, a subject which might have been of little interest to her. I steered the conversation to a close, thanking him profusely for the Chinese gooseberries and for showing us around. He raised his hands in a farewell benediction:

"I wish all our visitors had your harmony of spirit. One day soon you must tend your own garden. May God be with you."

As we headed back towards the wood, I sensed a slight impatience, even irritation, on Céline's part. I ventured:

"Is everything alright? Did you enjoy that?"

She smiled:

"Yes, of course. Narcisse was a sweet, interesting character. Imagine waiting fourteen years for a gooseberry!"

I was not convinced by her answer but did not press the point. She seemed to be walking a little faster than normal.

We reached the spot where there may or may not have been a weasel. Céline looked round and pulled me over into the clearing.

"This is what comes from eating exotic fruit."

Her kiss left me in no doubt. She was serious.

On the bus, the clothes of the other couples seemed more crumpled than I remembered, and they sat tired at the back.

Céline and I quietly held hands. A tiresome middle-aged couple with staffs and walking boots complained in loud and slightly querulous accents:

"Why does everyone want their properties to look as if they are in the Far East or the Transvaal? I see absolutely no need for Barberton daisies or Japanese maples. They are simply pretentious. Do you remember how gardens used to be clothed in gentle Swiss hues?"

16.
A Lunch and Two Obituaries

I remained thankful for all that the guardian and Édith had done for me, but it was time to follow my own path. I had started work and had visited them less frequently over the last months. They would occasionally treat me to a quick lunch to check that I was alright. The conversation would be pleasant but superficial. Now, however, I needed their help.

Armed with the appropriate coins, I found a telephone booth and requested the guardian's number. I could picture him putting down his book and hurrying over to the candlestick phone ringing in the hall:

"Sir, it's Jean-Marc. How are you?"

"I'm so pleased that you telephoned. But remember that you should call me Édouard now. How are you? What can I do for you?"

I explained that Céline and I had become close and that we expected to announce our engagement in the near future. The guardian was not totally surprised by this news. A diet of respectable concerts, exhibitions, and Mme Jodoin's charitable events had allowed us to get to know each other without scaring the older generation by appearing to 'rush into things'. However, I needed to ensure that I could get approval from my future father-in-law. This was not to be taken for granted, and M Jodoin had hinted strongly that he would prefer Céline to reunite with Olaf who was so clearly *de bonne famille*. Céline had shown her father a little malachite hatpin that I had found for her on a working trip to Montreux. He had responded:

"Yes, very nice. Have you met the people that brought up Jean-Marc *in loco parentis*? It is important that a boy has the right influences during adolescence. One needs to know that he was given a sound moral and ethical foundation."

I tentatively asked if the guardian and Édith would mind meeting Céline and her parents, maybe for coffee at a restaurant.

"Nonsense! They must come here. Don't worry, we'll try not to embarrass you too much."

He named a date some six weeks in the future.

I was walking up the guardian's drive as a stunning taxi pulled in. It was an unusual teal blue, highly polished and with magnificent chrome headlamps. Mme Jodoin and Céline, both in smart dresses and cloche hats, disembarked. M Jodoin leaned out of a rear door of the gleaming Peugeot 201 C:

"Come on, Jean-Marc. Get in. I'll ask the driver to take us to the bridge and back."

I had never suspected the severe M Jodoin of such enthusiasms. He explained:

"The car is built at Sochaux, just across the border from Neuchâtel, so it is almost Swiss. Surely many of the engineers must be from here."

It was on its maiden trip, having been collected that morning from the railyard. It had many exciting features: I did not understand the mechanics of its front suspension, but the passenger compartment had a rack for M Jodoin's fedora.

We returned a few minutes later to face a mild scolding from Mme Jodoin who was waiting in the drive with Céline and Édith:

"Really, what a way to arrive at a lunch party! Édith, I do apologize. Just like boys entranced by a new toy. Quite disgraceful!"

The guardian could not have picked a better day. The garden, which appeared gloomy and overgrown for fifty weeks of the year, was briefly a riot of rhododendrons, azaleas, and fruit blossoms under a cloudless sky. The interior of the house had just been repainted, explaining the delayed invitation.

As we entered with the Jodoins, Édith flashed me a warning glance. She had taken advantage of the redecoration to stage the main rooms. She had replaced the picture of an Egyptian scarab, which normally hung over the small side table, with the photo that M Boudillet had taken at the Institute for the Deaf. Next to the little girl, I resembled a caring army medic in my armbands. In the frame was the cutting from the paper naming me as the 'dedicated young volunteer'. The specimen debenture with my initials next to Étienne's was displayed in the dining room. The Romanian vellum was in the hallway. These advertisements attracted approving inspection from Mme Jodoin:

"Helping the deaf is such a good cause. My poor mother is already very hard of hearing."

And

"What an adventure at his age! One knows so little about Romania. Do you have a picture of Jean-Marc in his page's uniform? Is it similar to the Swiss Guards'?"

The guardian and Édith were excellent hosts, and I could see that Céline's father was very comfortable with them. It was warm enough for us to spend some minutes on the terrasse before we sat down to eat. The conversation turned to Édith's perennially disappointing floribunda roses and meandered to:

"Did you read about that principal who collapsed yesterday while inspecting the college azaleas? Apparently, he was quite famous."

An unusually mischievous smile crossed the guardian's face:

"I knew him when I was a student, and he was a recently-appointed professor. He was very clever and very ambitious. *De mortuis* and everything, but Alphonse was a good man while there were people around him who could bring him back to earth. Once he got promoted too high, he became a little pompous."

He paused.

"After that, Jean-Marc was the only person who ever put him in his place."

I had been distracted by an inquisitive mouse peering from the alpines in the rockery towards Céline's new sandal with its three different colours of leather.

"Sorry, what did I do to the principal? At the design college?"

"No. You remember, when you first started here, and he met you late one evening? The next day he called me spluttering that you told him that you knew how to tend an orchard, which was more practical than his Candide and '*faut cultiver notre jardin*'. Another man might have said '*touché*' and tried to understand your circumstances."

Turning to Céline's parents, he explained:

"I was a widower then. I asked a few people to meet Jean-Marc to give me their advice. It was a difficult road at times, but he hasn't turned out that badly. He was astonishingly well-trained in natural history and drawing, but he had a lot of ground to catch up in other subjects."

He glanced in my direction and teasingly admonished:

"But don't get the idea that you should go round being impertinent to professors."

Édith ushered us through to the dining room and the carefully laid table. It was the perfect menu for the occasion, high quality but not extravagant or pretentious. Each course was politely admired by Mme Jodoin:

"How clever of you to put that touch of mint with the *salade niçoise*! Was it from the garden? It made it so fresh. I must remember to try that.

"That was delicious. I've never been successful with rabbit terrine. The walnut and grape crust was pure genius."

The guardian and Céline's father contentedly engaged in a complex estimate of the hours needed by an Italian sardine to reach the fish market in Geneva if it were shipped through the Simplon tunnel using the new underground electric locomotives.

Céline's mother explained how she had to organize a charity event the following week. I did not pay attention to the many complications in coordinating this repast until I heard:

"I used to get excellent herbed rolls with dill to accompany the salmon. But when I went to see old Mme Beaulac yesterday, the shop was closed. The tobacconist next door said she had died overnight."

I let out an involuntary strangled "Mme Beaulac?" and was unable to pass it off as nothing.

M Jodoin looked at me as if I were a complete idiot. The guardian asked sharply:

"Did you even know the lady?"

"Yes. Please don't be angry. She was very kind to me."

There was a disagreeably long pause. It seemed that I was required to offer more detail. It seemed best to make my explanation to Céline's mother:

"When I first came here, I had a strong Amphoran accent. The guardian, I mean Édouard, was afraid that I would get mocked and held back. Sometimes I'd have to repeat myself in shops. One of the tram conductors laughed at me. I'd wait in the rain for the next one if I saw he was on duty. But it was very hard because the pronunciation was part of who I was and where I came from."

I did not look at the others, but Céline and her mother nodded sympathetically:

"Anyway, I went to elocution lessons in one of those houses on rue Martin Bellius. I understood why I needed them, but Mme Vaillancourt seemed to want me to declaim as if I were reciting Alexandrine verse. Or maybe she just wanted me to exaggerate the vowels as part of learning. In any event, she would get very vexed.

"Coming back after a lesson I passed the Boulangerie Beaulac. I don't know if you ever noticed, but the bread in the window is always in those baskets with little blue crosses in the wicker. That is an Amphoran tradition, one cross for each pot of honey that could safely be carried in the basket. I went in and talked to the lady in my natural accent. She had me sit down behind the counter and poured herbal tea blended just like we had in Amphora.

"My visits seemed to give her pleasure. I think she was lonely. Now that I sometimes leave the city for work, I send her postcards of the places even if they are not very far away."

I paused. I could not quite place the guardian's tone as he asked:

"How often did you see her?"

I glanced in his direction. The vein on his forehead had become prominent.

"At least twice a week until I started working and then normally a visit a week and a postcard. I really wanted to tell you. Often it was for no more than ten or fifteen minutes. But I was afraid you would have to forbid it as I was meant to be getting rid of my accent. I was still thirteen at the beginning. I didn't want to get her in trouble or lose my only link to Amphora. Everyone I knew was a child or grandchild of a family she remembered."

"So, all those times you were evasive and got in trouble for not telling me where you had been...?"

I nodded.

"And that explains those mysterious pastries and crumbs. I wish I'd known that you were taking tea with an old lady. It was very inconsiderate not to tell me. One day when you are a parent, you'll understand how much you worry about things that don't add up."

He was too well-mannered to pound the table in front of his guests, but I could see that his fist was clenched.

With hindsight, I might have found a different response to the guardian's question, but my instinct told me that an inadequate answer would only land me with a deeper problem. M Jodoin and the guardian would not be satisfied with an airy reply.

We finished the *charlotte russe* in silence after this reprimand. It was suggested that I escort Céline, her mother, and Édith on a short walk to the river. This expedition was a transparent device to take us out of the way while the guardian and Céline's father discussed my qualities, if indeed I had any. It was hard to see how my revelation of a secret relationship, however innocent, could enhance my desirability as a son-in-law. I was relieved to see Édith take the guardian on one side before we left. I did not know what she said, but I trusted her judgement.

Édith and Céline's mother followed the men's lead in setting up a private discussion. At the first bench they declared that they could not proceed further on the gently stony track in their current shoes. Céline and I were to follow a circular route that would take us some forty minutes before we would rejoin the ladies and accompany them back.

It should have been an idyllic afternoon. The insects were not yet a problem, and the river was at its best with enough water for the little waterfalls to be audible. The overhanging oaks and chestnuts had light green leaves but did not cut out the light as they would in mid-summer. I was with the girl who, against all expectation, had chosen to be with me.

Céline asked me as soon as we were out of earshot of Édith and Mme Jodoin:

"Do you think everyone is talking about us?"

"Of course. The guardian is acting as my representative in the dowry negotiations. We'll need a signed commitment before any engagement."

Céline caught me unprepared with a playful blow to my stomach.

"Ow! That's my lunch in there. Our demand has gone up by ten thousand francs."

I jumped to one side to avoid a repeat.

"But seriously, you looked a little anxious as your guardian and Father headed into that room and closed the door."

"Think of it from your father's point of view. What would you do if some nobody from some island wanted to marry your daughter, and you can't even make it through lunch without learning that he spent his teenage years being insolent and making up stories about how he spent his time?"

Céline put her hand on my arm.

"Look, those are things that you treat seriously when they happen, but you laugh about them later. The story about the principal wasn't to show that you behaved badly. It was about how you stood up for yourself."

"You may be right about the principal. But the guardian was not happy about Mme Beaulac. He looked really hurt as though I betrayed him. I got pretty good at reading how far I had annoyed him, and this was bad. You may not have seen it the same way as he restrained himself in front of you and your parents. Your father works in the magistrate's office. I just confessed to a sustained pattern of two or three half-truths a week for five years or so. Why should he trust someone like that?"

"Don't underestimate him. He growls and seems gruff, but he sees all sides to a story. I wouldn't be surprised if he were impressed by your loyalty to the old lady. Perhaps the guardian is jealous, if that's the right word. I don't know how my parents would react if I told them there was a secret third adult bringing me up. Did it get you in a lot of trouble?"

"Yes. It accounts for pretty much all of it, apart from the routine stuff like bad marks from the *curé* and cigarettes or forbidden books. I never understood why I was expected to know about Medea killing Jason's kids and Clytemnestra murdering Agamemnon, but a modern novel was considered corrupting. That all seemed very unfair, though I suppose I was warned several times. I had a copy of *Thérèse...*"[19]

---

19 *Thérèse Desqueyroux* by François Mauriac was published in 1927. Considered a masterpiece, it disturbed some contemporary readers with its perceptive portrayal of a woman who poisons her husband.

As we approached a smoother section of the path, our conversation was interrupted by a familiar voice:

"Céline, Jean-Marc, meet little Jean-Marc."

It was Laurent with Amélie and a very fine new infant in a wicker baby carriage with enormous wheels. This conveyance looked as if it had been handed down and modified over several generations and was equipped with pneumatic tires, a pump, brakes, a bell and a lamp. Laurent explained:

"Our Jean-Marc is named after Amélie's grandfather who is in great health at eighty. I liked the name. All the Jean-Marcs we know are good people. Different, very different, but good.

Do you like his carriage? One of Amélie's uncles had a bicycle workshop and wanted his children to have the best transport possible."

We congratulated the contented parents and continued on.

We had speculated that Édith and Céline's mother would be more sympathetic than the men. They had clearly formed a plan. Their inappropriate footwear notwithstanding, they strode back with determination. As we approached the house, Céline and I were again dispatched out of the way.

"Can you go and see if that stall with the different types of honey is open? You always ask such intelligent questions when choosing which one to get. We need a light flavour for a layer on the orange sponge cake."

It was a good hour before we returned with the requested ingredient. I was now in a more sombre mood as I digested the news about Mme Beaulac. Céline's mother managed to catch me alone and whispered that she would find out about funeral arrangements. She would be honoured if I would accompany her.

The guardian seemed a little subdued, but all parties looked in reasonably good humour as we assembled for tea and cake on the terrasse. Convention prevented anyone from telling us the decision about our engagement, or, indeed, admitting that the purpose of the luncheon had been to arrive at one. I was invited to enlighten the guests about beekeeping as practiced in Amphora.

The Jodoins departed, this time headed for the tram, with gracious thanks to their hosts. Édith accompanied them to the street and went to check on a neighbour, Mme Imbeault, who 'had not felt the same' since participating in two weeks of Renaissance madrigals in an ill-ventilated hotel overlooking Lake Maggiore.

As the guardian and I returned through the front porch, he uttered the only improper language I ever heard from him:

"What in God's name is this?"

White with anger, he pointed towards the framed letter of commendation from the organ concert. Édith had found it on the high shelf when preparing my old room for a guest. Naturally, she had no idea that I had kept it a secret. The letter was in the downstairs hall so she could ask me if I wanted to take it. Édith had shown it to Céline's parents, and everyone except the guardian knew that I had been recommended for the Conservatoire.

He continued in a cold tone:

"I'm not sure that you were ever honest with us. Is this even real? Did you enjoy mocking us as you played on the sympathies of an old lady? Weygand was absolutely right. I give up. We taught you nothing. Please leave."

I tried to reply but the words would not come. Eventually I managed an anguished,

"I never mocked you, ever."

I took the framed letter, which Édith had thoughtfully put in a canvas shopping bag decorated with the Genevan coat of arms.

I was utterly crushed. I had lost Mme Beaulac. The guardian's words hurt all the more because I had made it through those years still grateful and respecting him for rescuing me. He had often cautioned me with the old phrase 'Beware the anger of a patient man', but I was unprepared for so deep a resentment over, as he perceived it, my betrayal with Mme Beaulac. I don't know what he imagined, but she would never have permitted me to refer to any adult without proper respect. And I had no idea if our engagement would be blessed, though the omens were not good. Given the attitude towards such things in Geneva, it was very doubtful whether Céline could join me in an unsanctioned union where she would be estranged from her family.

When I changed out of my good shirt back in my cheap lodgings, the drawer stuck as it sometimes did. I angrily pulled with all my force. It suddenly came free, spilling the contents all over the floor. As I cursed and collected my possessions, I saw the three kopecks the guardian had given me when I first arrived. He had promised that he would always take two days to reconsider if I returned one to him. The intention had been to provide a safety valve for an overwhelmed thirteen-year-old, but the little coin might yet speak more effectively than words. I waited three days in the hope that his shock and anger might subside. My taciturn neighbour across the landing was a messenger. He had a motorcycle with a luggage sidecar, a peak cap, and a surprisingly steep tariff. The concierge had warned me that she had found a leaflet in his room about the monument at Champel erected in expiation of the burning of a heretic. The messenger could well be an 'antitrinitarian like that blasphemer, Michael Servetus'. His doctrinal sympathies seemed the least immediate of my problems, and I gave him an unsealed envelope with a kopeck wrapped in a letter. He was to hand the guardian the coin first and then the note which simply asked:

"May I come by on Saturday afternoon?"

The messenger was not to leave without an answer.

The response came on the guardian's favourite blue cambric paper and stated:

"Bring pyjamas and plan to stay for dinner and breakfast."

Édith told me later that she had been about to replace my picture from the Institute with the scarab. The guardian had gently stopped her with:

"Not yet. Maybe later. What if he never comes back?"

A few minutes afterwards, the messenger had arrived.

The proceedings of the meeting while Céline and I were purchasing the honey remained as rigorously sealed as if it were a wartime strategy conference. We extrapolated as best we could from the rare hints and nuances of the participants. Apparently, they decided that, if properly managed, I could be salvageable as a possible fiancé. The question then became whether Céline would be ready for such a commitment.

This theory would explain a series of discussions to which Céline was subjected by her parents and pastor. Did she understand that marriage required constant vigilance to overcome any defects in one's spouse? Would she request pastoral intervention if his moral virtues needed reinforcement?

The unfortunate, if tactfully unspoken, implication of the salvage hypothesis would be that the guardian had not had me under proper control. Given all that he had done for me, this would have cut to the quick and contributed to his outburst in the front porch.

There was a light drizzle as I approached the house on the Saturday. The guardian must have been watching out for my arrival and came down the path to welcome me:

"*Si tacuissemus, sapientes.* I think that is right? I've never heard it in the plural before."

If only we had stayed silent, we might have been considered wise. The guardian knew that I would understand his greeting and that the Latin would not seem forced. For the *curé* had expressed the same sentiment so repeatedly, albeit in the second person singular, that the phrase had worked its way into our vernacular. The guardian's version struck the right note. It was an admission that united us in our errors without apportioning blame. Relieved beyond measure, I extended my hand.

The guardian had shaken my hand when we first met in Amphora. He had once steadied me when, unused to the Swiss ice, I had lost my footing. But, perhaps conscious that I was someone else's adolescent son, he had avoided the smallest affectionate touch, not even a hand on the shoulder. Now, he accepted my offer with a firm grip.

We had arrived, however painfully, at a new relationship. Conversation flowed. Édith had replaced some of the furniture in the salon which now felt more inviting and less formal. I had sometimes wondered why the guardian had selected me for rescue, and finally asked the question. There were other children in the same need. He took a long breath.

"I never knew what to tell you. You didn't know it, but you selected yourself. I had no intention of returning with a child. I didn't want you to feel like a replacement."

He smiled slightly:

"Though you were too distinctive ever to be mistaken for anyone's replacement. You know that Marie, my wife, died suddenly of a heart issue. We had a son, Jean-Marc. He was staying with her sister's family and was just learning to walk when Lausanne was hit with a virulent strain of scarlet fever. I paid for the best nurse and doctor we could find, but it was no good. The city lost over thirty children that summer. I was not ready to talk about it for years afterwards. Jean-Marc would have been about six months older than you. When you told me your name and age, I had to ask if you wanted to come with me. Our team was worried that the crops would not see the island through the winter. There was something very sympathetic in the way you described how you had taken care of your mother. You were quiet but had character. I didn't want you to see my son's picture and ask questions. That is why I would not let you on the second floor. Did you ever sneak up there? It's alright to tell me now."

"No. I did many things but not that. Did you ever wish you had left me in Amphora?"

"Never! You make it sound like deciding whether to throw an undersized fish back in the lake! It was a total commitment, and you have to accept that some days will be better than others. You don't know how much it means to me to see the astonishing way you have developed."

I believed the guardian when he spoke of his commitment. One day in my first year I came home cut and bruised. At first, I was reluctant to explain, but he coaxed the story out of me. When I was switching trams, I saw a man with a similar build, coat, and case to my father. Perhaps he really was alive and had come looking for me. I had left a note in what remained of our old house to say that I was safe and headed to Geneva. I jumped onto the platform of the tram he was on when it was already in motion. I ran to him only to find that it was someone different and who gave me a sour look. I jumped off the tram, lost my footing, and hurt myself. The guardian could not have responded more sensitively. But there had been a momentary look of absolute dismay at the thought that he might have to give me up.

The guardian noticed that I was wearing my Saint Christopher:

"The medallion was a christening gift from Marie's father. He was a worthy man, a Catholic lawyer from Grenoble. I think he would have liked you and would want you to have it. It was made to order by a silversmith in Seville. Now I have a question. What was that letter of recommendation?"

I recounted the story about the organ recital and the professor's address but made light of my moment of panic.

"Besides, I'd have drowned at the Conservatoire. I can play the pieces I heard as a child. It's almost like speaking a native language. But everything else comes out without feeling as if a machine were playing the notes."

"That's a relief. I'd never have forgiven myself if I'd somehow stifled the next Berlioz or Debussy. But you should hang that letter up now. You deserved its praise."

The next morning, I tried to find out about the meeting with Céline's parents. Both the guardian and Édith reiterated firmly that they had all agreed to respect the privacy of the discussion. However, the guardian did reassure me that my medical records were no business of anyone else. I took this to mean that no reference had been made to Weygand, a well-intentioned omission which was to have strange consequences in later life. He also told me that I should not be embarrassed by my involuntary exemption from military service but would say no more. Certainly, Céline's father stopped asking when I would serve my term in the army.

After four or five weeks, I was invited to breakfast with M Jodoin. Even then Café Quis Custodiet seemed desperately old fashioned with dark blue wallpaper, heavy leather furniture and a conservative clientele from the neighbouring courts and police station. The preliminaries were extensive: Was my job going well, had I seen the red Peugeot cabriolet that often parked on rue de Candolle, were Édith's roses doing better with the new spray? Eventually we turned to more substantive issues:

"Do you like Étienne?"

"Yes, very much. He helped me a lot when I was new here. I trust him completely."

"That is good to hear. He speaks of you almost as a cousin or a little brother. I am sure he is a beneficial influence. I think it is very important for a young man to be guided by someone with such estimable personal qualities. I would like you to start seeing him on a regular schedule, two or three times a month."

"I'd be happy to do that if he doesn't mind."

"Perfect. It is settled. He is the type of person you should take with you when you select an engagement ring."

In other words, I would be monitored and managed, but our engagement could proceed. Céline and her mother normally got what they wanted. My excitement even impressed my future father-in-law:

"I've never seen anyone look so happy. The buckwheat crêpes seem to have a remarkable effect."

17.
The Engagement Party

The girls were facing away and stood several metres ahead of me as I waited in line for the tram. It was a calm, sunny, September morning and their voices carried clearly:

"Have you met him?"

"Not yet. I do like your blouse and that collar. It makes you look very aristocratic. Is he a handsome Viking like Olaf?"

"Heavens, no! When you first see him, you think she could have done better. You wouldn't notice him in a group. I'm sure you could find dozens like him in any college around the Mediterranean. But he's alright on his own. I think I could take a nice portrait shot against a plain background. He is rather sweet."

"How does she know him? Is he a friend of her brothers?"

"I don't think so. He's too quiet to be their type."

This evaluation reached me as I switched from a bus to a tram on the way to my engagement party. Fortunately, there was a crowd, and I could slip back without being seen. I would catch the next tram. I recognized the better dressed girl with an unusual high collar. She had befriended Céline in kindergarten and now aspired to be a fashion photographer. I could not see anything of the other one except for a plain shawl and a soft wide-brim hat.

The wedding was set for the spring, but Céline's parents were anxious to make our engagement more public. Prim neighbours were already commenting that their daughter was frequently in the company of an unknown young man. Mme Boucher, who patrolled the streets with her poodle, Ariodante, wondered if our hand holding and farewell kiss had been appropriate on a Sunday. The Jodoins decided to host an engagement party to explain their daughter's new circumstances.

To prepare for this celebration, I was invited into the back parlour which, as children, Honoré and Euzèbe had named the interrogation room. It was furnished with uncomfortable, upright wooden chairs, and a solid table illuminated by oversize desk lamps. It was lined with cactuses which would be joined in winter by moribund pelargoniums sheltering from the frost. Here I was carefully scripted by Céline's parents:

"You must let people know how you were brought up under your guardian's good influence. He is very well respected, as are his committees. When you talk about your printing job, there is no need to mention the more manual elements of your work. We don't want the guests to have a wrong impression. Will you be wearing that nice shirt with the herringbone weave? You must not spend all your time with Céline, or guests will tend to talk to her instead of to you."

Céline had not been summoned to the back parlour. However, she was given marginally more subtle guidance over dinner:

"People will be interested when you tell the story of how you first met Jean-Marc in Étienne's office and how he helped with the organ pamphlet. It shows a charitable side and helps avoid the impression that he has no ties here."

I am not sure that Céline took much notice of this advice. At least with friends our age, her version of our meeting focused jokingly on the day she called out to me as I diverted down that cold street.

"It was really thanks to a burst sewer that he ended up coming to our house."

Étienne happened to be at the Jodoins, with a gift of his mother's pickled cauliflower, when the idea of the party was first mooted. Mme Jodoin was exploring the possibilities:

"It will still be September. If we do lunch, we may be able to have it on trestles in the garden. If the weather is bad, we could fit a good number of people in the house. Jean-Marc, how many friends will you bring?"

"I have my friends from design college, Xavier and Louis. And Étienne will be there, of course."

"Only two?"

I had not given the right answer. M Jodoin explained:

"It won't look greedy if you ask for a few more places. You don't want everyone thinking that you are an isolated loner."

Étienne offered his assistance:

"Listen, I'm sure Laurent and Amélie would like to celebrate with you, as would Hervé, Renaud, and maybe Béatrice from the bookstore. Why don't you ask them?"

"Yes, that is an idea."

I could not express my real feelings on that particular suggestion until I was alone with Étienne. We were in the Jodoins' musty garden shed searching for some bunting for the party. Mme Jodoin thought it might be in a wicker basket somewhere on a shelf above the rakes and besoms. If the mice had not used it for nesting material, it could potentially be suspended from the gutter on the old stables over to the apple tree by the house.

"Étienne, I don't want to put you in an awkward position, but can I trust you absolutely to keep my confidence?"

"Of course. What is it? You look upset."

"I'm starting a new chapter. Nobody here except you knows why I had to go to the bookstore and all that story about needing mental discipline. What if Laurent or anyone from there brings it up at the party? I don't want to be cut out of photos like Philippe before I'm even in the family."

"Don't worry. Let me invite them, and I'll make sure they understand. But you're getting worked up for nothing. They were very discreet. They won't harm you. They really are your friends. Besides, except for Laurent and perhaps Hervé, I don't think anyone really knew anything anyway. I had some idea because I was close to you and Laurent. Most people just thought you were a guinea pig for that program with the Society. What a fiasco that was! We started making a little money from printing their materials and their new president made a deal with some university press.”

He paused before adding:

“You must put the comparison with Philippe out of your mind. You don’t know all the background. He often had good intentions, but he invariably chose the path that would get him in most trouble. Promise you’ll always turn to me if you are concerned about anything? The Jodoins are tremendous, but they can be a little intimidating until you get to know them.”

I was with Céline when she had her preparatory talk before the party with Honoré and Euzèbe. She had attempted to sit them down in the house, but we had somehow ended up in the vegetable patch where the brothers were cultivating muscle-building spinach and iron-rich beetroot. She finally got their attention:

“I want this party to be a success. Can you promise me that you won’t take it over? Last week I really wanted Anne-Marie to get to know Jean-Marc, but you monopolized the conversation with that silly argument about the clocks in the Olympics.”

Honoré looked up from inspecting the uneven rows of beetroot:

“If there was a problem, why didn’t Jean-Marc speak up? But alright, I promise that we’ll make you proud. I’ll ensure that Euzèbe employs his politest vocabulary and doesn’t ramble on.”

He returned to a close examination of the leaves:

“Jean-Marc, you know about these things. Do you think this is slug damage?”

Fortune favoured the prepared. It was a beautiful afternoon. The temperature was perfect as the visitors admired dahlias and potentillas under the bunting which had been washed twice to remove some of the more sinister stains. The remaining ones were optimistically ascribed to a leaking can of creosote. There were about forty guests, with the more senior ones seated at the trestle tables. The others stood and made polite conversation, breaking off from time to time to wave away some particularly persistent wasps. The older men sported blazers and boaters while the younger ones showed off their best cloth caps and shirts. The ladies, aware that the pastor's wife would be among the invitees, inclined to demure fashions ranging from the turn of the century to contemporary. The diners enjoyed a small glass of wine with no expectation of a refill. The tables were laid with large platters of smoked eel, cheese, and charcuterie at one end. At the other, intriguing aromas escaped from large casseroles. I could hear snatches of conversation:

"I want to know what is wrong with our Swiss sheep. My knitting pattern arrived with wool from Australia."

And

"If I were a young man, I would not stay here. I read that Brazil has much more potential. We can't survive on our banks and watches alone."

The Jodoins ushered me round to each group of guests who would greet me with lengthy explanations of where they fell on the family tree or how they knew Céline. As soon as there was a gap in the conversation, I would deliver my well-rehearsed remarks with the edited version of my background, interests, and employment status.

"I'm very pleased to meet you. So just to introduce myself a little more, here is a quick summary of my background..."

Mme Jodoin would supplement my lines with her comments:

"He is so modest. He plays the organ and could have gone to the Conservatoire. Étienne used one of his drawings in an engraving. What talent!"

M Jodoin took a different angle:

"I was very impressed by Édouard, his guardian. You can see that Jean-Marc was brought up with a solid moral structure. They had him tutored. Much more rigorous than idling at the back of a classroom!"

Even the brothers participated in my introduction. I still had access to the consul's pool where I had taken them separately. They had been more awed than I anticipated by the strange surroundings, and my attempt to find common ground was partially successful. Honoré advised the lunch guests:

"Don't be fooled by his look of gentle innocence. I didn't give him a head start, and he very nearly beat me at breaststroke. He knows a diplomat and swims in a pool with mosaics of goddesses as if he were a Roman emperor. Actually, he's a good man."

I was presented to M Sauvé, a recently retired neighbour who had literary pretensions after winning a prose competition in the local paper. He asked me a series of hypothetical questions: what would I have done if I had not been rescued after the earthquake, how might I have reacted if Céline were to have rejected my proposal? My answers met with his approval:

"Very few young men could have replied with such accurate use of the conditional tenses, and hardly any of them would employ the imperfect subjunctive as appropriately as you did. It is that kind of rigour which is lacking nowadays. I have no doubt that you will be a creditable addition to the Jodoin family."

A few of the gentlemen enquired about my military service. Although I was prepared for the question, I was aware that my voice betrayed a certain embarrassment. Weygand's recommendation was treated as gospel by the administration. Every birthday from the age of sixteen to twenty had been marked by a curt missive from the principal army surgeon confirming that I was 'of permanently unsuitable disposition'.

I would respond to the guests with:

"I was exempted. Technically, I was not a Swiss citizen until recently, and I am only just tall enough. But I'd volunteer for the ambulance service if there is a crisis. I used to help at the Institute for the Deaf and my manager has let me drive over a thousand kilometres for work."

I looked enviously at my companions from the design college whose laughter suggested that they were getting on well with Céline's attractive friends. Céline was trapped with an opinionated great-uncle in a fraying camel blazer who was explaining how morals and manners had deteriorated since the turn of the century. We exchanged supportive glances, but she stayed dutifully at her post. It was Étienne who finally retrieved me from the Jodoins:

"He may be the prize exhibit, but we've got to let him eat. He must have met almost everyone by now. Jean-Marc, come and taste the excellent cassoulet. We'll join Laurent and your bookstore friends over there. Or better still, come with me and see if we can liberate Céline. It can be a little hard to stop Great-Uncle when he is in full flow. He once lectured me for half an hour on how it is Napoleon's fault that all Europe does not drive on the same side of the road. Apparently, he reversed some convention from Roman times."

The girls who had been waiting for the tram came up to Céline and me. Louise, the one with the wide-brim hat, seemed taken with my friend Xavier and mumbled a few hurried pleasantries before rejoining more charismatic company. Sabrine, whose silk blouse did indeed look very stylish, continued the conversation:

"What a marvellous party! You two look so wonderful together. Will you let me take your portraits alone and as a couple before the wedding? Jean-Marc, what is your collar size? We'll borrow one of my little brother's Italian shirts, and we can get you looking like a film star. Don't worry about a haircut. I can take care of that. We want you looking natural, not as if you had just signed up as a police recruit. And both of you, no coffee, red wine, or staining fruit for three days before the shoot."

The guests had all left by late afternoon after considerable handshaking. They assured us that they looked forward to seeing me alongside Céline at the upcoming talks on the neighbourhood's architecture and archaeology. Once we had cleared the tables, we assembled in the back parlour. Thankfully there was enough wine left over for us to have a half glass. M Jodoin removed the cravat which he had reluctantly worn at his wife's insistence and reviewed the day:

"Overall, it went very well. We had the right dishes and in just the right amount. I think several people asked for the recipes."

He smiled proudly at his daughter:

"Céline, you worked marvels with Uncle Bartholomé. He hasn't approved of an engagement since Cousin Violette married that landowner in 1897. He thinks printing is an honourable profession and described Jean-Marc as your 'young Gutenberg'."

I managed a passing mark:

"Jean-Marc, you sometimes came over as a little unsure of yourself, but it is alright. Your shyness was not excessive, and some guests found it endearing. Do you remember Aunt Isabelle with her powder blue kid gloves? She was the lady to the left of the eels, with the lace bonnet and collar that she made specially for today."

He paused while I tried frantically to recall our conversation. I had not said anything outrageous, but perhaps she found my comments bland.

M Jodoin continued:

"She said that you have good social grace and posture. That constitutes high praise as she used to work at a finishing school. She taught embroidery."

He gave me an approving glance and went on:

"You made quite an impression, and she is going to send you *The Young Gentleman's Calendar of Moral, Ethical and Social Dilemmas*. Every night before bed you must read one of the three hundred and sixty-five dilemmas and determine the right course of action. Don't worry, it is the teacher's edition, so the answers are in the back. The students at the men's college where her late husband was a watersports instructor have to write a daily essay justifying their choices. You should take it seriously. I'm sure she'll ask you about it at the wedding."

18.
A Prophetic Image

Shortly after the engagement party, I was summoned to the Jodoins by an agitated note from Mme Jodoin. An early wedding present had been delivered, and I needed to take care of it. I was unsure why Céline could not simply store our gift in her bedroom, but I went as soon as I returned from a few days at a customer in the Valais.

It was an early October evening when an excited Céline, in sensible shoes and the practical clothes that she used for gardening or cleaning, greeted me with:

"Do you know what it is? Come take a look. We've been speculating all week."

Mme Jodoin, in a floral dressing gown and with a streaming cold, gestured towards the back parlour.

I had anticipated something on the lines of a tureen or a large Le Creuset casserole. Instead, there was a massive wooden crate which had been unceremoniously deposited by an uncommunicative delivery crew. It was five or six feet long, four feet high and just under a foot wide. The wood looked as if it had last been worked several years prior and was branded with signs indicating that the contents were to be handled with care. There was no indication of what was inside or who had sent it. It had been nailed shut and was too heavy for me to move from the floor where it was blocking access to the closet with Mme Jodoin's best tea towels and damask table cloths.

I was searching for a productive comment when Honoré, in wet and muddy rugby gear, returned from a match and announced:

"Jean-Marc, it won't open however hard you look at it with your sad Spaniel eyes. I'll help you carry it to the old stables where

154

I have my tools. Besides, it will be easier for you to clean up there if it is full of sawdust."

It was only just possible for Honoré, Céline, and me to lift the heavy crate and place it in a little workshop behind the brothers' gym. The narrow room smelled of gasoline mixed with mould, and pieces of a primitive motorcycle engine were strewn across the workbench. A feeble electric lamp gave just enough light for us to see what we were doing. Honoré removed several nails with a hammer claw, revealing packing material of wood shavings and crumpled newspapers from some fifteen years previously.

We finally removed enough packing to feel the structure inside and gingerly extract it, for it seemed to be made of antique wood with a heavy lining, which turned out to be a lead alloy. Honoré cleared the workbench, and we laid the object down. It consisted of a large wooden panel covered by two hinged flaps which looked as if they were designed to open out to the side.

I was about to lift the panels when Céline stopped me and laid out some of the sheets from the crumpled newspapers:

"Honoré, look at this. They are all from Montreux in 1920!"

This information meant nothing to me, but brother and sister urgently flattened out more pages. Céline observed:

"All from October and November 1920. How did he know that I am engaged?"

She turned to me and explained:

"You've heard of our cousin Philippe who used to stay with us? His parents died in 1920 while he was a teenager. I think a few family heirlooms were placed in storage for him when the house was sold."

A note of sadness came into her voice, and she avoided looking at Honoré as she added:

"We don't really keep in touch with him anymore. He once said that he was joining a French mining company exploring for nickel and phosphates in the Pacific islands."

Honoré seemed uncomfortable at the reference to his dismissed relative and instructed me:

"Go ahead. Open the panels. It is your present, whatever you've been landed with."

I opened a panel partway and realized that we were looking at an antique triptych that was meant to be standing vertically with the side panels supporting the main picture. We carefully lifted it and manoeuvred it into a position where it caught most of the inadequate electric light.

The central panel depicted the Eldest Son who was seated at a desk surrounded by an excess of artistic symbols. An almost golden pineapple signified prosperity while books, a globe, dividers, and compasses attested to his skills. A sword and spurs indicated military prowess. He seemed to be around nineteen or twenty, with a confident or perhaps arrogant air, dressed in green robes and a matching hat rather in the style of those worn at doctoral degree ceremonies. A jewelled disk was suspended from a heavy gold chain around his neck and bore the inscription *invicta veritas,* the unconquered truth.

Still in the wide central panel, a figure, helpfully labelled as *Pater,* stood to the son's right. He was more modestly clothed in browns and greys while a trowel, a branch laden with plums, and a sheepdog seemed to suggest that he might be a farmer. Other portions of the painting exhibited a certain exuberance, but the father seemed subdued.

The mother was clad in dramatic pink taffeta and looked proudly at her offspring. In one hand she held a pomegranate while the other clasped a jug with an elaborate fig leaf pattern which she appeared to be taking to the son. The background to the panel was almost black, but a shaft of improbably strong moonlight lit her long blonde hair, which flowed back as though in a strong wind.

The side panel to the son's left displayed the teacher who had so effectively informed the youth. He posed in front of a classical ruin whose remaining pillars were inscribed with Virtue, Morality, and Obedience. Attentive lion cubs and lambs lay at his feet. His billowing academic robes and hat had a faint hint of caricature, and his face was the least well-defined of all the characters.

The side panel to the right was more striking, even alarming. The son's physician held the medical symbol of the winged staff with two snakes whose eyes and forked tongues were shown in close detail. But one could make out an even more sinister viper lurking in the grass below. The doctor's spare hand held a vial while yellow roots protruded from a bubbling pot that was seemingly suspended in mid-air. More soothingly, leaves representing medicinal herbs bordered the frame.

The chill which descended on me came from the doctor's expression. His physique, short and portly, bore no resemblance to Weygand, but his face affected the same air of indisputable authority. Even worse, when the panels were set at the correct angle, he appeared to exchange glances with the eldest son. The father, by contrast, seemed a vacant bystander.

Céline and I were still only engaged, and parenthood was some way in the future. But the Jodoins had clear expectations of my duty: M Jodoin counted on a vigorous grandson. It was a source of embarrassment to him that his second son, Euzèbe, had been born left-handed. As was not unusual at the time, this condition had been discreetly handled by a specialist. Happily, the conversion process did not trigger any of the known side effects, though it perhaps explained his quiet nature relative to his extrovert elder brother. M Jodoin was relieved that I could confirm that the Montabeilles had been consistently right-handed. But in such an atmosphere I felt I had no choice but to suppress any hint that Switzerland's leading doctor had diagnosed potential delinquency which I might introduce into the family line.

Perhaps our circle of friends and relatives was not at the forefront of social change. After we moved to the farm, we would encounter a neighbour who had experienced some difficulties as a young man. Involved in a minor brawl and accused of stealing a cold frame, he had appeared in court in 1918. We were warned almost until the upheavals of '68 that the family was of 'bad seed' though, in fact, our interactions around drainage and boundary fences were entirely amical. If his friendly and polite children had been closer in age to ours, we would undoubtedly have spent more time together.

I was always on thin ice when it came to my exclusion from military service. The guardian had somehow satisfied M Jodoin on this issue when they first met. Nonetheless, I would feel uncomfortable as friends dismissed acquaintances as 'unwilling to do their part'. The bitterness increased as France was occupied, and there was a very real risk that the same fate might befall the Suisse Romande.[20] Honoré and Euzèbe never harassed me on this topic. Perhaps they could not picture me as a military comrade, but, for some thirty to forty years, they despised former school friends who had themselves declared unfit for service and 'did nothing although they were as healthy as oxen'. In time our own children would pick up on these attitudes from their classmates. Céline and I had to explain that:

"It would be very wrong not to play with Patrice and Vivienne. You must ignore the silly gossip you heard about their father's military record."

The triptych was to occasion much uncomfortable reflection on my part. As a gift from the absent Philippe, it was a reminder that rejection from the family could be real. He had broken the code with the affair of the 'stolen' bicycle and was now in self-

---

20 *Operation Tannenbaum* would have divided Switzerland between Germany and Italy. The Swiss may not have known the details of this plan, but they were deeply suspicious of the Axis powers.

imposed exile. I hated the picture as a reminder of Weygand and of the trap that I was in. If I spoke about Weygand, I could open the door to many unpleasant consequences. If I remained silent, the truth might be revealed in a way that showed me to be a coward and a liar.

A few weeks after we opened the crate, Céline was able to fill in some of the missing information. Isabelle was a dutiful Christian aunt to Philippe and had quietly gone to extraordinary lengths to keep in touch with him. She had informed him of our engagement in a note which she included with the leather-bound *Imitation of Christ* by Thomas à Kempis that she mailed *poste restante* to Nouméa for the thirtieth anniversary of his baptism. Céline and I both felt that a very full thank you letter was in order, but I struggled to find proper words of appreciation. We ended up with 'the particularly powerful image that you sent', but I am not sure that our words properly conveyed our feelings.

One of Céline's friends kindly researched what seemed to be 'Gu' abbreviation in the lower right of the central panel. She determined that:

"The work is by the Anonymous of Guingamp and probably dates from the late seventeenth century. He is not considered a master, and his oeuvre has been described as 'pastiche with infelicitous attempts at symbolism'. His use of sturdy frames meant that later artists would often buy his canvases with the intention of painting over them."

Once we were married and had our own property, Céline felt that we needed to display the picture out of respect to Philippe. We decided that it would be overpowering in any of the main rooms, and it eventually ended up in the 'library,' which might more accurately be described as some bookshelves in a long, open alcove under the stairs. It was positioned above another portent, the illustrated volume which the *curé* had given me with the unhappy tale of the farmer of flax and rhubarb who had not been honest with his son.

At first, I was prey to an almost superstitious dislike of the image. Céline did not know the true cause and would tease me:

"Don't be afraid. The viper is not real and can't bite you."

It seemed for many years that she was right. We were to prosper and enjoy a life whose aspirations now seem conventionally bourgeois with our acquisition of a refrigerator and a powered lawnmower. But we were contented and blessed with children who, while scarcely saints, gave us great joy. However, the serpent was patient. Undeterred by the brass mongoose bookends which Céline gave me one Christmas, it waited for the perfect moment.

19.
A Mystery Solved

Mme Beaulac had twice referred to a 'Massimo' in my presence but had never explained who he might be or why his name came so readily to mind. A few weeks after her death, a letter from a solicitor requested my presence at a meeting related to 'the testament of the late Mme Beaulac and the interests of the incarcerated Massimo Beaulac, formerly of Geneva'.

I knew that Mme Beaulac had left her shop to the friendly couple from the neighbouring tobacconist who had quietly watched out for her as her health became more fragile. In a nice gesture, they had given me the faded watercolour of Monastery Hill and the model fishing boat which Mme Beaulac had kept as souvenirs of her native land. I appreciated these and assumed that her simple affairs had been wound up.

Now officially engaged, I had invited Céline to accompany me to the solicitor's office. Neither of us had spent much time in such professional surroundings. I had a fresh pad in my leather writing case, and I had carefully polished the silver pen and pencil set which Édith had given me on my twentieth birthday. Céline was also prepared to take notes. Her writing case had an embroidered cover inspired by Mme Jodoin's collection of Malachite eggs.

The solicitor's office had many signs of past glories. The building had a fine stone façade from the nineteenth century, though corroded gutters and an uneven pathway suggested that the present incumbent was having some difficulty in maintaining it. Once inside, we could see that the solicitor's father, uncle, and grandfather had reached the heights of their profession, as evidenced by the framed awards and honours that covered the walls. The solicitor himself, a talkative, stocky man in his early sixties, had refrained from hanging any certificates beyond his original law degree.

The solicitor ushered us into an airy south-facing meeting room furnished with a fine walnut table and some slightly worn chairs. We pretended not to notice the discoloured ceiling where a leak had caused some of the elaborate moulding to turn brown and crumble. There was something in the lawyer's manner which made us wonder if we were his only company that day. Seeing Céline's writing case, he reminisced about his late, great-aunt.

"Jocelyne was a splendid embroiderer. Mottos, both sacred and profane, were her major interest. She would record them in a notebook as she encountered them in print or over school entrances or on public buildings. She would render her favourites in cross stitch. If only you could see her design for *Superna Quaerite*, Seek Higher Things. It is quite wonderful, with an ascending seagull on one side and a lark on the other. Sadly, she never fulfilled her ambition to inspect the Tapestry of the Apocalypse in Angers.[21] Have you selected a motto to live by when you are married?"

We confessed that we had not.

The receptionist brought tea in an enormous silver pot. The solicitor explained:

"My uncle was president of the Association of Anglo-Swiss Jurists. You can see from the inscription that he was presented with this tea set by Dorothea, Lady Beckermet, to mark the accession of George V *Rex et Imperator*. She nearly caused a diplomatic incident by declaring that, biblically, countries should only be ruled by anointed kings."

As we sipped our Earl Grey, the solicitor enquired:

"Are you familiar with the history of artistic colonies in Italy?

---

21 *La tapisserie de l'Apocalypse* woven in the late fourteenth century for the Duke of Anjou.

Our faces must have betrayed our ignorance. The solicitor reached for a cutting from a magazine:

Massimo Beaulac was an immigrant from Amphora whose parents lived in Geneva. He was naive and overly anxious to ingratiate himself with the more exotic residents of the Florentine artists' colony. His paintings certainly had sufficient merit to give him an entrée. He lacked the wealth of the American and French members and repaid them for his board by running errands. The group was notorious for its libertine mores. A police raid discovered drugs and elicited muddled stories of extramarital relations. The other artists found Beaulac a convenient scapegoat. Their errands were cast as his drug trafficking, and their seductions were transformed into his aggressions. Confused and betrayed, Beaulac lashed out, breaking an artist's hand, and punching a police officer in the jaw. The artist needed surgery and nearly lost his fingers. This assault was portrayed as attempted murder, and Beaulac was sentenced to permanent detention. Interestingly, his best canvases display stylistic tendencies that foreshadow ......

The solicitor continued:

"It was a severe sentence. I don't know the details, but I gather that Massimo was provoked into a fight four years after his imprisonment. I understand that has closed off any chance of a pardon or conditional release. In any event, Mme Beaulac instructed me to contact him before sharing this with you."

The lawyer reached for a sealed envelope which he opened with a paper knife advertising a new and convenient toaster powered by electricity. He read the document before handing it to us.

Mme Beaulac had written:

My son Massimo was a good boy but corrupted <u>by others</u> in early manhood. I pray he will be absolved in the next world. He is now in an Italian prison from which he will *probably never be released. He is too broken to communicate much with me, but I arrange for a small allowance and monthly food parcel to reach him as permitted by the authorities. My solicitor will explain the details. I have suggested to Massimo that our old farm be transferred subject to certain conditions to Jean-Marc (whom I trust <u>completely</u>) after my death. During Massimo's lifetime, Jean-Marc may not sell it or rent the room where Massimo's belongings are stored. He must continue the allowance and the little food parcel. In the event of an amnesty or pardon, the farm <u>must</u> be transferred to Massimo. We have been advised against putting the farm wholly in Massimo's name for fear of <u>unjust</u> seizure by the authorities...*

The solicitor explained that Massimo had simply responded to Mme Beaulac's suggestion with 'Please do what Mother wanted'. The farm could be ours if we accepted it. Céline was unsure:

"Wouldn't it be like living with a ghost? Could we really be happy in a home where everything depends on Massimo remaining behind bars? What if he has changed and really deserves another chance?"

I did not have a ready answer to her questions. The circumstances made me feel uncomfortable. But perhaps I owed it to Mme Beaulac to assist her son in any way that I could. In any event, the first step was to inspect the property. The solicitor cautioned us:

"Don't expect anything grand. Most of the fields were sold long ago. The farm is too small and will never be profitable. My cousin inherited a property like that which took all his energy and drained him financially. He sold it and is now invested in government securities."

Honoré and Euzèbe had accepted me as family to please their much-loved sister. They accompanied us on a grey day in late autumn as we set off beyond city limits to find Massimo's farm. I was glad of their company. They still lived at home and spent much of the day in physical exercise. But they were starting a building renovation enterprise and knew much more about properties than I did. We had trudged a long way on the road before turning off onto a muddy farm track, which, lacking a signpost, might or might not have been the right one. A short burst of stinging ice pellets turned into intermittent sleet. We finally came upon a house with a large barn whose sign proclaimed '*Fruits Beaulac*'.

Céline looked with dismay at the peeling paintwork and the dirty, rotted windows. I was more depressed by the unmanaged fruit trees. Most of their leaves had already fallen, but I could make out some varieties. In better times, Mme Beaulac's tarts would have been filled with the freshest greengages, cherries, pears, and apples from the grounds.

I felt Honoré's hand on my shoulder.

'Jean-Marcot, don't look so glum. The structures look to be in good shape. If Euzèbe pulls his weight, we can turn this into paradise regained."

We went into the main barn. It had been solidly built and had survived intact over years of neglect. It contained some shears, scythes, and other implements that were in reasonable condition having been used and oiled by a relatively recent tenant. Over the workbench there was a framed picture of a radiant Mme Beaulac standing next to a vigorous and grinning young man who must have been Massimo. The legend explained that they were accepting a rosette and special commendation for their pears at the agricultural show. I wondered how soon after this Massimo had decided to pursue his artistic calling in Italy.

The farmhouse looked to have once been a terrace of three sturdy, stone cottages, each with its own front door. Combined together, they formed a good size property, but nothing extravagant compared to other working farmhouses in the neighbourhood. The solicitor had given us a bunch of large rusting keys. We eventually found the right one and entered a kitchen whose enormous range could easily handle the catering for hungry farmworkers. The bottom floor had been knocked through all three properties and the kitchen opened into a refectory and a communal living area. A locked door concealed a staircase which took us to the private living quarters of the first and larger cottage. The dust sheets covered old fashioned but serviceable furniture. The windows looked out over the fruit trees and, on the other side, the mountains. It was a little difficult to make out the exact boundaries of the property, but the orchards covered the equivalent of two or three fields.

We unlocked a door which looked as if it might lead to a closet. It was a small room with Massimo's possessions. Céline was near tears as she examined the wooden yachts and sketchbooks of the once happy boy who was now trapped in prison. I noticed an easel and some playful drawings of squirrels and hedgehogs. One image of mice and a cornucopia stayed in memory—it was not until I was at an exhibition of surrealist art that I understood its genius.

We returned downstairs and briefly examined a fruit cellar that ran the length of the property. In the middle cottage we found another staircase. It led to a substantial steel and wood door which bolted from the inside. The room behind it was full of bunk beds. Some crudely printed leaflets indicated that this space had served as a dormitory for female seasonal workers working here and at neighbouring farms. Readers were assured that the ladies could 'sleep and wash with the greatest propriety'. A minister would come by on Wednesdays to conduct a short evening service. On Sundays they would be escorted to their choice of French, German, or Italian worship.

The staircase at the far end of the building led to the men's accommodations. The layout was similar except that the bolt was on the outside of the door. Their leaflet had a paragraph to remind the gentlemen to eschew spitting, uncharitable language, and unkempt beards. More positively, married men were entitled to a pencil and one stamped postcard per week to keep in touch with their spouses.

As we locked up, Euzèbe turned to Céline and me:

"Promise you won't make any decision until you've talked to me? "

It seemed unlikely that we could be persuaded to move to such a building.

Regardless of our determination on the property, it was important to renew the arrangements for Massimo's allowance and the food parcel with its olives, chocolate bar, and cacciatore salami. The permitted limits were so low that I could afford them without difficulty from my junior salary. The posts worked with extraordinary speed, perhaps as the result of a pilot experiment with airmail. Massimo seemed to have taken my gesture as a sign that we had accepted his offer:

"Dear Jean-Marc,

Thank you so much for the allowance and the food parcel. They make a very real difference to my condition here!

You do not know what pleasure it gives me to imagine the revival of the farm! I am unsure how much it has changed, but I enclose a map of the orchard. The trees marked with an 'A' are from seeds or grafts from Amphora. The water supply from the stream is normally adequate, but the 'B' indicates a capped well that you could use in an emergency. The pears include rare varieties that I list on the back. Mother's recipes involved layering the different types of pears to have contrasting consistencies and an appetizing aroma when the tart was warmed. She taught me to poach some of the fruit overnight in wine in the slow oven to the side of the main range.

Mother would mention you, at first very briefly, in her letters. But your visits came to mean a great deal to her. I respect her judgement. I, too, hold you in high regard and thank you from my heart for providing her with companionship in a way which I have not been able to manage.

Please do not be concerned that I may ever reclaim the farmhouse from you. I do not expect to be released. I have found some purpose in life under the guidance of our visiting priests. I create contemporary illuminated manuscripts and would continue with this mission if my circumstances were to change.

You may rest assured that the farm was bought legitimately, before my errors, as the deeds will show. You will live there with a clean conscience.

May you and your fiancée be truly blessed as you restore the familial happiness which once abounded on our little property.

I was surprised at the length and feeling of this correspondence. It was, perhaps, easier for Massimo to open up to a stranger than to the mother whom he felt he had let down.

Céline was impressed by Massimo's letter, but we continued to have reservations. Private cars were still a luxury, and we certainly could not afford one. Our lives promised to be spent in walking along the track and then down the road until we could connect with the buses.

Céline enjoyed her work as an assistant to a lawyer who specialized in conveyancing disputes. He was in his early forties but, following rheumatic fever, was under strict doctor's orders to work no more than six hours a day. He was tall, thin, and extremely sensitive to cold. Céline warned me not to comment on the scarf, heavy cable-knit sweater, and beret which he wore on the mildest of days. He was a good man, and she shared our dilemma with him. He pulled out some maps and advised her:

"Put your fiancé to work! Look at how the city is going to expand. Within a few years, you will be next to an exclusive residential area with schools and shops. Imagine the increase in value! Tell Jean-Marc that he has to buy you a bicycle and fix the windows before you'll marry him."

He paused and then added:

"I didn't tell you this before, but I'll be moving the office to the north of the city in a year or two. It will be closer to your farm, and you'll still be able to work with me. My work is much less tiring when I have you as the best assistant in the city."

I was growing to like Euzèbe. He good-naturedly allowed Honoré to tease him as the quiet, younger brother. But Euzèbe had drive and would do anything for his sister. He had vaguely mentioned some plans for the property, but I was unprepared when he shepherded Céline, Honoré, and me into the back parlour after lunch at the Jodoins'. His tone switched to the professional, he was ready with estimated costs and work plans, and he had a vision:

Euzèbe and Honoré would renovate the house for us. In return, we would let them use the barn for ten years to store materials for their business and park a truck. For two years after we moved in, they would need access to the farm to showcase their work to potential customers. They would make sure that the renovation was good quality, but it might take a little longer as they trained their team. Euzèbe continued:

"The great thing is that you really have three houses joined together. So, at any time, one will be undergoing renovation, Céline and Jean-Marc will be in another, and, as needed, we and some of our crew can stay in the other. Have you counted how many bunk beds there are?"

A few weeks previously, I would not have contemplated such an arrangement. I bore no grudges, but I had not completely forgotten Honoré's mocking comments at the fair. I was now considered a friend, albeit a junior one, but I was not sure how well our relationship would survive any misunderstanding about the property. On a long journey to a customer, I shared my concerns with Timothée, our salesman who acted as my manager. Our subsidiary was small, and we worked well together without a rigid hierarchy. Timothée was in his late forties, genuinely enthusiastic about our products, and proved an excellent mentor. Dark-haired, he had a slightly wolfish smile with conspicuously white teeth, which he attributed to a baking soda-based tooth powder. He advised me against toothpaste:

"Don't be lazy and waste your money. It is much cheaper to buy tooth powder and add the water yourself."

He had started his career just before motorcars were generally available to salesmen and, efficient and coordinated in other spheres, his primary weakness was an inability to master double declutching on the car. Following a journey undertaken entirely in second gear, I volunteered as his chauffeur. His grasp of theory being better than his practice, he gave me a quick driving lesson on a deserted country road and had me accompany him to almost all his meetings. The clients invariably decorated their offices with their best published illustrations. I would comment on their different styles and techniques, which pleased the customer, and I would support Timothée with some of the technical details related to the sale. He had a practical perspective, and I appreciated his advice.

"Jean-Marc, you remember when that press in Lausanne was down for four days while we waited for a part from Gothenburg?"

This question seemed irrelevant to the problem of the farmhouse, but I agreed that I did recall this unpleasant incident in which the customer's wrath had been directed to me as the company's representative. He went on:

"This is not official yet. But we are going to change how we do things. You will have to stay on site longer after the equipment is installed to make sure there are no hidden defects. Instead of a raise this year, you'll get a little van stocked with components.

Within limits, you'll be allowed to take it home and use it as yours. I think I have convinced management that you'll need the expensive heater accessory, but don't tell that to the French team."

It took me some time to digest this news. I had worked hard and counted on my raise to pay the rent for an apartment when we married. But the van would make it more practical to live on the farm.

We opted for the small holding. The next day the brothers took down the sign over the barn. *Fruits Beaulac* would now be *Entreprises Jodoin.* I rescued the old sign and the picture of Mme Beaulac and Massimo and hung them in the fruit cellar.

20.
A Dog and a Hedge

"Do you understand your duties here?"

Achille, our tiny new black Labrador puppy, cocked his head as he listened to my question. I had been playing with him on the floor, and he came and nestled next to me. I could hear Céline and Honoré discussing the evening meal in the farm kitchen. I continued:

"When no one is here, you must guard the house. If those two by the stove take the wrong bottling jars from the fruit cellar again, you should stand like a brave ancient warrior and growl like this: grrrrrr... We can polish up your epic over the next few days:

> *Le grand Achille, chien fort, doué et brave,*
> *Sait chasser les voleurs fructivores de la cave.*
> *Admiratifs, les chiots chanteront sans cesse,*
> *Ton courage canin, ta vigueur et tes prouesses.*
> *Les dieux eux-mêmes..."*

A wet sponge flew towards me. I could not see who had thrown it, but Céline's laugh was clear:

"That is quite awful! Achille, don't listen to his nonsense. Your job is to keep him in order. Jean-Marc, can you do something with these pears? There is no room for the casserole."

"Alright, I'm coming! Sorry, Achille, life is not easy as an in-law of the Jodoins."

We had moved into the farmhouse a few weeks after our wedding. Our accommodations were primitive, as we slept in the former women's dormitory on two bunk beds pushed together. There were no wardrobes, only thin pine lockers. Honoré and Euzèbe had spent weeks turning the large barn into a combination of storage, workshop, office, and garage. But now that they were properly set up, they had switched to a vigorous renovation of the old private quarters. It seemed that at least one of the brothers was always in our house. Honoré would summon me to impart the latest developments:

"Jean-Marc, come and congratulate Euzèbe on his certificate in residential sanitation! Tomorrow, we can show you how to maintain the drains to avoid back-ups. Don't wear long sleeves."

Some of the team would stay in the men's dormitory and would expect breakfast, a sandwich lunch, and a full evening meal. We were struck by the remarkable appetites of three convivial carpenters from Liechtenstein. Euzèbe had given them free rein to demonstrate their carving skills, with the result that every beam, lintel, and window sill carried a shield with a design of bees around a mountain. This detail impressed the brothers' prospective customers and endowed the renovation with a wholly misleading suggestion of noble heritage behind the Montabeille name.

Céline and I were finally alone. Honoré, a mason, and two plumbers had retired for the night. They planned to cut the water at five-thirty in the morning for a major rerouting of the pipes and the stove stack which helped heat them. She asked:

"When you were talking to Achille, was that a true word in jest or whatever the phrase is?"

"About the fruit cellar? Of course, not. I'll just label the jars properly so that Honoré doesn't feed damsons in gin to the roofers."

"I understand that. But also, what you said about it being difficult to be our in-law?"

"That wasn't serious. I mean, it would be nice for us to have more privacy, but then we'd be living in a cheap apartment worrying about the rent. We'll get this place fixed, and everything will be alright."

It was true that my remark to Achille had been entirely frivolous, but it did betray a measure of insecurity. The Jodoins meant no disrespect when they took a close interest in my activities – on the contrary, they genuinely wished to be supportive. The problem was that they asked many questions, and I worried that I was judged on the quality of every response.

I was sincerely grateful to the brothers, even if I might have preferred to access the kitchen without finding one of them in an undershirt reheating the leftovers. They would make friendly enquiries about my day, but I had the impression that my answers were reported back to M Jodoin. When we visited for our bi-weekly Sunday lunch he would make remarks referencing conversations from earlier in the week:

"Jean-Marc, is it true that you enquired about getting a telephone line installed? Are you sure you could afford that on your salary? It would be expensive to run telegraph poles to the farm. Telephones are overrated. Most communications are expressed better in person or in a note with proper syntax and good penmanship. Are you still using the calligraphy set that we gave you for Christmas?"

In that particular case, I was able to reassure him that we did not intend to proceed with such an extravagance. And to his defence, his interventions could be benign. After hearing of a gruesome trip on winter roads with Timothée, he presented me with a set of tire chains:

"We installed them with excellent results on the van that takes guilty defendants to jail. The shackled passengers were not much help in pushing it out of snowbanks."

The same might have been said of Timothée, who in three-piece suit and patent leather shoes, would move into the driver's seat. I would hear a grinding as he attempted to engage gear while I applied my weight behind the rear axle.

I had little cause for complaint as a newcomer to Céline's family. Nonetheless, I met up with Xavier, my friend from design college whose uncle owned a nursery. Their surplus cypress, elderberry, and quince would form a dense hedge separating the house from the *Entreprises Jodoin*.

21.
A Mixed Report Card

I remembered M Jodoin's words exactly:

"I think it is very important for a young man to be guided by someone with such estimable personal qualities. I would like you to start seeing Étienne on a regular schedule, two or three times a month."

I had readily accepted his terms. But, at one of our early encounters, I was exhausted, having helped with the installation of a press over the night shift and most of the following day. I was earning my own living, soon to be married, and it suddenly irked me that I should have to report to my fiancée's cousin. I tried to postpone, but I could not reach Étienne.

I had innocently suggested a beer in a bistro by the train station. It proved conveniently situated but characterless, with faded gingham tablecloths, and filled with business travellers carrying briefcases and raincoats. They all looked stressed and irritable.

Out of respect for Étienne, I attempted to be upbeat and friendly. But I really needed to return home, complete the post-installation paperwork, and go to bed. After we had talked for a while, Étienne began questioning me:

"Jean-Marc, are you monitoring your health properly? It is absolutely essential. Do you carry vervain lozenges with you? My mother swears by them for headaches and insomnia."

I grunted something to the effect that I felt alright. Undeterred, he continued:

"Is your job secure?"

"I suppose so. No one else would put up with the hours."

 Do you follow a disciplined routine to get enough sleep?"

I snapped:

"Of course, I'm not getting enough sleep! I've just worked twenty hours straight getting a new press installed. And I was on my own. In Sweden and Germany, they send a team of two people to oversee it. But my manager trusts me even if no one else in Geneva does."

I had spoken too loudly. A waitress ceased emptying ashtrays into a bucket and turned to stare at us. Étienne looked uncomfortable and slowly put down his stein.

I was immediately ashamed of my outburst:

"I'm so sorry, Étienne! Please forget that I ever said that. It's been a very long couple of days. You know I respect you. But how does this work? Do you fill in a report card on my adequacy as son-in-law? Do I lose points for insufficient sleep?"

For a second, I could not tell from his expression how he might react. But his tone was friendly though concerned:

"Don't be an idiot! It's not like that at all. Look, I'm new to this too, and my questions came over the wrong way. Think of me as a species of brother. However annoying you are, you are always my friend. I'll even let you take that last olive."

Then he added drily:

"Besides, I could never give you a satisfactory grade if we keep frequenting places like this."

I looked around. The businessmen had left, only to be replaced by ladies with a little too much makeup.

We held future meetings at a café run by Vincent, Étienne's old school friend. He would collect unsold stock from his mother's florist shop. Depending on her sales, diners would converse over a little wilting gypsophila or peer at each other through abundant arrangements of roses. Broad-shouldered and with a mop of unruly dark hair, this friendly giant would tower over us:

"Jean-Marc, I am prescribing a complimentary side of endive with cumin. You must eat it slowly to bring tranquillity to your mind and digestion."

I now looked forward to my meetings with Étienne, although I was aware that the Jodoins occasionally asked him about my progress. However, my affection for him was to be sorely tested in the unfortunate affair of Achille's kennel.

Together Céline and I could just about cover groceries and expenses on the Beaulac farm, and we urgently needed to set up a joint account. We had arranged a time when we could both see M Labrie at the *Banque des Alpinistes.* He was semi-retired but had previously set up a savings account for me. One of the guardian's committees had helped his disabled sister, and he ensured that my meagre funds earned an interest rate normally reserved for the most privileged private clients. The bank, an imposing building with classical pillars and polished teak, was conveniently opposite the bookstore.

The appointment was in the afternoon. I just had to finish training a customer in Trois Cruches, a town known for its calcium-rich mineral waters and prisons. I could leave at midday and be back in plenty of time. I had just concluded the session when we heard shouts and loud whistles.

The young officer, with rifle and fur earmuffs, was polite, but firm. I was not to drive the van. There had been a rock slide. The mayor, who was renowned as a geologist and didactic poet, had declared an emergency. The valley road would be closed until engineers confirmed that there was no further danger. The higher, alternate route was impassable due to snow.

The limited telephone lines from the town delayed the operator in connecting me to Céline. A crossed wire with an angry farmer disputing the auction fees for his bulls made conversation difficult. I explained that I was delayed. Céline had another appointment near the bank, and we agreed that she might as well see if the account could be opened without me.

Céline, arriving a little early for her meeting, had filled the time by visiting Étienne. He needed to deposit a birthday cheque from Aunt Isabelle, and the two cousins had met M Labrie together. The banker courteously enquired:

"Your husband is otherwise engaged in Trois Cruches and not immediately available? That does not present any problem. There is no need to explain, this sort of thing happens all the time."

My signature was already on file, and M Labrie would set up the joint account immediately.

The affair of the kennel unfolded in a pleasant market town where Timothée and I had met successfully with a customer. My presence was not required while Timothée and the accountant discussed financing options, and I explored the little high street which still had traditional shops including a fishmonger, a butcher, a wool shop, and a hatter. A carpenter's store with a wonderful scent of fresh cedar sold kennel kits at a very reasonable price. We had already planned to build a shelter for Achille on the little hillock in our orchard. He would be safe there, it was south-facing, and he would enjoy watching me as I worked on the trees.

I went to the local branch of the bank and wrote my first cheque on the joint account. The friendly teller with a bob haircut explained that she would need to call Geneva to verify the balance. As I waited, I exchanged greetings with a garrulous director from the customer.

I waited even longer. Doubtless there was a problem with the switchboard. Eventually I saw the assistant emerge from a rear office accompanied by a sturdy colleague. M Bolduc did not match the standard image of a bank manager. Square and solid, he would not have looked out of place in a group of heavy-weight boxers. His bass boomed through the glass partition to the entire customer hall.

"Sir, you must know that your signature is not valid unless countersigned by Étienne Levasseur. Perhaps you could ask your wife to write the cheque?"

Reddening, I explained:

"The account was set up with my wife's cousin when I was away at a customer's. There is clearly some mistake. I'll take care of it as soon as I get back to Geneva."

These excuses did not convince anyone. The once-amiable teller gave me a look of withering disapproval as she stood at a safe distance behind her manager. I overheard her sotto voce comment to a passing colleague:

"It's probably to stop him smoking opium. He's from the city."

The director seemed to listen closely and would doubtless retail the story at the customer site.

As I retreated, my embarrassment ignited a rare anger. How could there be a mistake? What if Étienne was party to a scheme which would allow the Jodoins to control me if I did not conform? How dare they deny me the right to spend the money I had earned? Maybe I had never really been accepted. Had they somehow involved Céline, and what did she know? I reflected bitterly on the potential schemes of the smiling group which had recently gathered for Ascension Day lunch at the farm.

Furious, I strode to the post office across the street and spent my remaining cash on an ungrammatical telegram to Étienne:

"Why my cheques require your signature?"

Timothée calmed me down as we drove back. He explained:

"That was a major sale. We're well above quota and you'll get a nice commission. Don't worry about the kennel. I built one for my mother-in-law who wanted a Dalmatian puppy. I was inspired by that new art-deco cinema, and the entrance has ornamental sphinxes. Anyway, she changed her mind and got an annoying ginger cat. Bring the van, and I'll help you transport it."

It was dusk when I arrived home. As Achille sprinted across the grass to meet me, I realized that I did not want to go indoors. Céline and I had experienced very few misunderstandings and no really serious arguments. I did not know what I would say if it turned out that she had agreed to this limitation on my banking. I was still very angry, but increasingly and uncomfortably aware that I had not taken the time to reflect before transmitting my accusatory telegram. Did I really believe that Étienne would have betrayed me? What if I had jumped to a wrong conclusion and destroyed a deep friendship? I stroked my faithful Achille.

"Let's go and see where we'll put your grand new kennel. You'll be able to survey the whole terrain."

Achille and I were sitting on the rocky outcrop when we heard Céline calling him. I replied:

"We're coming. We were just inspecting the orchard."

I was distressed as I saw the effect of my impatient query. My telegram had reached Étienne, who had made the inconvenient trip to the farm. My action had clearly upset him, and he seemed exhausted. Céline looked deeply worried. It was Étienne who spoke first:

"Jean-Marc, I'm so dreadfully sorry. I spent the afternoon in the bank trying to understand what happened. I wanted to speak to M Labrie, but he has retired to live with his daughter in Perpignan. It is all my fault for not reading the paperwork more carefully. It went on for fifteen pages of legal terms. I promise you we'll get it fixed. I'll pay the fees."

Étienne was less composed and coherent than usual. I gradually understood that M Labrie's delicate and euphemistic queries about my failure to appear had led him to a wrong conclusion. The *Banque des Alpinistes* had a reputation for preserving the funds of dissolute and incarcerated clients, several of whom were detained in Trois Cruches. Accounts were set up in their names, but they could not access the monies without the countersignature of a responsible party. It was relatively easy to open such an account, but expensive legal and medical attestations were required to allow the customers to withdraw a single franc on their signature alone.

Mollified, I apologized:

"Sorry, I feel really bad. I should have waited to talk things over with you and not stirred things up with my stupid telegram. Look, it's late. Why don't you have dinner and stay the night? Céline, are we having that dandelion and pepper salad with the anchovy quiche?

I never did ask Étienne to pay for the attestations. I was busy with new installations at work, and Céline managed our finances more effectively than I could. It did not trouble me that he would receive our statements and, perhaps, share them with the Jodoins. Timothée and I made a good team, and I earned a little more than expected. I did not anticipate that one day my inability to withdraw my own funds would be held against me by my own son.

22.
Visitors and a Singular Offspring

"Did you hear that Dr Rossignol won first prize for his amaryllis? He inserted the same iron tablets in the soil that he prescribed for your convalescence from pink eye."

I had not been apprised of this information, and I was happy to see the guardian and Édith looking relaxed as we drank coffee outside on a beautiful day in late May. I had been a little nervous about this first visit to the farm which we had delayed until after the renovations were completed. The guardian showed no sign of discomfort that I was living in the Beaulac property. On the contrary, he and Édith were appreciative of almost everything from the moment that I picked them up in the van:

"You drive so well! You know how to respond to the needs of the motor."

I was negotiating a charabanc, which had stalled on a hill, when Édith remarked:

"Don't let me forget my bag in the van. I have a present for you of *saccharomyces cerevisiae Amphorae*. It has fascinating characteristics."

Seeing my vacant expression, she continued:

"I'm talking about the type of yeast used in Amphoran bread. Prof Chassé is retired, but I was sure that he would have some in his home laboratory. He had a theory that the right combination of yeast and mineral supplements in bread could reduce treatable cases of indigestion by twenty percent. He ran a popular course where the students ate four large bread rolls in five minutes and made notes on the after effects. I'll show you how to manage the yeast so that it will supply you for years."

After finishing our coffee, Céline and I took our guests on a tour of the house. Neither of us was excessively house proud, but we kept our part of the bargain with Honoré and Euzèbe. One of us would sweep and polish on alternate days and, for two years, the house was uncomfortably clean and tidy, always ready to be shown to their potential customers. Our visitors were impressed with one exception. The triptych did not appeal to Édith:

"What a peculiar scene! One feels quite nervous for the Eldest Son and the Father. It would have been much more agreeable to show a cockerel in the grass instead of a snake."

We had given away half the bunk beds from the overcrowded dormitories, but we were still left with three in each room. The guardian performed the calculation:

"Three beds times two rooms times two bunks per bed. Perfect! We look forward to meeting your twelve children in due course."

We failed to meet this playfully suggested quota. Without realizing it, Céline and I were ahead of our time. We both worked, and she quickly progressed from being an assistant to what would now be termed a senior paralegal. Sympathetic friends regretted that she was unavailable for social events during the week and concluded that her husband must be a poor provider. An older lady in a farmhouse nearby was the mother of thirteen adult children. She would bring us pies and recipes.

"These served me well, and all our children were healthy. But a mother can't work in an office and take care of them."

We exasperated M and Mme Jodoin by delaying children until we had the farm under control and felt more financially stable. But after five years we entered the world of cribs, nurseries, and schools.

Marguerite, our first born, was a beautiful, outgoing girl who had her mother's looks. She was followed in two years by Mathieu, whose appearance and manner betrayed from the youngest age that he was my son. His younger brother, Olivier, soon grew taller than his sibling and was never happier than playing catch with Honoré and Euzèbe. Élisabeth, our youngest, was delicate but always very sweet and thoughtful.

Mathieu was unquestionably the most idiosyncratic of the children. Rather like an overzealous sheepdog, he decided that it was his mission always to know where I was and what I was doing. As a very young child, he would insist on taking his blue toy bus into the hallway in the early evening so he could meet me as soon as I got back. Once he had confirmed that I was safely in the fold, he would return quietly to his normal occupations.

We became friends with several neighbours who were bringing up children in the surrounding small holdings. The Bouchards were particularly sociable and would organize activities for the children while the adults talked or played cards. Mathieu would play happily with the others of his same age. But roughly every hour, he would excuse himself to 'check on Papa'. He would come and touch my hand before returning to his playmates.

The robustly built M Bouchard was very kind but excitable. In discussion his voice could become a little loud. He would turn slightly red-faced, and his wife would discreetly move his glass in case his hand gestures became too expansive. We were discussing the relative engine capacities of Renault and Citroën vans when I mixed them up. I was immediately put in my place:

"Other way round! That makes no sense."

Mathieu, who had overheard, held my arm before taking his leave with a stage whisper:

"Papa never wrong!"

We never entirely understood Mathieu's eccentricities. There was a time when I would often take him for a walk in the orchard while Céline and Marguerite readied his younger siblings for bed. He liked to say goodbye to Céline before we set off on these little promenades. She would respond with:

"Take care of Papa." Or "Bring Papa back safely."

Perhaps these light-hearted injunctions had a subliminal impact on his juvenile mind. One of his earliest drawings was a sticklike Papa standing ineffectively while a heroic dog chased away the neighbour's goat, a creature which would sometimes startle us with a loud bleat from the other side of the boundary fence.

Mathieu's performance at junior school placed him unostentatiously in a lower quartile, except in geography where he managed some tepid compliments from the austere Mme Vézina. He would interrogate me about my trips and ask to be shown my route on the road atlas. Soon he was acting as an unofficial planner.

"If you don't need to take any heavy parts with you on Wednesday, you could take the early train and get back before my bedtime. On Thursday, you can take the mountain road if there is no snow and have lunch at that place with the good spätzle and *saucisson vaudois.*

I tried to prevent his enthusiasm from becoming too intrusive. I already had to fill in an annoying trip form for some accountant in Sweden who would compare my planned route to the one actually expensed. We would correspond weeks after the event about the variances, how a bridge had been washed away, or the train driver's appendix had needed urgent attention.

We might have pushed Mathieu to try a little harder at school, but we were disarmed by Mme Trifonov. She was a white Russian *émigré* and the mother of his friend, Anton. Elegant and with an alarmingly imperious manner, she recognized me one summer weekend at the outdoor swimming pool in Cologny where I had taken the children. I was in trunks. She was dressed in a cobalt blue ensemble with diamond earrings, a matching bracelet, and several strings of pearls. She began:

"I have been looking for you! We need to speak about your son. He talks with my Anton in the back of the class."

I braced for a lecture. M Jodoin had already made it clear that he believed that I was too soft as a parent. Perhaps she felt the same way. The sun sparkled off her earrings as she continued:

"He understands Anton better than any of the teachers. My son is working in a second language, the Roman script is new to him, and he cannot hear well in one ear. He would drown if Mathieu did not keep checking that he was alright. You have brought him up with the proper values."

She retrieved her reluctant son by tapping on a rose gold watch to indicate that it was time to leave, and withdrew to the adjacent taxi rank.

I concluded that Mathieu was on the right path despite the acerbic M Corbin's complaint that 'he explores null values in algebra lessons.' I was glad that Mme Trifonov had passed on her information, for Mathieu never used helping Anton as an excuse for his indifferent results, and rarely mentioned him except in an anecdote about a stray kitten which had disrupted a German vocabulary test.

Céline and I held a theory that the children plotted at the start of each school session to make life as exhausting for us as possible. Two of them would do well and require equipment and transport as they participated in their clubs and teams. One would perform badly, requiring coaching and discussions with agitated teachers. The remaining child would hide in the middle of the pack until a perceived lack of attention led to an outburst. At the start of the next session, they would swap roles.

Our hypothesis may have been ill-founded, but the exhaustion could be real. Céline had taken Olivier and Marguerite to her parents. Olivier would return talking of weights and spinach leaves that would allow him to grow up like uncle Honoré. Marguerite would help with mittens or cakes for Mme Jodoin's charities. I was at home with Mathieu, then aged thirteen, and Élisabeth, who had just turned nine. We had finally installed a telephone with financial assistance from the company. It rang at two-thirty pm on a Saturday afternoon in June. There was a problem at a press, and I needed to get there immediately with a replacement part.

As it happened, none of the neighbours were at home, and I did not want to leave the children alone. There had been some thefts in our normally placid sector and reports of a long-haired lady with green cigarette papers. The Jodoins were on the opposite side of town from the press. In desperation, I called the guardian. Although now officially retired, he had just returned from Bern where he had spent several months assisting a government committee. I gave a rapid summary of my problem:

"I'm so sorry. The repair may take five minutes, or it could take fifteen hours depending on what we need to disassemble."

"Of course, you can bring the children! We have beds if they need to stay the night."

I bundled Mathieu and Élisabeth into the van with a little overnight case. The Jodoins were relatively frequent visitors to the farm, but the children saw less of Édith and the guardian, whom I normally met alone. I offered some parental advice:

"It is very kind of them to take you children at such short notice. Try not to be too loud or tiring. If you get bored, ask the guardian if you can look at the pictures in Doré's edition of *The Rime of the Ancient Mariner*."

I urged the children out of the van and, with a wave to the guardian and Édith, headed to my customer.

I was not certain that a short delay in printing *A Moral Approach to Sales and Merchandising* justified the urgent interruption of my family's Saturday afternoon. Keeping these reservations to myself, I remedied the customer's problem while tactfully pointing out that the issue could have been avoided by following the pre-run inspection procedure. The printer was delighted to be running again:

"Your company offers the best service in the industry. You don't have children, do you?"

I confessed that I did.

"I was going to offer you a copy of our *Illustrated Vases of Europe,* but some of the classical examples might not be appropriate for a home with younger readers."

I let myself into the guardian's house around six pm while there was still light. For a moment I thought I had penetrated the wrong building. While the guardian was in Bern, Édith had installed large windows on both sides of the vet's room. One could look right through it from the hall to the garden, which, having been properly thinned and pruned, was now colourful and welcoming. The vet's table had not moved but was covered in clay pots with a lush array of exotic plants which I could not recognize.

An excited Élisabeth came by, holding a guide to butterflies and moths.

"Papa, can we have a room like this? Édith is so nice. She showed me all her flowers. That one is *Mimosa Pudica.* If you touch the leaves, they will close and pretend to be dead so you don't eat them. She grew this palm from a date. But I have to go to the rhubarb patch. We think we've found a moth that normally lives in Libya. It may have blown here in a storm."

I looked briefly for Mathieu and the guardian. Through a window, I saw the guardian sitting by the cannas while Mathieu sketched his portrait. The guardian appeared relaxed, and Mathieu had a look of deep but contented concentration. It seemed a shame to disturb this scene, and I rested on a comfortable wicker chair. It replaced the wooden one on which I had endured so many dreary hours as I wrestled with the demands of the *curé* and Stéphane. Then I must have fallen deeply asleep. It had been a long week.

I awoke to the sound of Mathieu and the guardian clearing space for my dinner tray.

The guardian explained:

"We didn't want to disturb you when we ate earlier, but Mathieu and Élisabeth are about to go to bed. They wanted to be sure that you would not go hungry. We reached Céline, and she is not expecting you until morning. Is it alright if I give this to Mathieu? It looks so remarkably like him."

The guardian was holding that picture of me playing the organ with which Étienne had taken artistic liberties over twenty years ago. He was right. It had never seemed entirely accurate as my image, but it resembled Mathieu exactly, a little taller, stronger, and more confident than I had ever been.

23.
The Conman

"Papa, why did Uncle Philippe call you a brilliant conman?"

The thirteen-year-old Mathieu sat beside me as I drove back from the station after seeing off Philippe, who had passed through Geneva on expatriate leave from his mining company. Our relative had only stayed one night, but that was enough.

Aunt Isabelle had died well into her nineties. She had owned a strip of land, of no great value, where her husband had taught canoeing in a pond and on a short stretch of river. This once charming meadow was now overlooked by the cement works and bisected by electricity pylons. Covered in old mattresses and discarded stoves, the property had been left to Philippe, Étienne, Céline, and her brothers. They were all to meet with the lawyer and sign documents selling this wasteland as additional parking for the cement trucks.

Céline and I were to pick up Philippe early on the Friday evening. His train was delayed some seven hours by subsidence on the tracks. I drove Céline back home and returned alone. I had never met Philippe but had formed a sympathetic picture of him as the child who had stood up for a bullied friend in the affair of the 'stolen' bicycle. He would now be in his forties and visiting the family for the first time in over twenty years. I was determined to make him feel welcome.

The train finally pulled in after midnight with an unpleasant odour of binding brakes. Most of the descending passengers rushed towards the exits, anxious to conclude their disagreeably extended journey. I started to approach a figure who looked like a possible candidate. He sidestepped me and threw his arms around a stern, soberly dressed woman who had earlier offered me a pamphlet, *The Imminent Demise of Swiss Capitalism.*

A tall individual in a trilby, carrying two large suitcases covered with shipping labels, approached me:

"Excuse me, did Mme Montabeille send you?

"Philippe? I'm Jean-Marc. So happy to meet you."

He did not seem seized with my answer and continued:

"Jean-Marc Montabeille? Really? Céline Jodoin's husband?"

I extended my hand in greeting. Perhaps he genuinely misunderstood my gesture, but he passed me the largest suitcase as though I were a hotel valet.

I could not make out Philippe's tone and was unsure if he was just teasing or simply being inappropriate. He had a certain family resemblance to Honoré, but his complexion was darker and, while well-built, he was less conspicuously muscular. His slightly irritating stare lasted a fraction too long after asking a question. I essayed some bland, welcoming pleasantries as I led him to the van. Unimpressed by the news that we had aired his bed and warmed it with hot water bottles, he responded:

"Jean-Marc, you know that your left lace is becoming untied? Have you tried loafers? They are much simpler for some people."

Céline and I had both taken the day off to ready the house for Philippe's arrival and prepare a memorable dinner. Tired and cold, I reacted to his query by slamming the van door shut and coaxing the damp motor into life. We travelled in silence while he peered at the city, which had welcomed and then rejected him. I reflected bitterly that, in adult life, my laces had remained properly attached until some two weeks prior when I had acquired a pair with a shiny, frictionless coating.

Arriving at the farm, I saw that Céline had left the light on by a side door. As I led Philippe inside, I realized that she had carefully placed a lamp so that his wedding present, the triptych, would be better illuminated and seem a more prominent part of our décor. It caught Philippe's attention and he murmured:

"I'm glad that Céline has the picture on display. It's good to remember that snakes lurk everywhere. *Latet anguis in herba.*"[22]

I wondered if this comment was directed at me, but my train of thought was interrupted. Our second Labrador, the tirelessly friendly Ulysse, had sensed the friction. He crouched by me, emitting a low growl at Philippe, who returned a disdainful look at both dog and owner.

I awoke much puzzled by the events of the previous night. I had no involvement in Philippe's past history and had tried to be companionable. It seemed unlikely that he would have received ill reports of me from Aunt Isabelle who had been his main correspondent. Maybe he had reached an immediate decision that I was not good enough for Céline. After all, it had taken me months to win over Honoré and Euzèbe. I descended late and reluctantly to breakfast. Céline and Philippe were clearly enjoying each other's company and reminiscing about a trip which they had taken in the little cogwheel railway that goes up Mont Blanc. Céline, then aged ten, had been scared and had clasped the teenage Philippe's hand throughout the descent.

Philippe rose upon seeing me:

"Jean-Marc, I never thanked you properly for waiting for me last night. As you probably realized, I was in a foul mood after being trapped in that infernal compartment with two French couples who argued about political philosophy for ten hours straight. Do forgive me. It was so very ill-mannered. Can I pass you a slice of the brioche?"

I projected a hospitable smile:

"No harm done. You are safe here. Céline and I couldn't sustain a ten-minute discussion on politics. Did you try the honey? It's from our hive."

Ulysse, unpersuaded by this rapprochement, would not leave my side.

---

22 Virgil Eclogue

Mme Jodoin, now in her seventies, was engaged with a charity which sponsored Swiss youths with equestrian backgrounds to spend summers in England working as grooms and learning the language. This laudable exchange scheme had apparently worked well except that several of the team failed to adapt to the diet and returned several kilos lighter. Mme Jodoin resolved to address this issue by acclimatizing the next year's intake to British cuisine. She would learn how to prepare pork pies, scotch eggs, and tapioca pudding. And what better audience to test these delicacies than our family when we were all gathered at the farm for lunch with Philippe?

Étienne dropped off Mme Jodoin and her baskets of food before collecting Céline and Philippe to meet the other signatories at the lawyer's office. I stayed at home with the children. The solicitor's building happened to be opposite the photographers where we had posed on Céline's birthday for a family shoot arranged by Mme Jodoin. The proofs would now be ready. This innocent coincidence was to prove unfortunate.

I have tried to see the events of the day through Philippe's eyes. After an absence of twenty years, he may have felt entitled to be the focus of attention. And he would have expected, perhaps, some different gestures of respect and reconciliation given the circumstances of his removal from the centre of the family.

The afternoon started promisingly. The documents had been executed without any problem at the solicitor's office. I greeted the returning party with a Chasselas blanc accompanied by goat cheese and fruit *hors d'oeuvres* which the children had sculpted into little mice. Honoré, in his finest white shirt and with rare tact, raised a toast to his cousin. M Jodoin, who was a little breathless with his advancing years, expressed the wish that:

"You will always feel welcome in your native country and will return soon and often."

Étienne, Euzèbe, and Céline had carefully selected snapshots from Isabelle's album, excluding any with bicycles or other possible reminders of difficult times. While I helped Mme Jodoin with the lunch, I could hear a running commentary:

"Look at how young Aunt Isabelle looks in this one! Is that when she gave you the jam spoon that belonged to her great-uncle Pierre-Philippe? Wasn't he the one with the wig who sold potted liverwurst to the Swiss mercenaries?"

Philippe's replies were relaxed.

The late train had meant that Philippe never tasted the *boeuf bourguignonne* which had been carefully prepared for his arrival. Mme Jodoin explained the unlikely lunch menu:

"I hope you don't mind. It is for such a good cause. If the exchange children can acquire the taste now, they'll be happier and not return so thin."

No one objected, but I thought I saw disappointment in Philippe's eyes as he was offered a pie with a gelatinous substance visible through a crack in the crust.

The lunchtime conversation was polite, but it never flowed as it might among old friends. Mme Jodoin did a good job of questioning Philippe and how he had a house by the sea although he spent much of his time in mining camps. Various past relatives were discussed and provided a minute or two of reminiscence. Honoré and Euzèbe gave abbreviated accounts of their sporting and business ventures:

"One of our first contracts was a shed for the rowing club. Their boats are really expensive so we fitted one of those electric alarms."

Philippe responded with a quizzical look before commenting:

"Really? European competitive rowing seems so pointless compared to canoeing by the Pacific islanders."

The silences grew longer as we finished the meal, and it was clear that the next two hours before I could take Philippe for the train would be heavy going. I suggested:

"Would anyone like a walk? Philippe, we could show you the orchard and head down to the little waterfall by the next farm."

The patter of heavy raindrops put an end to this option. It was then that Mme Jodoin asked to see the proofs from the photographer.

The *Studio Si Monumentum* had caused a sensation when it opened. Glamorous Hollywood-style photography would replace staid black and white family photographs. The owners, a French brother and sister, whose portfolio even included celebrities from Detroit and Des Moines, could make Genevans look as if they had just stepped off the red carpet. Mme Jodoin was delighted with the results:

"Philippe, do look! Aren't Céline and Jean-Marc wonderful in this one?"

In truth, we could scarcely have looked more phony. Wishing to please my mother-in-law, I had accepted whatever indignities might be demanded by the photographers. With greased hair, a tuxedo, a clip-on bow tie, and a smile showing many teeth, I resembled the well-scrubbed lead singer in the *Trois Grenouilles de Besançon*, a popular band whose lyrics spoke of fragrant maidens encountering kindly unicorns. Céline fared slightly better. She had resisted the proposed bouffant hairstyle though she had to contend with a wide red belt 'like in the musicals.' I was placed on a platform next to her as 'it would be normal for the man to be taller than the wife'.

Seated on the sofa next to Mme Jodoin, Philippe was subjected to all sixty proofs, with parents and children pictured in every combination and from every angle. Mme Jodoin offered continuous commentary:

"Doesn't Mathieu look like the image of his father? We are so blessed that Céline chose Jean-Marc. Isn't he good with the children?"

I could see that Philippe was struggling to suppress a certain irritation at this endless paean to our family. A break in the rain offered a chance to escape:

"It looks a little drier. I'll take Ulysse to check that the brassicas did not get battered. Would anyone like to join me?"

Mme Jodoin responded:

"You should take Honoré and Euzèbe with you to check on the broccoli. You have such green fingers. We never have any success with it. I still need to catch dear Philippe up on everything that has been happening here."

Once out of earshot of our guest, Honoré confided:

"Thank heaven you got us out of there! Philippe still has that annoying way of peering at you after he talks. It's murder trying to keep the conversation going."

At four-thirty, to the brothers' barely concealed relief, I helped Philippe load his luggage into the van. Mathieu, looking smart in his matching jacket and cap, was going to accompany us to see the trains. He had earlier run into the dining room and spilled two portions of treacle sponge pudding with custard over his sister's chair. By the time Céline and I emerged from the kitchen to investigate, Philippe had risen to his assistance:

"Don't worry, Mathieu. I once dropped Aunt Isabelle's *crème caramel* on her favourite carpet with the strawberry pattern. Let me help you clean it up."

Philippe clearly had a kind side, even if it was often frustratingly hidden. Mathieu never forgot his cousin's gentle gesture.

We arrived at the station in good time. Philippe had donned a smart raincoat with wide lapels and double buttons, which, with his trilby, made my cap and cardigan seem distinctly provincial. I slipped Mathieu a few francs to buy a newspaper for our relative and some chocolate for himself. As he ran down the platform to the kiosk, I apologized to Philippe:

"I'm sorry. You got rather a full dose of our family's news. Mme Jodoin tends to get a little over-excited by photographs of us and the grandchildren."

He nodded before replying:

"I'm used to it. Aunt Isabelle would have made an excellent propagandist. You don't know how many letters she sent me extolling your family's virtues."

He paused, as though debating whether to continue, before remarking:

"I'm full of admiration. How did you do it? Don't take this the wrong way, but, although you're nice and everything, you don't really stand out. I mean you're not the handsome son of a millionaire with a big automobile. Not everyone could have penetrated the Jodoin fortress. I couldn't even keep my place there. And yet, you won over the brothers and married the girl."

We were briefly interrupted by a loudspeaker announcement before he continued:

"I never fully understood the story of the old lady and how she came to leave you her son's little farm. I don't know how you worked that, but I'm not judging. You have a very nice place for a print mechanic."

I flashed Philippe a warning glance as I saw Mathieu approaching with the paper neatly rolled into a baton and held by a rubber band. Perhaps Philippe did not care, or maybe he did not realize how well his voice travelled:

"Don't misunderstand me. Everyone seems happy with the result, which is the mark of a true professional. You are a brilliant conman."

I did not want to discuss this topic with Philippe in Mathieu's presence, and we made small talk until the train pulled in. He shook my hand:

"Thank you for everything Jean-Marc. And don't take anything I said too seriously. I was just joking around."

He put his hand on Mathieu's shoulder before handing him a little vial:

"Take this. Those flecks are gold samples that I panned in Australia."

Philippe disappeared into the compartment and, in a mercifully short interval, was transported out of sight.

Mathieu was distracted for most of the way back by his precious vial, but eventually he asked his question about the term 'brilliant conman'. I answered:

"Philippe did not mean it. His humour is a little different. That is why he said we should not take anything too seriously."

Mathieu seemed satisfied and started asking whether we could pan for gold in the stream by the orchard. But Philippe had planted a seed of doubt which would germinate in its own time.

24.
The Second Raincoat Incident

Mathieu and Élisabeth's visit to the guardian and Édith gave such pleasure that I would leave them there several times over the next couple of years. Élisabeth and Édith visited the university biology department, traded cuttings, and studied bees and butterflies. The guardian had mellowed, or at least he did not feel that it was his duty to guide Mathieu in the same way that he had trained me. Mathieu loved him as a grandfather, and they spent hours working on little projects, including a present for me of a *papier mâché* paperweight in the form of the island of Amphora. This faithfully followed the contours of the island and Monastery Hill. They had personalized it based on a sketch map that I had made as decoration for my room shortly after I arrived in Geneva. As a result, the main features were our house, Paul's house, and the rock pool.

As I contemplated this thoughtful gift, I reflected that our children had never been to the sea although we had taken them on the lake steamers. Marguerite was seventeen and Mathieu fifteen. We needed to take a family holiday before it was too late, and the children dispersed. It was not possible to go to Amphora. Depopulated and still heavily mined from the Second War, it now consisted of desolate ruins inhabited only by seabirds and feral pigs.

Céline considered my suggestion of a holiday:

"It will be expensive, but I think we should do it. Can we go to the Atlantic coast? I badly want to see Aunt Yolande and Uncle Germain."

I looked puzzled as I had never heard of these relatives. She continued:

"We are not really related, but they looked after us during the dark period."

I understood. Céline had a younger sister who had died at age four after a difficult illness. Mme Jodoin's own health had been compromised by this awful experience, and the kindly neighbouring couple had supported the children.

I was not allowed to take the company van across the border. We now had a little car, but it was old, second-hand, and could scarcely transport the family up the incline to our house. We would take the train to a station a few miles from the hamlet of Saint Zotique de Comana, a low-key holiday destination entirely overshadowed by Biarritz some fifty kilometres away. We would pick up a rental car and drive to a holiday cottage. Here, according to the brochure, we would find 'sand and facilities that will delight the most exacting of families with their sophisticated ambience'.

In truth, the sophisticated ambience proved to be a marketing flourish, but we did not mind. The resort consisted of twenty little self-catering bungalows forming a crescent around a central clubhouse and sports facilities. The children swam like dolphins and made friends with families from Toulouse, Paris, and Brussels. They played tennis, badminton, and *pétanque*, learned the guitar, or read in one of the crumbling gazebos overlooking the shore. Céline and I pursued a more sedate regime including trips to the excellent fishmongers in the port villages. The resort hosted the Choir of Public Sector Retirees in the off-season and boasted a reasonable organ. I was a little rusty but managed to impress the children with some of the livelier Handel pieces.

I was alone when I made the mistake of reading one of the papers in the clubhouse. I had not been able to forget Weygand entirely. He had a gift for publicity and amassing honorary degrees. He had apparently lost interest in delinquent youth and, I reluctantly admitted, had performed some valuable services. In particular, he had identified industrial chemicals and practices leading to clusters of respiratory diseases. For this he had been rightly honoured. Now well into old age, he was setting up a foundation. The article explained:

Truly a twentieth century hero, Dr Auguste Weygand is generously ensuring that his legacy will be perpetuated. The Weygand Institute will be based in Montreux and provide scholarships so that students in the French-speaking lands can undertake research that will result in mass benefits to mankind.

I could see Mathieu playing volleyball on the beach with Olivier and their new Belgian friends, and wondered how Weygand would have evaluated him. Mathieu was definitely an improved version of me. Perhaps it was the absence of my alleged defects that had allowed him to flourish. In any event, I had no worries, for I was a proud parent.

We had enjoyed many happy days at the beach, but we needed to see Aunt Yolande and Germain. They lived in a somewhat inaccessible area and had sent us detailed maps and instructions along with their invitation for dinner. The day before our visit, Céline and I drove to the nearest village and bought them a decorative pot of prunes in Armagnac. I turned the motor. There was a loud, crashing thump on the floor pan. The crankshaft had detached from the rental car.

The local garage was a branch of the one in St. Zotique. They would repair the car for us. In the meantime, the only vehicle available was a little Italian two-seater—and it was a two-seater. We could scarcely have carried a terrier as a passenger.

We researched the buses. Céline and I would take the car to Yolande and Germain and visit a regional art gallery en route. The children would take a bus which, after two hours of meandering through the countryside, would drop them opposite a path of a few hundred meters that led to the house. Céline explained the arrangements, stressing that bad weather was predicted. The children should take coats with them.

Yolande and Germain were thrilled to see Céline. I relaxed with an excellent white wine while they caught up on old friends. Their house was well-appointed, furnished with expensive white and turquoise carpets complementing high-class chair coverings with equestrian scenes. Our hosts were in their eighties, very lively and hospitable. Yolande wore a canary yellow dress and a fascinator, Germain a navy-blue bow tie and gold cufflinks. I glimpsed the elaborate place settings and polished silver in the next room. They had clearly gone to enormous trouble.

Germain had closed the windows against the rain some twenty minutes before we heard a knock at the door. The bus had kept to its schedule. Marguerite was, as always, dressed elegantly, and her primrose coat and hat could have kept her dry on a North Sea trawler. Élisabeth and Olivier had been protected by their jackets and caps. Mathieu was soaked to the skin and had carelessly walked through a deep puddle. Removing his squelching shoes, he left wet, grey marks from his socks on the carpet. He explained:

"Sorry, my tennis game was just before the bus left, and I didn't have room for all my gear and a jacket. Besides, it was such a beautiful day until it rained in the final set."

I watched the normally patient Céline's temper rise as the evening focused on Mathieu. Yolande produced two heavy towels and led him to the bathroom.

"You must get warm straight away. We have a therapeutic bath system. Let me explain the six taps to you."

Germain took him hot tea, pyjamas, slippers, and a heavy dressing gown. The wet clothes were hung in front of an electric heater in the pantry.

I could see that Céline was having to exercise considerable self-restraint. We finally sat down to dinner. Mathieu was robed in white terry cloth and seemingly quite unperturbed. He started to tell us about his tennis match, but I cut him off:

"You can tell me about that tomorrow. Your mother needs to talk with her friends."

My comment did not seem to affect his appetite as Yolande fussed around making sure that he had sufficient Béarnaise sauce:

"It is important for a young man like you to eat enough to stay warm. Let me refill the gravy boat, and I have more dinner rolls. I'd have brought them earlier, but they get cold quickly in these copper baskets."

I kept a close eye on the time and was eventually able to send Mathieu to get changed and ready in time to take the bus back.

We did not experience a good night. We had left Yolande and Germain after presenting apologies on behalf of our eldest son. The rain had affected the car's ignition, and it needed a push-start. I missed a signpost in the dark, and it was well after midnight when we reached the resort. Our bedroom had an outside door to the patio and a transom window which we used for ventilation on warm nights. It had blown open in the storm, and the bed was soaked. I attempted to close it with the rod and hook provided, but my efforts were not entirely successful; just after we finally fell asleep, it re-opened with a loud clatter. It was not long until the alarm sounded, for we needed to rise early for a planned trip to a nearby island. Here we were to enjoy a picnic and inspect the medieval chapel of St. Acisclus, erected in gratitude by a merchant from Cordoba who had prayed to him for rescue as his ship foundered.

Céline and all the children except Mathieu were already up and ready to tackle their coffee and baguettes. I had just poured my coffee when Mathieu entered with a cheerful greeting. Céline got up to attend to something at the sink. Mathieu unthinkingly sat in her place and drank her coffee.

Céline's vocabulary was more contemporary than that employed a quarter of a century before by the guardian in the bookstore, but many of the adjectives were the same. Mathieu was thoughtless, self-centred, and lazy. He had ruined the evening with friends that she had waited years to see. She continued:

"I don't even want to go on the trip with you today. I'll stay here and clean up the mess in the house. Do you know how much sand you trail in with you?"

I jumped in with a voice that was unusually firm:

"No. Mathieu will stay here with me. He'll clean the place and get dinner ready. I'll go to the garage and retrieve the bigger car. Marguerite, the tickets for the boat trip are on the hall table. Why don't you run and see if those nice Belgian girls would like to use the spare two tickets? Make sure their parents are alright with that."

Everyone left apart from a subdued Mathieu who was doing the washing-up. I barked some instructions about the cleaning and took the two-seater to the garage. It was again difficult to start, and I was glad to be rid of it. To my annoyance, the other car would not be ready until midday. The garage was not far away, and I walked back to the resort.

My temper did not improve when I attempted to resolve the transom problem. I almost had it in position when the hook fell from the rod, hitting me on the head. I reattached it and was eventually successful. I emerged from the room scowling, and with my pride wounded, to find a nervous Mathieu shyly asking me to inspect the swept floors.

I made Mathieu write a detailed shopping list. We were to pick up the car and drive to the stores in one of the bigger villages to get food for dinner and the next day.

The trees kept us at a comfortable temperature as we walked from the resort to the garage on a path through the pine woods. I felt Mathieu slip his hand into mine as he used to do when a child. Becoming self-conscious, he withdrew it almost immediately before asking:

"Papa, what is wrong with me? Why am I so different from everyone else? I never meant to hurt Maman."

He caught me off guard:

"Listen, the problem is not that you are different, it is that you are too much like me. I once made the guardian very angry by not taking my coat when he told me to."

This did not seem the right approach, and I instructed him:

"You must try to be much more sensitive to other people's feelings. You should have seen that your mother was upset. If you had apologized straight away, you would not be in so much trouble. We don't have too many days left here. Try to make sure that you are more thoughtful."

"I understand. You don't know how sorry I am."

I put my hand on his shoulder:

"I think I do. You'll be alright."

We reached the garage:

"M Montabeille, I have unexpected news. Your car had vibrations when we tested it, but I think you'll be very happy with the alternative."

I was sick of car problems and was about to start complaining when the attendant opened the door to the shop.

We had never seen such a vehicle. It was something from the future, aerodynamic, elegant, and with class. There had been rumours of a dramatic new Citroën, but it seemed entirely improbable that St. Zotique should have one of the first examples. The pre-production model had been used for nocturnal testing on the rough forest roads of the Landes when it struck a deer. Attempting to limp back to base, it had stopped here. Now repaired, it was ours for the afternoon. In a few months fashionable French drivers, and eventually the President, would catch up with us and make the Citroën DS an unofficial symbol of the country.

I could not sustain my stern image. I was excited, and Mathieu was delighted. This was better than studying the stained glass of some medieval chapel. He explored the different controls, and we experimented with raising and lowering the air suspension.

I drove cautiously and was unworried when a police motorcycle pulled us over. The rider, as enthusiastic as a schoolboy, simply asked if he might sit in the driver's seat and examine the dashboard.

A small crowd gathered around us as we parked in the village. I dispatched Mathieu to the grocery while I chatted with admiring motorists and completed a few errands in the pharmacy and post office. Eventually, I went looking for my son, who seemed to be taking an inordinate amount of time to buy a few ingredients.

The store was still traditional with no self-service. One of three generations of the Desrosiers family would assemble your requirements on the wooden counter. Armchairs were provided for older customers to sit comfortably as they discussed their orders. A kindly lady with a cloth bonnet was serving Mathieu while the other customers waited with exemplary patience.

"Don't worry. This will make your Maman happy, and you won't be in disgrace anymore. I've given you a sachet of herbs to put with the pasta. I won't charge you extra, but you mustn't use packaged linguine. I've substituted fresh. Give me a moment and I'll write down the cooking times for you. And you really should have a lemon. Put thin slices on top ten minutes before you take it out of the oven. Here's a good raspberry tart for dessert. My grandson always makes more than we can sell."

We handed back the Citroën and returned to the resort in our more modest vehicle. I cautioned Mathieu not to talk too much about his automotive adventure, and he complied. We were about to sit down to dinner when Céline noticed that he had not set a place for himself:

"That all smells delicious. Did you miscount? Aren't you going to sit with us?"

"It's alright. I'll eat in the kitchen and get the *crème fraîche* ready to go with the dessert."

She kissed him on the forehead:

"Don't be like that. You went off-course. You didn't get sent into exile."

She took a couple of mouthfuls:

"What a perfect choice of herbs! I must send you and Papa to do the shopping more often."

25.
In Memoriam and New Danger

It had been a difficult and very painful winter. The guardian had passed away, peacefully in early retirement. I was grateful, and respected him when I was younger, although he could be exasperating. I grew very fond of him later as I saw how happy Mathieu and Élisabeth were in his presence. His well-attended funeral was held in the cathedral of St. Pierre as a soaking, cold January rain lingered on the coats of the mourners.

At Édith's request, Mathieu and I were to read the lessons. As we nervously awaited this duty in our black suits, I was strangely comforted at the thought that my twenty-year-old son would surpass his father in this task and in much else. I could always draw strength from him and Céline. His voice was clear, respectful, and in just the right tone as he delivered Luke 10:33-37 telling how the Good Samaritan had taken care of an unknown stranger.

I only made it through the first verses of Psalm 46, *God is our refuge and strength*, by looking to Céline and Mathieu for support as I struggled to keep my voice from quavering.

The eulogy was delivered by the guardian's successor as chairman of one of the committees. I had been seated next to him many years previously at a particularly dreary dinner with the sub-committee on cereal ergot fungus. He was then a clean-shaven junior administrator. The guardian had given us a disapproving glance when he amused me by using a teaspoon to draw a fish on his *crème caramel.* Now a dignified professional with greying temples and a tidy beard, he set the stage:

"Édouard d'Egremont allowed himself no peace until he had led his committees to a solution. He did not seek glory or to compete with larger organizations where they were better equipped to help. His focus was on effective relief of the smaller and forgotten emergencies."

He went on to read extracts of letters he had found in a file in the guardian's office. Refugees, the injured, and famine victims wrote movingly of grim situations which had been mysteriously resolved by a committee of which they had never previously heard. Residents of a remote village destroyed by a forest fire recalled the unexpected arrival of a doctor, a nurse, and tents. Parents recounted how their daughter had been rescued from a flooded peninsula when radio messages from the committee had caused a yachting couple to look for their little five-year-old waving desperately from the river mouth.

The service ended with a haunting Slavic choral benediction performed by two families who had been at the point of starvation until a call from Switzerland persuaded the local commander to allow the committee's supply truck into their hamlet. The guardian had performed his duty without ever telling me of these details, and I cringed at the thought that my petty teenage concerns had competed for his attention against such dire emergencies.

I helped Édith answer the many letters of condolence whose envelopes bore stamps from at least eighteen countries. This process contained some moments of relief as we heard from former dinner guests whose survival of the Second War was not to be taken for granted.

Mathieu and Élisabeth had both become close to Édith and would find time to visit her in her bereavement. She kept up a large correspondence, but many of her colleagues from the university had moved to other institutions, leaving her with relatively few companions in Geneva.

I was also moved by the death in the same month of a very different character, Stanislas, my breakfast companion with the eyebrows, whom I had met in the Consul's swimming pool. He had emigrated to Argentina where he lived under an assumed name, revealing his true identity only in a draft obituary which he left for his fourth wife to publish to selected acquaintances. I felt honoured to be on the list.

Always irrepressible, he had survived imprisonment over the affair of the education budget. Sentenced to forced labour, one of his connections was able to ensure that he ended up driving a narrow-gauge train through sheep pastures from the marble quarry to a branch station. This proved a relatively safe occupation, since the various regimes all prized the marble for both their private accommodations and for civic buildings. He finally escaped back to Switzerland where he discreetly 'attended to business' before disappearing to a villa outside Buenos Aires.

I had remembered the codes which he had taught me and had gone to the bank as agreed in 1950. An enormous transfer had been made from the bank account a year earlier, but he had generously left a sum roughly equivalent to the value of a new car. The bank had also been instructed to hand me an envelope with a key to a large security deposit box. The package was labelled as "Extremely Fragile—Handle and Open with Supreme Care".

I parked the van at the bottom of the track. Its suspension had never been compatible with carrying delicate goods. I walked as slowly and carefully as if I had a bomb in my hands and called to Céline to open the door. We carefully unpacked it, removing the small balls of cotton wool protecting the contents which gradually emerged, first ceramic water lilies on long and delicate stalks, then stunningly realistic fish and frogs. It was a three-dimensional ceramic sculpture with a message which we could not fully interpret. On one side of the sculpture, the frogs had their normal, natural appearance, but on the other their faces were clearly caricatures, though we were not sure who they represented. I explained to an amused Céline how my unlikely friend had reprimanded me for using bad language by quoting the verse from Ovid about the frogs speaking ill under the water.

This impractical *objet d'art* did not seem destined to survive long in a house with children. Mathieu, then aged around nine, was fascinated by the colours and wanted to embellish it with a toy seahorse. We contacted a curator from the museum who reluctantly ventured to the farm to inspect the artifact. A grey and solemn man, he did not enjoy his trip outside city limits.

"How on earth do you get anything here along that dreadful track without breaking it? Do you realize that you have one of the most unusual and spectacular pieces of late eighteenth-century ceramics exposed on your windowsill? There is a dead gnat on one of the fish."

He suggested that we loan the piece, which had no maker's markings, to the museum while they established its provenance. There its striking glazes and composition proved a source of lively discord with competing catalogue entries at its exhibition, and were the subject of at least three doctoral theses, each contradicting the other. One theory held that the faces represented Diderot, D'Alembert, and other Encyclopaedists. Other dissertations argued that they mocked unpopular city counsellors in Munich or Italian antitrinitarians.

We let the museum keep the piece for many years. Both Olivier and Mathieu, as teenagers, took their girlfriends to see it. Unimpressed, they would steer the boys to an outside courtyard where they could talk by a real pond with goldfish and water lilies.

I wished that my absent friend might have contacted me before he passed. I would have liked to thank him and learn what he knew of the sculpture's history. He would certainly have appreciated the 'Migraine Montabeille' as our puzzling ornament was termed in an acrid exchange of articles between Swiss and Dutch experts.

After this unbearably dismal winter, we were excited that all the children were with us for Élisabeth's sixteenth birthday in early May. Marguerite was now married very happily to an immigration officer at Cointrin Airport. He was a lean, slightly serious young man, though he adored my daughter. He was shocked by my passing comment that I had spent my first five years in Geneva without proper documentation. Olivier was training as an architectural engineer. Mathieu wanted to be a doctor but was struggling with the examinations.

The party had been a Saturday evening to remember. The children were still young enough to be overflowing with fun and energy, but sufficiently mature that we could converse as adults. We had finally repainted the kitchen and dining room. With new sconce lights and better floor mats, they seemed much more bright and cheerful. Élisabeth was in perfect form, always brilliant, pretty, happy and laughing in her chambray blue dress. The others had clearly put thought into her homemade cards and gifts and were enjoying themselves thoroughly. They had come early and helped us with the preparation of the meal, reuniting and teasing each other as they seasoned the ducks or tasted the carrot and ginger soup.

The evening was getting late and I noticed Élisabeth looking at her watch. I knew a writer from *The Journal of Helvetic Horology,* which was published using our presses. Through him, I had arranged to have a watch face engraved with the Montabeille mountain and bees motif. It was discreet, it would not mean anything to anyone outside the family, and Élisabeth was thrilled with her present.

I saw Mathieu walk over to his sister. He inspected the watch and then asked:

"I know it is my wonderful sister's evening. But would you be alright if I made an announcement? It is a nice one."

"How exciting! So long as it is nice."

Mathieu took a deep breath:

"I've been offered a scholarship, and I think I know what I want to do for a career. I had to write an essay on how I could best help patients if I had funding for nine months. I wrote that I wanted to investigate where there are high concentrations of people with partial deafness and to see if there are common causes. I mentioned Papa's work with the voice magnifier at the Institute for the deaf. I used Anton from school as an example of when partial deafness is not properly acknowledged and treated. They said my essay was the shortest submission from Geneva but the most persuasive and heartfelt. I don't want to spend the next six years studying every part of the body. I want to be an audiologist. The new hearing aids mean that they can really do a lot of good."

I was delighted, for I had feared privately that Mathieu might not make it through the full medical program, but had kept quiet for fear of discouraging him. Pursuing a passion for a narrower specialty seemed ideal.

He continued:

"The program director will contact the relevant offices in Paris, and possibly Brussels, so I can go there and have access to their records after I have compiled data in Geneva and Bern."

I turned to Céline:

"I think this news calls for a toast?"

"Of course, shall we have the bottle the client gave me after the hotel boundary case?"

I set off towards the cellar. I was just leaving the room when I heard her ask:

"Is the scholarship from the university?"

Mathieu replied:

"No, not directly. It's from the Weygand Institute."

I must have hesitated a second but continued on my way. Once in the cellar, I felt drained and confused. I sat down and covered my eyes as I tried to come to terms with the unwelcome ghost of Weygand. I would not say anything. Surely Weygand could not hurt my son even if he recognized the resemblance to a father with 'all the indicators of potential delinquency'. He would be an old man by now, and certainly too senior to take an active role with junior researchers. My records would be lost deep in the archive, and they were probably filed under the guardian's surname rather than mine

For the first time in my married life, I felt desperately alone. The guardian was dead, and Weygand's diagnosis was the only secret that I had from Céline. Mathieu and I were sufficiently alike that she might find a decades-old medical opinion based on 'physical and mental characteristics' to be relevant, or even compelling. She could also be distressed that I had not been honest and forthcoming with her and her father.

A gentle knock alerted me to a presence in the doorway. I didn't know how long Mathieu had been there. His look was sympathetic and worried. I should have known that my human sheepdog would have come quietly looking for me.

"Just checking on Papa. You look exhausted. Are you alright? Are you feeling any pain?"

"No, nothing like that. I just needed to rest a moment. It was a long week at work, and even wonderful evenings can take a little energy. I'm so very proud of you. Would you mind getting that bottle from the right of the top shelf?"

Over the coming weeks, I learned to put my memories of Weygand in a separate compartment from Mathieu's enthusiastic letters and visits. He had been entrusted with valuable equipment which measured decibels and frequencies. He was collaborating in a study on the effect of acoustic baffles in certain industries. A noted statistician, whose brother was deaf, was showing him how to interpret the data from all of Switzerland. Surely, I should keep quiet. If I told Mathieu how Weygand had wanted me treated, he would be quite capable of leaving the program. I decided to let sleeping dogs lie, *quieta non movere.*

26.
The Certificate of Achievement

We would not let Mathieu down. Olivier and I had polished our Peugeot 203 with the finest automotive waxes. We had soaked the tarnished hubcaps overnight in a patent fluid and applied tire-black. We had disassembled the lights and cleaned them on the inside. Céline had made me buy new suits for myself and Olivier. She already had an appropriate hat and dress from a recent wedding, but Marguerite and Élisabeth needed to replace their shoes 'which were only good for taking the dog out'.

Our preparations seemed less excessive at a time when the term 'smart casual' had not yet reached our family. Mathieu had thrown himself into his research project with the deaf. His results were meaningful and well laid out. He was to be rewarded in a ceremony at the Weygand Institute where he would make a short presentation before receiving a certificate of achievement. This honour was accorded to only five or six of each year's twenty scholarship recipients.

After a journey punctuated by stops for coffee, fuel, lunch, and tea, we rounded the northern shore of Lake Geneva and reached Montreux. Mathieu, who was already there to finalize his conclusions, had arranged for us to spend the night before the ceremony in the optimistically named *Château Espérance*, better described as a hostel for visitors to the Institute.

Mathieu's association with the Institute earned us a twenty percent discount at the hostel as well as access to the preferred visitors' lounge. This salon was lined with portraits of Weygand, complementing the ones in the bedrooms. Free pamphlets were available on the good work which he had accomplished and on how one might leave a legacy to the Institute. A map of the world showed, in imperial purple, those countries where grateful governments had thanked him for his lifesaving contributions.

Mathieu joined us for dinner, which was served at a communal table in a student-style refectory. It was a little primitive, but we were seated with a charming family whose lively daughter, Claudette, had won the scholarship offered to students in Bern. She had also qualified for a certificate and would present her work on avoiding chemical burns in certain industries. We chatted amiably over the nutritious, if meagre, portions of salad and chicken with prunes and olives before Mathieu and Claudette had to leave for a final rehearsal. As we neared the end of the meal, I noticed a young man across the table who had said nothing. I originally thought he might have been Claudette's brother, but he seemed to be alone. He was pencil-thin, tall, with heavy glasses, and had a distant look as though his mind were handling issues more abstract than the *gâteau Breton*. I asked:

"Are you here for the ceremony tomorrow?"

His face suddenly became animated with a look of delighted surprise.

"How kind of you to ask! No, I could never win one of the scholarships. I am here to compose an opera. Do you like Handel?"

I admitted that I appreciated Handel's organ fugues. He moved to be directly opposite me and continued:

"Dr Weygand has been celebrated in print and in portraiture but never as he deserves in music. He has led such a wonderful life that it lends itself to lyrical interpretation. Most of the opera will be my original composition, but I plan to work in some of the tunes from Handel with my own words: *See, the Conquering Hero Comes* and *Rejoice O Judah* are obvious candidates. Perhaps I'll also use *O Thou Bright Orb, Great Ruler of the Day.*"

I had been successful in suppressing my more hostile thoughts about Weygand for Mathieu's sake, but I winced inwardly at the prospect of choruses extolling the doctor from La Scala to Covent Garden. I responded:

"What an interesting project! Do you know my son, Mathieu Montabeille?"

"You're his father? How wonderful! Yes, I didn't want to intrude now while he is enjoying time with the family, but we often eat together. He is an inspiration. He works so hard and truly believes in the Weygand methodology and philosophy. I haven't finalized the libretto, but I can maybe build in some recitative and an aria for a character based on him."

Although Weygand's image loomed over Céline and me in the bedroom, I had been relieved to learn from Mathieu that he was now almost permanently based in Antibes where the climate was less challenging for his rheumatism. Nonetheless, his ghost seemed to hover over Montreux, and I was discomforted by the cult-like devotion which he seemed to inspire.

The next morning, we parked in front of the Weygand Institute. To Olivier's satisfaction our vehicle was the most conspicuously shiny, though far from the newest or most expensive, and we ascended the impressive steps leading to the enormous classical portico. Above us, reliefs of Hippocrates, Galen, Harvey, and Weygand reclined in the pediment. We met up with the family that we had encountered the night before and, in a blur of hats, polished shoes, and new ties, entered through the temple-like doors. A guide led us across a marbled chamber, past a series of displays of Weygand's work, and into a well-appointed auditorium. A grand piano stood on the stage, and crystal chandeliers hung above us.

Perhaps a hundred people were in the room when Weygand's deputy, Dr Trépanier, made a brief announcement. One of the winners of the certificate was a nephew of the French consul, who was present in the audience. Would we please stand? A lady in an emerald evening gown swept on to the stage and delivered a fortissimo rendition of the *Marseillaise* on the piano. The lights then dimmed, and a cinema style projector lit up.

A sultry voice informed us of the benefits of smoking cigarettes lightly laced with pyrethrum to repel bacteria-carrying insects in tropical zones. This advertisement, showing a glamorous couple relaxing after a jungle expedition, concluded with the information that the product had been developed in conjunction with the Weygand Institute, to which two percent of the revenue was donated.

The next reel showed a white-haired Weygand, surrounded by potted palms on a terrasse overlooking the sea. Old age had given him a more benign appearance, and he congratulated the winners of the certificate as if he were a fond uncle. He then proceeded to talk of their obligations:

"Physicians have sworn oaths from the time of Hippocrates. You will shortly make a solemn promise to be faithful to your new intellectual homeland and to follow its best practices. You will support the Institute and, in the fullness of time, become mentors to future generations. Every year we give opportunities to young men and women who think of themselves as Parisien, Genevois, or even Montréalais. They leave us proudly as Weygandoises and Weygandois."

I scarcely had time to reflect on the prospect of a Weygandois son when the screen showed the sexagenarian heiress to a mining fortune speaking from her suite in one of the most expensive hotels in Geneva. Dr Weygand's team had been instrumental in reducing the incidence of malaria and cholera in her mines. This resulted in increased dividends, leaving her able to make substantial quarterly donations to the Institute. Her cousins had 'benefited from expensive educations and good marriages' and she planned to leave her fortune to the Institute. She concluded in cultivated tones:

"There is no more solemn duty for anyone associated with the Institute than to support its admirable endeavours. I beg you, while you are still in the Institute building, to collect a form with the postal and banking details for your regular donations."

The lights came on, and Dr Trépanier announced that there would be an interval for us to enjoy coffee and biscotti while collecting the forms. The biscotti were excellent, though Céline was surprised at my curt refusal to commit to a donation:

"I'd rather increase our contribution to one of your mother's causes. Her committees won't spend it on marble and statues."

Dr Trépanier returned to the stage after the interval and subjected us to a prolonged slide show. He must have been in his forties, but he retained a certain boyish enthusiasm as he waved his arms and pointed to the screen. As he gestured, the arms of his suit jacket and white shirt of the finest Egyptian cotton would fall back, exposing a large stainless-steel watch. It had some seven crowns, leaving Olivier and I to pass each other notes speculating on the functions that they might control. The presentation could have been summarized in the sentence that Dr Weygand had saved innumerable lives. However, Dr Trépanier did not arrive at this conclusion until he had taken us through maps, bar charts, Weibull distributions, and slides covered with formulae and Greek characters.

"Even the most rigorous analysis won't give us a precise answer because the underlying trend data are recorded so erratically. But we can say with certainty that very many lives have been extended in numerous French-speaking countries."

The winners of the certificates had rehearsed well. Claudette spoke of preventable incidents involving components dipped in hydrochloric acid. Mathieu pinpointed clusters of deafness associated with certain infections and industries. Their presentations were short, well-researched but comprehensible, and ended with clear recommendations. Some of the proposals for noise baffles, sterile jars, safety guards, and ventilation might seem a little elementary today; the principles of personal and industrial safety were not as well developed at the time, and each winner fully deserved their applause.

The lady with the emerald dress reappeared on stage after the presentations and played a pleasant, if somewhat unnecessary, Beethoven sonata in G minor.[23] Dr Trépanier then delivered an encomium to Weygand whom he described as 'one of the most positive forces for good since the Enlightenment'. His voice cracking with emotion, he announced that it was time for the awards and that perhaps 'a Weygand of the next generation will be found among this group'.

Mathieu, looking smart, proud, but a little nervous, advanced on stage after Claudette. He raised his hand, looked at Trépanier, and swore:

"I will be loyal and faithful to the principles, methods, and values advocated by the Institute and Dr Weygand."

I squeezed Céline's hand for it was a moment which meant a great deal to both of us. But it was not only paternal pride which caused a tear to form. The pianist, who we subsequently learned was Weygand's great-niece, handed Mathieu his certificate, and he bounded off stage to come and sit with his sisters.

Our small car could not hold Mathieu in addition to the rest of the family. We gave him and Olivier money to stay the night, have a celebratory meal in a restaurant by the lake, and return by train the next day. I overheard Céline taking her leave:

"I'm so proud. Goodbye my little Weygandois—though I won't call you that in front of Papa. You mean so much to him that I think he is somehow jealous of Weygand. You men have such strange thought processes."

---

23 Sonata No. 19 in G minor, Op 49 No. 1

27.
The Return of the Curse

Céline and Élisabeth were away for a few days in Lausanne. They would attend the tapestry exhibition with Céline's fashion photographer friend and stay with a distant cousin who, for our wedding, had given us an antique set of silver apostle spoons. Sadly, these tarnished on the smallest exposure to most ingredients. We only used them at Easter when the Jodoins would visit *en masse* to admire Céline's tulips and sample our simnel cake.

Olivier and Mathieu spent most nights in student lodgings. For the first time in over twenty years, I would be alone in the farmhouse. I would be able to play Handel as loudly as I liked on our new gramophone. I could make Amphoran spiced fish sausages, a formidably aromatic dish which everyone outside the island found overpowering. I had already ordered the fresh sardines and a blue cheese. The little spice chest in the kitchen was full.

I had some responsibilities. The roof and ceiling over the private quarters needed attention following a series of storms and leaks. I needed to meet the workmen who would come on the Monday. I would sleep in the men's dormitory, now the bedroom for Olivier and Mathieu. We had often offered to convert it into two rooms, but our sons would turn hesitant. It was large enough that, with the strategic placement of two large wardrobes and a dresser, they each had their own space.

I had retired late, slept well in Olivier's bed, and was struggling into consciousness. I was comfortable and had two days off, having worked the weekend on an installation. I stretched out and felt the presence of a body that was not my spouse. I murmured:

"Mathieu, go away!"

He was sitting on the bed and burst out laughing:

"You're no fun."

I looked up and saw that he was holding two wires. These were from an ancient field telephone system of the sort where one wound a handle to generate a current. It had previously connected the dormitories, the private quarters, and the barn. We had reinstalled it when the children were old enough to sleep in the dormitories. The boys believed that they could administer mild electric charges from the circuit.

He continued:

"I'd pretend to wake Olivier with a shock on his ear. He'd turn all red and threaten that he'd tell on me to you and Maman."

I growled:

"I knew we should have shipped you both to Stéphane's school in Mozambique. What are you doing here?"

"Just checking on Papa. I've got to go, but can I come this evening and next? I need to talk to you."

I looked forward to Mathieu's return, though I suspected that he might need money. A short extension to his scholarship for further research covered the necessities, and we gave him an allowance. But Paris, and now Brussels, were not cheap, and we did not grudge him a few tourist expenses. In any event, I modified my plans. Instead of listening to my new thirty-three rpm records, I gathered raspberries for his dessert and early leeks for his vegetables. I went ahead with the Amphoran sausages but toned down the herbs and spices.

Mathieu would have made a fine assassin, for he could appear unseen and noiselessly.

"Papa, is everything alright in the kitchen?"

"It is an Amphoran test of manhood. If you can't eat it, you owe a hundred hours of work in the orchard. But don't worry, I have some ham in case you really don't like it."

Mathieu passed the test with flying colours, and I would not be troubled with leftovers. Nor did any dry cider remain to go flat.

We ate at the solid kitchen table. This had survived many mishaps, including being hit by a full coffee pot when the pewter handle broke off. We had thought of replacing this primitive furnishing until Céline's friend had declared it:

"A wonderful antique, with such history and patina. One can just feel the spirit of ancient diners."

Mathieu, sitting to the left of a dark ring which a teenage Olivier had made with a hot pan of haricot beans, finally broached his subject:

"Papa, do you remember the Belgian girls that were next-door to us in St. Zotique?"

I could not recall their names, but I could picture them laughing as they headed to the badminton courts with Marguerite and Élisabeth.

He continued:

"Marguerite gave me their number before my first trip to medical records in Brussels. I met Gisèle and Annette for lunch. I kept quiet because I didn't want Marguerite to get all excited, but I felt something immediately when I saw Gisèle again. I know we are in love, and I want to get a residence permit so I can spend more time in Belgium."

I offered congratulations. I had never entirely warmed to his previous friends. His last girlfriend, Henriette, seemed to have mapped out his future: he would rent her a television and escort her parents to ornithological slideshows.

He continued:

"Would you and Maman be alright if I moved to Belgium? Will you always let me know what you are doing?"

"We'll miss you very much. But there are trains, and I read that jet aeroplanes are making it cheaper to fly. We'd just need to buy tickets nine weeks in advance. It's not as if you'd be moving to New Caledonia like Cousin Philippe. I'd rather you were happy in Brussels than disappointed down here."

He digested my comment, took a chocolate truffle with his coffee, and went on:

"My visa application needs a lot more paperwork. Do you have anything that documents the nationality of your father and mother, and preferably of their parents? There is a fee of twenty francs. Gisèle's father is a fairly well-known businessman. He says I can use his name as a reference."

The guardian had encountered extreme difficulty with my Swiss naturalization. I did not have my parents' birth certificates, or my own, and our applications were rejected over several years. I was finally considered old enough to swear affidavits which then had to be endorsed by the Swiss government. Happily, the guardian knew one of the most senior officials who happened to serve on a committee for refugees. The endorsement was signed by the relevant minister himself with a hand-written note instructing that the naturalization was to be concluded without delay.

For my twenty-first birthday, the guardian gave me the code to a safety deposit box in which he had placed these precious documents along with the details of a pension savings plan to which, without telling me, he had generously contributed from the first week that I stayed with him. The fees for the box were pre-paid for the next half-century.

Céline and I had occasionally accessed the box when the children needed passports or visas for school trips. I gave Mathieu the code:

"Just root around in there and see what you can find. And here is a cheque for the fee and a little extra. Just ask Étienne if he can countersign it."

I knew something was wrong when Mathieu returned that evening. He lacked appetite and just mumbled a few responses when I asked about his day. I assumed that he was worried about Gisèle and his permit. I refrained from questioning him.

We sat in uncomfortable silence at the kitchen table. There were some extra portions of schnitzel, but neither of us were interested. He shook his head when I offered dessert and percolated the coffee. I asked if he would mind if I put on the gramophone. I had found an excellent recording of Chopin's Raindrop prelude and Minute waltz.

My fall was not the consequence of a trust gradually eroded by suspicion. It was an instantaneous crash into a special section of hell. The viper had struck. I had never heard my son snarl:

"Yes, I do mind. I can scarcely bear to be with you. How could you lie to me?"

I did not have time to recover before he added:

"I found the red envelope. I used to think you were the best father in the world. How can I propose to Gisèle if our children could be like you?"

"What red envelope?"

He looked as if he were about to explode at my question:

"You know, the big one at the bottom of the box. It came out on the table."

It slowly came back to me that the deposit box had been lined with red paper, the exact size of the box. Neither Céline nor I had ever imagined that it was anything other than lining. Mathieu had taken the box to the little table in the vault and turned it upside down to sort through the contents. The large red envelope fell out.

I floundered:

"I thought that was lining. Why are you so upset? What was in it?"

The reply was chilling:

"Three things. A certificate from Dr Weygand that you were mentally unsuited for military service. All that had nothing to do with your height or the status of your nationality! A letter from the army surgeon, and worse, the report of a follow-up visit. I think the exact words were:

The youth who sits outside my office retains all the indicators of potential delinquency that I first observed. He will experience a delayed and dangerous transition to maturity, as amply evidenced by the fate of others with his mental and physical characteristics."

Many years ago, the guardian had mentioned to me that, if necessary, I had proof that I had not voluntarily evaded military service. He was doubtless referring to these documents. I later saw that he had labelled the envelope 'Weygand—destroy unopened if not needed'. The ink had faded over time and was almost illegible against the red envelope.

I reached for my coffee. I had to use both hands to steady the cup. Mathieu gave me an unsympathetic glance before asking:

"Does Maman know?"

I shook my head.

He continued.

"So, you betrayed her too? Everyone says that I look like you. What if I develop symptoms or pass them onto the next generation? Remember that day in St. Zotique when I was in trouble. You said that it was because I was too much like you. You have ruined everything. What do I say to Gisèle?"

The attack was not over.

"So many things fall into place now. Do grandfather and Étienne suspect something? I've noticed how Uncle Étienne seems to check up on you. And what is that ridiculous story about your cheques needing his signature? Philippe understood something when he called you a brilliant conman. You live in a house transferred from a drug dealer so vicious that he got life. And I never understood about that weird sculpture thing from Stanislas. Was that bought with stolen money?"

I took a breath, ready to tell him to leave Massimo's name out of this, but he was faster.

"I haven't forgotten the day I told you about the scholarship and found you hiding your eyes in the cellar. It wasn't because you were tired. It was because you were afraid that you'd be found out."

Mathieu, now red and flushed as I had never seen him, finally paused. I said carefully:

"Listen, nothing bad is going to happen to you. None of Weygand's predictions came true in my case, and they are even less likely to apply to you. You were so much stronger and more mature than I was at the age when he saw me. Surely..."

He interrupted me:

"I can't have been that different, judging by that picture on the organ pamphlet. And if you didn't believe in Weygand's methodology, why did you say nothing when I got offered the scholarship? Are you trying to tell me that you know better than the best doctor in Switzerland? You watched as I swore to uphold his 'principles, methods and values'."

It was no good arguing. Unprepared, I had no reasoning that would have convinced Mathieu in his current state. Anything else would simply have enraged him further. I offered:

"We're not going to agree on Weygand. I can't forgive him, ever. Where do we go from here? I don't want your mother to be hurt."

"Alright, I won't mention this to Maman."

"Look, I can keep out of your way until you go to Belgium. Timothée is having an operation so I'll be picking up some of his work. I'll make sure that you won't see very much of me, but we'll act normally when we do meet."

He stood up.

"I'll go that far for you."

He walked out of the door and, still reeling, I heard his motorized bicycle as he headed down the track.

28.
The Wedding

I had no direct contact with Mathieu after he left for Brussels. Céline, Olivier, and Marguerite spent a week in Belgium to visit him and meet Gisèle. Élisabeth and I sent our greetings. She had college commitments, and I used the pretext of a major equipment overhaul at a customer in Neuchâtel. We exchanged seasonal greetings at the end of a pre-booked Christmas telephone call before being cut off by the operator. Céline and Marguerite had used up most of the minutes in thanking Gisèle for a book of lace patterns. Céline would send a weekly letter. Mathieu replied with accounts of his adventures. I only intervened once in this process by adding a postscript.

I had been one of relatively few parents with a vehicle and would help shuttle the children to team events. Placide would always try to travel with us and would thank me politely. I sensed that he felt safe in our company. On the few occasions that he opened up, I was impressed by his unassuming intelligence and gentle humour. He wanted to work for the Red Cross and travel. I never learned what went wrong. There were few mourners at his service, and it seemed inappropriate to probe too deeply. In my paragraph to Mathieu, I mentioned that his devastated parents had recognized our old Peugeot with its distinctive fog light and approached me with extraordinary gratitude for our modest services. Mathieu replied to Céline:

"Thank Papa for his note. Poor Placide. He never said anything unkind about anyone. He told me Father was not like the other parents."

A few months later, a date was set for the wedding. Élisabeth had a critical exam. The rest of the family would take the express on the Wednesday to meet the in-laws. Élisabeth and I would catch the first train on the Friday. We would have time to go to the hotel and be ready for dinner with Gisèle's family.

Our plans were disrupted when a freight train derailed near Mannheim. We were rerouted through damp and grimy industrial sidings while the loquacious couple who shared the compartment congratulated us.

"You are so very lucky! There is nothing more wonderful than a family wedding. Our Léopold married a delightful girl last year. He still cuts our lawn and brings roses on..."

The extent of Léopold's filial piety remained unclear. The guard opened the compartment door to interrupt with the news that we would not move for another two hours. We were welcome to exercise on a short industrial platform along the rear of the train.

The guests were into their second course by the time we arrived, and the seating plan had been rearranged. I offered apologetic greetings to our hosts and acknowledged Mathieu. He returned an adequate gesture of welcome, and we avoided each other for the rest of the evening. I found a place next to a distant middle-aged cousin who owned a trucking business. Preoccupied and with an inelegant goatee, he did not seem to notice that I had scarcely spoken to my son. As I tackled the mussel chowder, he described in painful detail how the Walloon socialists had formed an unholy alliance with the Flemish capitalists. There would be implications for the tax on diesel.

"You have no idea what this will do to our cost per kilometre at full load. I can scarcely break even as it is. Did you read how the French and the British control the supply of raw rubber from Vietnam and Malaya? Then they sell us tires that shred on farm roads. We might as well go back to ox carts."

I had been well trained at the dinners with the guardian and expressed just enough interest to keep the conversation flowing. However boring the topic, it was better than appearing to be a silent outcast or having to disclose that I had not talked with my son since he moved north. I felt an unexpected respect for the cousin as he explained:

"I'm sorry. I'm sure you did not come all this way to listen to our political problems. But if this insane legislation passes on Monday, I may have to lay off two of my workers. Manfred was forced to witness dreadful things in the war and has not really recovered. But he refuels and guards my trucks at night. He keeps them so well-polished that we could enter them in a *concours d'élégance.* Mathilde had a difficult time, too. But she takes care of our drivers' uniforms and gives them haircuts. She won't hand over the keys if the men would not look sufficiently respectable for her mother to let them into the house. She provides cheese and gooseberry jam sandwiches if they are scheduled for a long day. I don't know how you explain all that in the profit and loss, but the customers really do trust our employees. Have you tried the pork carbonnade yet?"

The dinner came to an end, and I wished my companion good luck as he departed.

I heard:

"I do hope you enjoyed the meal? Our cousin is really very sweet, but he can be a little intense at times."

It was Gisèle. I had been worried about meeting her. She would surely have detected Mathieu's coolness towards me. She seemed friendly, very attractive, with auburn hair, and, based on the laughter from her end of the table, very personable.

"It was excellent. I apologize for trailing in late. Your cousin has some interesting perspectives."

"That is a nice way of putting it."

She touched my arm.

"I can't believe how alike you and Mathieu look. You must tell me what to expect."

The conversation switched as her parents came over with Céline to discuss the plans for the morning. But I was sure that I liked my new daughter-in-law. I surmised that Mathieu, finding himself in the same dilemma that I had faced, had omitted to tell his bride of the defects which, according to Weygand, might accompany his mental and physical characteristics. I took no pleasure in his uncomfortable situation, but I could see no way of broaching the topic or expressing my sympathy.

Gisèle's parents had spared no effort for their elder daughter's wedding. We were taken by coach to a village where the family had originally lived. Our luggage would be delivered to the hotel, *Le Château des Orangers*, adjoining the splendid fourteenth-century church with its white spire.

I had toffees in my suit pocket. This was a mistake, for I kept thinking about them during the service. We had been served a light breakfast. The lengthy ceremony was conducted in French but with elements in Flemish to accommodate part of the family tree. Gisèle's father was a benefactor of the local choir which expressed its appreciation with, it seemed, every anthem ever encountered by the Belgian people. During one particularly ambitious piece, I thought Mathieu shared an amused glance. Perhaps I was wrong. When I looked for confirmation, his regard was cool.

The reception was held in the sixteenth-century hotel dining room with its timbered walls and ceilings. I was seated next to Céline, who always managed to liven up tables at these events. The *Châteauneuf du pape* and the Charolais beef were excellent. I forgot the toffees and managed to enjoy the proceedings. We then had the speeches. The best man, whom I had ferried to almost all his soccer games, recounted some appropriate anecdotes before observing that Mathieu grew up with a wonderful mother and siblings. Mathieu made some vague remarks in the passive voice concerning the opportunities that had been offered to him. He expanded on this with tributes to his grandparents, uncles, mother, brother, sisters and in-laws. He concluded with:

"I have never met one of my benefactors. Dr Weygand's wonderful foundation has allowed me to play a small part in his good works. I will never save lives in the same way as he could, but I am sure I can help with the hearing problems of many patients. Thank you, everyone"

He sat down to general applause.

The band was excellent. Céline was a wonderful dancer. Perhaps she was too good, for we attracted some attention and a little clapping. Mathieu looked faintly irritated. I suggested that Olivier should have a turn with his mother. I would take up Gisèle's great-aunt on her offer of a tour of the hotel.

Mme Legrand was a sprightly octogenarian. Her pale green sequin dress might not have suited everyone, but, trim and vivacious, she carried it with aplomb. I had only seen the front of the hotel, which faced west overlooking a stream and gentle waterfall. She led me to a large and well-stocked orangery. We continued to an extension stretching nearly a kilometre with all the common varieties of citrus. She explained:

"The hotel was occupied. The local commander was worried about vitamins in the diet for the troops. He had seen scurvy in the first war. His family had pioneered some greenhouse techniques. He got approval for the extension by presenting it as a pilot for a massive, glorious initiative. They even featured it in propaganda films. We all said he was mad, but at least it gave him a pretext to keep people here instead of shipping them off as compulsory labour. The work was finished in time for the liberation. The allied platoons were greeted with baskets of clementines."

I made sure that we did not hurry through the tour.

"Are these lemons the same as the ones we just passed? The leaves look a little different."

My timing was right. The newlyweds were just leaving as we returned to the main orangery. I doubt if they saw us as we waved from behind King Albert's favourite variety of tangerine.

29.
A Book with Two Themes

Dr Weygand died a few weeks after Mathieu's wedding. There was talk of a statue and renaming a street by the hospital. Citizens were invited to make donations to the Weygand Institute. Radio Suisse Romande broadcast a two-hour tribute.

A few months later, I needed to mail some warranty documents to Gothenburg. I called out to Céline:

"Do you need anything from the post office?"

"Yes, I'll be right down."

She came bearing a large book.

"Look what I found for Mathieu. He will be thrilled."

I examined the volume while she hunted for brown paper and string. It appeared to be a hagiographic biography of the late physician. It was based on his unfinished memoirs and had been rushed into print. It was amply illustrated, with a photo of the villa where I had shivered in the cold corridor. There was also a shot of the gardener, chauffeur, and chef whose conduct had so shocked the Weygands. They looked alike, youthful, short, and dark-haired. I wondered if my similarity to them had contributed to Weygand's adverse judgement.

I kept my feelings from Céline but placed the packaged book in the back of the van. I did not want it near me in the passenger compartment. I had to apologize when I laid it down a little heavily in the post office after completing the customs declaration. My only consolation was that Mathieu was not a great reader. He would thank his mother for it politely, but he would not wade through its full turgid text.

In October Mathieu asked Céline:

"Would it be alright if we come for Christmas? I would love to show Gisèle the farm."

I studied the calendar at work. I could keep my commitment to Mathieu. I would suggest to our customers that we bring forward more maintenance work to the quiet period between Christmas and New Year. He would hardly see me except on Christmas Eve. The house would be so crowded and busy that we would only have a few hours when we needed to be polite to each other.

Timothée tried to keep Friday afternoons clear for a meeting where we would wrap up the endless paperwork for Gothenburg and a new manager, who created an endless stream of forms, which did nothing to help us sell or maintain the presses. We would also plan out the schedule for the next six weeks. We met in our office, a small number of soulless rented rooms in a larger building.

It must have been the first week in November. We had finished the Friday meeting. I was killing time before my haircut reservation, or more officially, I was studying the revisions to the technical overviews. The intercom from the reception desk rang.

"M Montabeille, your son is here to see you. I'll escort him up."

The connection went dead before I had a chance to say that Olivier knew the way. He would sometimes come by at this time, to plan a surprise for his mother's birthday or to see if I had time for a soda before heading home. But M Piguet, the building's stern sentry, who otherwise passed his day criticizing detective novels, did not accompany Olivier.

My heart broke as I saw Mathieu. He was ashen, untidy, and looked crushed. One lace was undone, and his shirt was not properly buttoned. He had dark rings around his eyes and carried a battered leather bag which we had given him years ago. I had been sheltered from such things, but I wondered if he might be suffering from the effects of drugs. I gestured for him to sit down and poured him a glass of the sparkling water that we offered customers.

I tried to be reassuring:

"Mathieu, are you alright?"

He did not respond.

I continued:

"Listen, if you are worried about Christmas, I can show you my schedule. I need to be at home with everyone on Christmas Eve but otherwise I'll be away at customers'. You and Gisèle will scarcely know that I exist."

My offer seemed to make things worse. He shook his head vigorously.

I tried a different tactic:

"I've got a haircut in ten minutes. Why don't you come and have one too? Then we can talk afterwards."

This plan seemed to suit him and he nodded.

I asked:

"Can you stay the night with us?"

He looked uncertain.

"Alright, we don't have to decide that now. I'm happy to pay for a hotel."

Fortunately, M Robert had a spare chair. I felt I needed to offer some explanation:

"You know my son, Mathieu. He is tired and needs to rest after a long journey. Can he get a full haircut, wash, and shave?"

I had often taken the boys with me to the barbers. M Robert was a motoring enthusiast, and his establishment resembled a child's bedroom with little models of French cars and pictures of various races on the walls. He would talk to every customer about the Monte Carlo or East African Safari rallies, managing to express fresh interest even though he must have held the identical conversation a dozen times that day. I was comforted to overhear Mathieu advance some appropriate opinions on the relative merits of the Peugeot 403 and the Volvo Amazon as contenders in the East African race.

Mathieu seemed a little revived, and I guided him from the salon to a café, where I ordered tea and petits fours. Neither the food nor the service was particularly good, but there were booths where we could speak privately while studying the extraordinary array of decorative china dogs.

I tried again to communicate.

"I don't want to pressure you. But talk to me when you are ready."

He said nothing but opened his bag and pulled out Weygand's biography. He opened it to a page marked with heavy underlining.

The chapter was entitled *A Rare Misstep* and seemed to have been researched by the author rather than just copied from Weygand's memoir. It recounted how Weygand had begun his initiative to prevent delinquency with the best of intentions. His impatience with bureaucrats and their data had served him well in the past. He had saved countless lives by cutting through red tape. But, overconfident, he had ignored advice to engage a statistician on his team. It was left to a courageous PhD student to prove that his methodology was flawed:

> *Armand visited fifteen seminaries and fifteen centres for young delinquents. He established that Dr Weygand's methodology would have been as good a predictor of a young man's chances of becoming a juvenile saint as of falling into delinquency. In other words, it was useless.*
>
> *These findings met a chilly reception, and the thesis was never published. Nonetheless, the data were incontrovertible, and Dr Weygand quietly moved onto other areas where he accomplished a great deal for mankind.*
>
> *The one stain on so great a man is that he did not acknowledge his error. For example, he had prescribed a regime of the severest discipline for an orphaned boy from an obscure island in the Mediterranean. His diagnosis was never rescinded and one wonders....*

I reached over to Mathieu.

"Thank you for bringing me that."

He was near tears as he responded:

"Can you ever forgive me for what I said?"

"I already have. But it was never your fault. Everyone except that Armand believed in him as an expert."

"You don't know how much I hate Weygand. I feel sick that I took his scholarship."

"Don't feel that way. He made a mistake like we all do. But think of how many people you'll help if they can hear clearly again."

I was surprised to find myself absolving Weygand, but a great weight had been lifted. Given our relative standing in the world, I had never before managed to convince myself fully that I was right and the doctor was wrong. Continuing bitterness would serve no purpose, and I did not want Mathieu to go down that route.

I called Céline from a public telephone as Mathieu listened.

"I'll be a little late. I'm just setting off now. I'm bringing someone from the office to dinner. We'll have enough with that chicken? He's an unusual character, but I think you may like him."

Mathieu filled me in on some details as I drove. He had skimmed the book and had overlooked the short chapter referring to the Missteps. Gisèle had read the text more carefully and, in a passing remark, had mentioned Weygand's error. Two days later, Mathieu's office had closed for an extended weekend to allow for repairs to the plumbing. Short of money for the train, he had embarked on the lengthy journey to Geneva by bus.

I agreed that Mathieu could tell Céline the whole story the next day. I let him out while I positioned the van. Timothée, with a little poetic license, had advised the European Regional Manager that 'it is always fuelled and facing outwards, ready to rush to any emergency.' Joyful cries from the kitchen indicated that mother and son had successfully reunited.

It was a busy Saturday. Céline had committed to helping Mme Jodoin, who remained vigorous and active despite her years, with a charitable event. Mathieu came with me to some kennels in a little village in the mountains. Our Achille and Ulysse had passed many years previously. The house seemed empty as the children began to live independently, and we had arranged to adopt a new Labrador puppy.

Hercule left the litter to greet Mathieu, who spent the rest of the day playing with him and making sure that he was comfortable in his new surroundings. It was only after dinner that we managed to have our discussion with Céline. Mathieu began:

"Maman, there are things that we want to explain. Did you know that Dr Weygand saw Papa when he was a boy?"

I recognized that flicker of an expression on Céline's face. It usually indicated that she was planning to cut a child or husband down to size, gently but firmly. She asked:

"No. Really? Did he have some exciting, exotic disease?"

"No. It was because Weygand's study showed that he might..."

The words would not come out. Mathieu struggled before continuing in a low voice:

"...might become a delinquent."

I was about to jump in to help him, but Céline motioned me to silence. Looking serious, she observed:

"I had reached the same conclusion, but the cantonal Inspector of Jails and Prisons himself reassured me that he was alright."

I was about to ask about this improbable conversation, but an astonished Matthieu was faster:

"Papa was in prison as a boy?"

His mother responded:

"Maybe. It was all so long ago. He was leaving our house for the first time when the Inspector came to discuss a possible miscarriage of justice with your grandfather. He saw Jean-Marc leaving and whispered to me that he was of 'fundamentally sound character'. I remember the phrase. It sounded like something that a defence advocate might say."

She motioned me to keep quiet, looked at Mathieu, and continued:

"I was young and—but don't ever tell your sisters—intrigued at the thought of being with a boy with an exciting history. The next time I saw Papa was at a fair where he was carefully dressing a china elephant in daisies and a bracelet of semi-precious stones."

Mathieu's eyes grew wider as he learned the behaviour of his future parents.

"On the tram coming back, Honoré, who could still be a little juvenile in those days, and our friend Olaf, made crude remarks about Jean-Marc as they got off. Étienne was with me, and I thought he was going to turn blue. He said that they didn't know what they were talking about, and that Jean-Marc had more fortitude than all of them together, but refused to tell me any more. I was confident in my assessment of Papa. I listened closely to his stories of Amphora, but I never probed too deeply into his past in Geneva."

She sipped her coffee while holding up the other hand as a sign that Mathieu and I should stay silent. She went on:

"There was an exhibition of Lucas Cranach. I invited the mysterious Jean-Marc. We had tea afterwards. I enjoyed the music, Schubert's Trout Quintet, and went on seeing him. It turned out that he led a double life where he got bread from an old lady as well as food from the guardian. That caused a lot of complications and nearly meant that we could not get engaged. But, I suppose, it turned out alright. We already made it to our silver wedding."

She paused. Mathieu and I looked at each other. She concluded:

"Sorry, so what is all this about Weygand?"

I indicated to Mathieu that he should let me take the lead.

"Mathieu is right. He found papers from Weygand when he was looking for documents for his visa. You already know that the guardian asked a number of people for advice after he brought me to Geneva, but they included Weygand and the Inspector of Prisons. The Inspector was nice, and I told him about my friend Paul, but Weygand came up with a theory that I might become a delinquent because I had similar characteristics to some valet in Monaco. He wanted me treated severely. It put the guardian in a very awkward position because of Weygand's reputation as the best doctor. Mercifully, he mitigated my regime, much to Weygand's annoyance. Mathieu and Gisèle found the chapter in the book you sent them which proves that his theory on delinquency was entirely wrong."

I studied Céline's expression before adding:

"I'm very, very sorry. I know I should have told you long ago. I was afraid that your father would never approve of our engagement. It was the real reason I was not eligible for military service, and that was a very sensitive topic at the time."

She looked thoughtful as she contemplated my last remark.

"You could be right. Attitudes were very different even twenty-five years ago, and his approval was a very close-run thing. But then, after we took the farm, he never stopped asking me if I was taking proper care of you."

She reached for her coffee and went on:

"I don't need a doctor to tell me that you two are equally strange and alarmingly alike. But you have your good points."

Mathieu asked:

"So, we are all alright then?"

She kissed him on the forehead.

"That depends. I'm still waiting for the recipe you used that night in St. Zotique."

www.ingramcontent.com/pod-product-compliance
Lightning Source LLC
Chambersburg PA
CBHW070416310726
48977CB00003B/716